GHETTO FLOWERS

THE EARLY YEARS

Francis O. Lynn

i

GHETTO FLOWERS
THE EARLY YEARS

First Edition: June 15, 2008

Editor: Randy Istre

Author Photograph by Hazel Hankin

Special Note

The characters and events in this book are fictional. The story represents life as it was lived for thousands of people from a generation that experienced an unusual confluence of circumstances in a world that existed within inner cities all across the United States.

DEDICATION

I have deep appreciation and admiration for all the Ghetto Flowers who helped free each other from the chains of fear with the power of love. Their seeds of love have sprouted over the earth, and yet their roots remain firmly grounded under the red brick, row homes, concrete and asphalt jungle of South Philadelphia.

LOVE IS THE CURRICULUM OF LIFE

The past isn't what it used to be, never was and never will be, and as we learn to let it go, perhaps we can see life as it truly is in the present moment - and begin to heal, turning our wounds into lessons of love.

Francis O. Lynn

CHAPTERS

LITTLE PANTHER

When I was five years old my mother took me to the city zoo. I stood in front of a Black Panther's cage. The cat paced his prison with nervous agitation. His once sleek muscles were flaccid, and loose skin flapped as he pranced back and forth. I cried. Taking me in her arms my mother said, "There's nothing to fear son, the panther is locked in his cage. He can't hurt you." I looked into my mother's eyes and asked, "Mama. Why do I feel like that big cat?"

The red brick back alleys were narrow – three and one-half feet wide passageways stretching the length of a city block, one alleyway connected to another by intersecting cross streets – a labyrinth spread throughout inner city Philadelphia. The fences were made of wood, some painted, and others weathered grey and a few were made of cinder block. People kept their slop cans (compost) and trashcans in their small rectangular concrete-paved back yards, along with miscellaneous partially wanted things. These alleys were home to feral cats; cats that at one time were house pets but had tasted freedom, never to fully return to the sanctuary of the family home, choosing instead to roam the streets and alleyways. The boys had recently developed a passion for hunting them, using homemade spears fashioned out of branches or old brooms, sling-shots made from coat hangers and scraps of rubber from bicycle tire inner tubes, and of course by simply throwing rocks and stones.

The cats were awesome creatures: independent, efficient hunters, graceful and agile. They provided hours of entertainment to me, watching them from my bedroom window as they leaped from fence to fence, searching for prey and garbage cans with loosely fastened lids. They would challenge each other for dominance – stand-offs on the fence tops, hissing out threatening sounds for hours before striking each other with razor sharp claws; ultimately the weaker one would back down. Their late night mating cries were hauntingly beautiful, even though they kept awake many a disgruntled human, who would toss hot water on them to end their love ritual. I wanted to convince the other boys to stop hunting these marvelous creatures, but I went along with them, doing my best to protect the cats while pretending to be a hunter.

We moved with stealth as our eyes scanned the alley fence tops and nooks and crannies of dark corners in search of feline prey.

"I saw it, the big black cat went up the tree in Mrs. Hines' back yard," whispered Liam.

"Quick, let's get closer and try to hit her with our sling-shots," Butch whispered urgently.

When we were within range, we zinged pebbles into the branches. They zipped past her as she leaped from tree to rooftop – she was safe. Liam would not give up. He climbed the tree and on to the roof as we followed. We saw no signs of the black cat but we did see an expanse of rooftops stretching throughout the city, and on distant roofs we saw cats scurrying along their house top haven, plus countless pigeons perched along the highest roof edges and electric wires. Pigeons were preyed upon by these hunting masters. These birds were the most abundant animal life in Philly, known less for the beauty of their design and the grace of their flight than for the filth from their defecation that was everywhere throughout the city, spreading stench and germs. The cats never made a significant contribution to reducing the bird population, for they were far too numerous, and flight was their perfect defense. (City officials would later decimate them through a massive poisoning campaign.) Killing pigeons was an easy game for the boy hunters, many taken from their flight by well-aimed stones hurled from slingshots. My father forbade me the killing of birds. Once, while sitting on my front steps, I killed two pigeons in flight with a single shot. My father saw this happen and I was punished for my deed, my father making me swear to never kill another bird. He enjoyed sitting on the front stoops of our home on Saturday mornings feeding the flocks in the street stale bread crumbs. It was one of his favorite activities. The killing of birds made them afraid to gather in the street in front of our home. My father attempted to rescue baby birds that had fallen from their nests or were left abandoned, although he was never successful. He had no contempt for alley cats, but he had no fondness for them either.

2

"She got away," I calmly stated, trying to hide my satisfaction.

"Yeah, but look at these rooftops. We need to come up here to hunt. We should try it at night – surprise them by waiting. I bet we'll catch the big black cat that way. I'd sure like to have its hide hanging in the clubhouse. She looks like a miniature panther," said Liam. My stomach churned at the thought.

"Liam, you wouldn't take its fur, would you? Besides, you don't know how to skin a cat," I said.

"No I don't, but my father does. He hunts up in the Pocono Mountains and he has deer, rabbit, skunk, raccoon and squirrel skins hanging in the mountain hunting trailer," he proudly stated.

Liam could be quite aggressive and impulsive, which sometimes led to violent action. I was worried that he would take this pursuing of cats too far and that he would actually skin one. He was an adventure-seeker extraordinaire, with a personality that was charismatic enough to convince others to follow his lead into performing deeds that expanded their horizons. He had a powerful, athletic body, a handsome Irish-German face accentuated with thick black hair and startling blue eyes. Liam possessed a keen intellect and a moral code consistent with that of most boys in our neighborhood: do what's fun and don't get caught. There was a strong streak of cunning and mischief running through his veins. He truly enjoyed exploring the neighborhood and its outer limits – he was a thrill seeker. People had a slightly uneasy sense of apprehension when around him because they never knew what he was going to dream up next. During my early childhood it was his friendship that I valued highest above all the other kids in the neighborhood – we were best friends. It was difficult to convince him to curtail the tendency to take things too far, which he often did while enlisting the help of others, including me. Indeed, life was far more exciting when Liam was around – a lot more fun, perhaps because of his astonishing sense of daring.

The hunting of cats disturbed me. I was the youngest in this gang and didn't want to risk rejection. When we threw spears, stones, or used our slingshots to hurt them, I would aim near the cats, hitting a close target, giving them warning. The boys were irritated by my poorly timed and inaccurate shots. I wasn't always successful – cats would get injured and occasionally killed. I wondered what drove boys to hunt and kill like savage animals. I too felt the surge of energy in the thrill of the hunt, yet something else would then take over, stopping me in that crucial moment from choosing to inflict harm.

I never told them that the black cat came to my backyard to eat. I vowed to do everything I could to stop Liam and Butch and the other hunters, but I didn't know how.

Several months later, shortly before sunrise on Christmas morning, my brother and I quietly went downstairs to peek under the Christmas tree. Our parents were asleep on the sofa as the multi-colored tree lights blinked and twinkled, casting holiday radiance through the room. As we stared in wonder at the colorfully wrapped presents, particularly the two red bikes that came straight from the Sears & Roebuck catalogue, my brother noticed a very large black cat make its way from the kitchen and slip through an opening in our basement door. Our attention immediately went to the cat and we followed in quick but quiet pursuit. It was crouched on the edge of the cellar stairs. My brother picked up the cat by the hair of its neck. It swiftly spun around and clawed his chest with several deep scratches. He yelled, causing our parents to awaken.

"What the hell is going on?" cried my mother.

"It's a big cat Mom, the one I told you about. The one that is as big as a baby panther," I said with excitement. She ran to my brother to comfort him and examine his wounds, while my father and I went in search of the cat. "Don't hurt it, Dad. It's very cold out and it probably just wants to be warm," I said.

"Yeah, and she's pregnant. Look at the size of her belly. She's big all right," he said.

"She must have come through the backyard door during the night when we were putting out trash. Lenny, I told you to fix the latch on that door. She was looking for a warm place to have her kittens," my mother explained.

The decision was made to keep her in the basement. My mother took my brother upstairs to clean his wounds. My father placed an old wool blanket and a bowl of milk near the coal chute where the cat was hiding. We couldn't go back to sleep. We decided to make breakfast (it was still dark outside) and then we opened our presents. Afterwards, my brother and I went to the basement to check on the cat.

"Wow, Bill, look at that, she's having kittens. She's pushing them out of her butt and they're all wet and so small," I said.

"Yeah, weird, they're cute and ugly at the same time. Let's count them," Bill suggested. "One, two … I count 7 so far, and look she's pushing out another one! Hey Oliver, isn't she the cat you put food out for on the fence tops?" said Billy.

"Yeah, but don't tell Mom or Dad. They'll get mad and say that's why she came to our house to have the kittens," I replied.

On this Christmas day she had 13 kittens of a variety of colors and markings. We named her Little Panther. Since Panther was an alley cat, she was not tame and would not allow anyone to pet her. She came and went as she pleased through the 'cat door' my father installed in the cellar window. She was a good hunter, although prey was harder to find in the winter, so we provided extra food for her. She was the queen cat among the neighborhood alley cats; she was larger than all other cats and fierce in her battles with rival felines. My peers knew Panther very well, she was artful in escaping them during the hunt; they respected her and they enjoyed the challenge she gave them. The story of Panther's thirteen kittens spread quickly throughout the neighborhood and the boys visited my basement to watch her and her litter.

A few weeks later I walked into the kitchen and saw my father, accompanied by my Uncle Nathaniel, sitting on a chair with a kitten in his hand about to dip it into a bucket of water. I screamed, "No!"

My father yelled, "There are too many kittens. The neighborhood is overrun with them. And I have heard rumors that Mr. Nasty has poisoned cats that go in his yard. We both know Panther goes in there. These kittens will surely follow her. The best thing is to drown them."

"No!" I screamed again, and kicked the bucket, spilling the water over the kitchen floor. "You can't do that. You're a monster. I won't let you kill them. I'll take care of all of them!" I stood there with tears streaming down my face and fists clinched in angry defiance.

"You're crazy! So you think you and your hoodlum friends, who hunt cats, are going to save them? Those boys would just as soon kill them," he yelled.

"I'm going to take them to our clubhouse and give them away to the boys. I know they'll learn to take care of them. They must." I responded with determination.

"Oliver, you have the wackiest ideas, those street boys aren't going to take those kittens home, you know darn well they'll never be able to take care of a single one of those wild creatures. No home will contain them. All they'll want is the food they can get and then turn over the garbage cans for more, making smelly messes all over the alleys, increasing the mice and rat population."

"The cats kill mice and rats, and people should attach garbage lids better. Besides, look how Panther allows us to feed and shelter her, and she still roams through the alleys. That's where the alley cats belong, and they hunt rodents that live in the sewer, and they hunt pigeons as well. I'm going to save these kittens, Dad."

"Go ahead then. Take them to your clubhouse and see what happens. The parents of those boys won't go for it. You have one week to get them out of here. And we're not going to keep a single kitten."

"What about Little Panther? Can she keep coming here?" I asked.

"I'll leave the opening in the window. If she brings any other cats in that basement, then the cat door comes out," he said with finality.

The boys were thrilled by the idea of having personal alley cats; ones they could have relationships with, look after with minimal responsibility, and allow them their freedom. (They'd take it anyway.) Most of the parents weren't keen on the idea, so we took all but two to our clubhouse, an old abandoned two-story brick shell that we claimed as our own, complete with secret entrances, furniture, flags, and other paraphernalia useful for our adventures and cultural rituals. The kittens were well fed and free to come and go as they pleased.

"Hey, this is almost as much fun as hunting them," Butch said, laughing sarcastically. Butch was my elder cousin. He was tall with a slender, muscular, quick and nimble body, curly brown hair and light blue eyes, a face of strong sharp features and smooth skin dusted with freckles across his nose and cheeks. He was popular among the girls, and he enjoyed the role of teen idol – he was thirteen years old, a few years older than all the kids in our peer group. He loved to run, climb, jump and direct us into adventure. Butch had an intelligent and imaginative mind that he applied to creating excitement within the confines of our city world. Contrary to me, our neighborhood was not a prison to him, not a land of limitation but of abundant opportunities for excitement and adventurous exploration. He created and initiated the playing of games - games that we engaged in playing for hours in the streets and on the playground. The hunting of cats and pigeons was one of his pastimes. He had the tribal mind of an inner city boy, organizing our younger group into performing rituals and creating cultural symbols that unified us into a cohesive group with a sense of

6

belonging that each of us enjoyed as a member of the gang. He played an integral role in shaping our tribal mentality.

"Yeah, and we have our own army of cats to keep the clubhouse free of mice and rats," Liam added. "If Panther ever dies though, I would still like to have her skin. It would look great hanging in the clubhouse," he continued.

"Never!" was my reply.

"Just kidding," said Liam.

Spring arrived and the kittens had grown quickly, as kittens do, and since we weren't consistently available to take care of them, they soon became full fledged alley cats, occasionally visiting the clubhouse, some of them using it as a part time shelter. As time went on they became ever wilder, although never completely distrustful of their former human caretakers. Panther occasionally visited the clubhouse and our home, coming through the cellar window, and she never allowed other cats to come with her. This was a good thing because my parents would have closed up the opening.

It was the middle of June when I noticed that Panther had not been around for a few days. I asked if anyone had seen her and no one had. We decided to search the alleys.

"She's not in any of the alleys and we haven't seen her on the roofs either. Let's go check out the nasty man's yard," I suggested. We walked along the edge of the roofs looking down into the yards. When we came to Mr. Nasty's yard we saw something lying in his garden, slightly camouflaged by plant leaves. "That might be her," I said. We climbed down the drainpipe, jumped onto the kitchen roof and then into the yard. "Oh my God, it's her. She's dead!" I cried.

Her limbs were fully extended, her tongue was hanging from the side of her mouth and her eyes were open and covered with a light white film, obscuring the color of her green eyes. I picked up her stiff body and held her close to my chest. Anger surged through me and tears streaked my cheeks. After handing Panther to Butch, I kicked the nasty man's back door and I screamed, "Come out you murderer. How could you be so mean? Come out now!"

"Get out of here you little hoodlums. What do you want with me?" he yelled back from the second story window.

Butch lifted up Panther to show the man a full view of her large stiff body, as ugly in death as she was beautiful in life.

"You killed my cat. You're a murderer!" I screamed.

"That cat was always in my garden and destroying my tomato plants with its mess. I didn't kill her, but I'm glad it's dead. It's just a freakin' alley cat. What's the big deal?"

"What's the big deal with your stupid tomatoes?" I hollered as I ran into his garden and stomped all over his plants. He yelled a curse and disappeared from the window and within moments he was at his back door with a walking cane in his hand.

"Get the hell out of here you little snot-nosed vermin," he screamed while shaking his cane and threatening to hit us.

This man was truly nasty: long greasy black hair streaked with white, a forehead with lines etched by anger scrunching his eyebrows to where they almost touched. Snot dripped from his long sharp nose and spilled onto his moustache. Foam formed on the edges of his mouth, and his beard had remnants of his most recent meal. He wore a trench coat that was torn and covered with patches. His feet were bare and hairy, and the fingers of his long hands replete with uncut, dirty fingernails clutched the cane. As he spoke his mouth revealed few teeth stained yellow and broken. Above all else it was his eyes that caught my attention: they were pale blue and glassy, glaring out of sunken sockets. They looked like tombstones with an unwritten epitaph of a life filled with fear and suffering.

Butch put down Panther, picked up a board and threw it directly at the man, hitting him on the shoulder. "Take that you crazy old man," cried Butch.

The man screeched in pain and quickly went into the house, slamming the door behind him. Mr. Nasty was mean and crazy but he wasn't brave. Butch didn't stop there.

"Take this you freak," he yelled as he threw a rock smashing one of his kitchen windows.

"Butch! Stop!" I yelled, as he was about to pick up another rock. "Put it down and let's get out of here," I said, fearing that Mr. Nasty would have a gun.

"Well, it looks like he kept his promise," my father said.

I was determined to make him pay and begged my father to do something. He knocked on the nasty man's door. The man looked out his window and seeing my angry face glaring at him, he refused to answer.

"There's nothing we can do Oliver. Panther is dead and there's no proof he killed her. Come on lets go home."

"Dad, you heard him say he was going to poison Panther and she was found dead in his yard, that's proof enough for me. He did it and he needs to pay!" I exclaimed.

"There's nothing to be done. Forget about it, and I don't want to hear another word. Do you hear me?" I didn't reply.

Butch carried Panther's body to the clubhouse. The boys gathered around her in an atmosphere of disbelief. There lay Panther, stiff and dirty. She hadn't begun to rot. She hadn't been dead for long. Then Butch spoke in a mournful and eerie tone: "She is a black cat and she gave birth to thirteen kittens on Christmas Day. She was the queen of the alley cats and an evil man poisoned her. We need to give her the right kind of burial; otherwise we may all get seven years bad luck."

"Mr. Nasty deserves the bad luck," I replied. "How do you know this is what we have to do, Butch? You're just making this up, aren't you?" I asked.

"No! I am not just making it up. I just know. So let's do it," he commanded.

"So how do we bury her?" I asked.

"We make a casket and get dressed up in costumes. We will walk through the streets so everyone can see Panther. Then we burn her on a bonfire in the clubhouse yard." Butch was clear and direct in his instructions, convincing us that he indeed did know what he was talking about.

That same day we had a funeral procession through the neighborhood streets. We poured water over coal soot to make black paint to cover our faces and we dressed in black clothing with green headbands made of rags tied around our heads to represent Panther's remarkable green eyes. We made drums and a white flag with a painted image of a black cat. As we walked down the center of the streets, parents and their children watched from the sidewalks and front stoops with looks of curiosity, amusement and, in some cases, sadness. We made our way back to the clubhouse through the alley, stopping at the nasty man's fence. As we stood there I decided to pee on his fence and all the boys followed my example. Fifteen boys peeing on his fence – that made me smile.

When we reached the clubhouse we placed Panther in her open casket on top of the prepared bonfire. We stood in a circle as I poured lighter fluid on the wood, struck a match and simply said, "Goodbye Panther." I threw the lighted match on the pile and the flames jumped up in a roar as they licked Panther's body. We danced around the fire, making "meow" cries and other weird sounds, trying to imitate cats. The smell of burning hair and flesh filled our nostrils, making my head spin with dizziness. I suddenly felt sick and started to puke.

The fire finally went out. We took Panther's ashes and placed them in a bucket and walked to St. Aloysius' Catholic Church. We opened the cemetery gate. The cemetery had only one headstone and that was of the founder of the church. We dug a small hole and poured in her ashes. Fortunately there weren't any priests or nuns around to stop us.

As we placed her remains in the shallow hole and each of us threw handfuls of dirt upon her ashes, I said with tentative authority, "Guys, you have to swear a solemn oath to never hunt alley cats again. Panther's kittens, our kittens, are now roaming the alleys and no one should hunt them."

"You're right, Oliver. Guys, what do you say? If you agree not to hunt cats anymore say 'Aye!'" Butch shouted.

"Aye!" everyone said in unison.

We finished filling in her grave and patted down the earth. We decided not to have a gravestone because she wasn't supposed to be there and we didn't want her grave disturbed. We had given Panther a proper burial – but I wasn't finished.

"Butch, Liam, I want to talk with you," I said with a slight quiver in my voice.

"Yeah, so what's up?" they asked as I gestured for them to step behind the six foot high gravestone.

"I have a plan to get even with Mr. Nasty. My grandfather went fishing down to Stone Harbor this weekend and brought back lots of fish. He gave my mother some. I want to climb Mrs. Hines' tree, get on the rooftop and put a few fish down his chimney. Will you help me?"

"Sure! But I'd rather break all his windows; it was fun tossing that rock. It scared him real good," said Butch.

"Count me in," Liam replied.

That night we climbed Mrs. Hines' tree and dumped smelly fish and a sack of cat poop down Mr. Nasty's chimney. We then threw fish into his yard and along his fence in the alleyway. Cats were soon all around his house eating dead fish and defecating all over his property. A month later the nasty man had some workers come to his house to get rid of the smell that spread throughout his home from the chimney flue. They discovered the source, opened the bottom flue and cleaned it out. Two days later we put more garbage down his chimney. Three weeks after that he moved out.

Rumor had it that he went to live with his sister in Southwest Philly for a short while before going crazy and being committed to a mental hospital. A part of me believed that justice had been served, but I found no satisfaction in this thought. Little Panther was gone forever and I realized that getting back at Mr. Nasty offered me no comfort. To my surprise, I felt a twinge of sorrow for the man.

Little Panther

Boy hunters of the Alley Cats could never catch you
Glowing satin sheen
Light glimmering black richness
You're Highness of the felines
Roaming narrow walls under starry skies
New, full, quarter and crescent moon
Echoes your soprano meow-cries
Stalking for rats in backyard habitats
Moving without sound, catching your prey
Challenges from rivals, showdown on the fence
Electrified hair, straight fanged teeth and ivory razor claws
Erie dazzling subterranean green piercing eyes
Panther of the Alley Cats
Wisest of the Wise
Ninth life played out in the human designed maze
Roof-top to roof-top leap
Feline stretched elongated eloquence gracing the air
Balance unmatched by nature's beasts
Landing on padded paws
Moving through the alleyways seeking your feast
Rats and mice and tipped garbage pails
Friendly boys treat – daily leftovers strewn in a trail
To tame was not his intent, only closer appreciation of wild beauty
Cat scratch fever, heat running through her veins
She finds a mate and the ritual begins
Singing the cats' meow, they jam all night
Creators and hunters joined as one
Passion spent and new life begins
Christmas morn cold blowing snow
She enters the backyard door
Into the warm basement she goes
Two boys, brothers, chase after to see
And discover she is pregnant on this Christmas day
Thirteen kittens came to be, a gift to the boys in the 'hood
Queen Mother of the Alley Cats
Wisest of the wise
Final life spent, poisoned by Nasty Man
Boy hunters laid down their weapons
In honor of thee
Our precious Little Panther

WHITE SHEPHERD

"Let's play half-ball on Second Bambrey Street. I cut off the straw part of my mother's worn out broom and made a bat from the stick. It's a real nice one. I think it's made of oak. Does anyone have half-balls?" I asked.

It was Saturday morning and we were hanging out on the front stoop of our clubhouse: Luke, Liam, Bones, Johnny Boy and myself. I was in the mood to play half-ball. Recently I had developed a good swing and was able to hook the cupped side of the half-ball on the tip of my bat, causing it to spin like a flying saucer high enough to go over a three-story roof. I was determined to become the best player in the neighborhood, which meant beating my cousin, Johnny Boy. I was a good pitcher too, zinging, spinning and curving the half-balls with a twist of my wrist, holding two fingers folded under the cupped side, two fingers on the curved outside and my thumb on the back – and my pitch was fast. Few were able to hit it, but when they did, it moved fast and hard in a line drive, making it difficult to catch. Johnny Boy was one of the few to consistently hit my pitches, but he never got more than a double. The spin, curve and dip of my pitch didn't allow the batter to hook it on the cupped side, which was the only way to get good height from a hit. This frustrated all the players, especially Johnny Boy.

"I cut six pimple-balls in half. That gives us a dozen half-balls. I have a stick-bat that is perfect for my swing," added Luke.

"I have a few smooth air-balls I'm willing to cut in half," said Bones.

"Hey guys, I'm gonna bring along my trusty stick-bat," said Johnny Boy. Johnny Boy was two years older than most of us and he was the best half-ball player in the neighborhood. He was sort of a loner, but he always joined us in playing ball. He was only interested in sports, and whenever we engaged in adventurous activities involving mischief, he stayed away. Because of this he was often referred to as a sissy, but no one called him that to his face because we all knew that he could easily kick our asses. Johnny Boy was one of my many cousins; one of the sons of my mother's oldest sister. On several occasions he tried talking to me about the kids I hung out with and our questionable activities, wanting to convince me to avoid trouble. I never listened to him. My friends were important to me – I couldn't live without them – and Johnny Boy's life as a loner wasn't appealing.

"Let's stop gabbing and head on down Pie Street," said Liam. Pie Street was the name the black kids gave to the 1600 block of Bambrey Street. My home, along with Liam's and Johnny Boy's, was on the 1500 block of Bambrey Street. The blacks called it Pie Street because the entire block was a pie-making factory, and it provided jobs for mostly black folks. There were no cars or crowds of people.

There was only one residential building that shared an alley on Pie Street. It was on the corner of Tasker and Pie Street. There was a dead–end ally running behind the backyard. We passed this backyard every time we walked down Pie Street. A huge German Shepherd lived in that backyard. She was owned by Nicky Milano, a roofer by trade. His yard was triple the size of most yards. He kept his roofing equipment there. The Shepherd was his guard dog. For years we had walked past the wooden fence that penned in the dog, and it would always growl and bark menacingly. We had gotten into the bad habit of scraping our stick-bats along the vertical boards of the wooden fence to tease the Shepherd. On this Saturday morning our unfriendly habit of teasing the dog lead to a disaster.

As we approached Pie Street and the Shepherd's fence, we heard its familiar growl. Luke started scraping the fence with his stick-bat, causing the dog to become more aggressive. He then began poking the stick-bat through the cracks between the wooden boards, trying to touch the Shepherd. The dog grabbed the end of the bat in his teeth and wouldn't let go. Luke pulled as hard as he could and landed on his bottom – the Shepherd got his stick. This infuriated Luke. Without asking he grabbed my new bat and began poking at the dog once again. This time the dog ignored the bat and began tossing her 100 pound body up against the fence over and over again, as we had seen her do many times over the years. In spite of the Shepherd's excessive aggressive behavior, Luke continued to poke my stick-bat at her. The boards had become weakened from years of wear and tear, and suddenly the Shepherd broke through the fence. We were startled and began to run. Bones tried climbing up a drain pipe; Liam successfully climbed on top of the wooden fence; Johnny Boy ran like a bolt of lightning down Pie

Street and I just stood still, frozen – partly out of fear and partly because I had heard that if a dog attacks you the best defense is to stand motionless. The Shepherd first went for Bones. The dog caught his pant leg as he scurried up the drain pipe. Bones started screaming and crying, saying: "Let me go, let me go." The dog tore off a piece of his jeans, which allowed Bones to climb higher and out of the Shepherd's reach. Johnny Boy, by this time, was around the corner and out of the Shepherd's sight. I stood like a statue in the middle of the street. Without the slightest hesitation, the Shepherd ran up to me and sank her teeth right into my buttocks. I screamed from the pain. The Shepherd held on tight. Fortunately for me, I was wearing heavy jeans and a thick sweatshirt so her teeth mostly had hold of my clothing and only the sharpest part of her fangs pierced my skin. Johnny Boy ran back up Pie Street with his stick-bat in hand. He was screaming like a banshee that had gone completely mad. He ran up to the Shepherd and started beating her on the head and body with the stick-bat. The Shepherd would not let go of me. Johnny Boy's stick-bat splintered with each blow. The Shepherd was flinging me around like a rag doll. I had strong legs and an exceptionally good sense of balance, which kept me from falling to the ground. If she brought me down, then she could go for my throat and kill me.

Just as Johnny Boy's stick-bat splintered into useless pieces, the owner of the dog, Nicky Milano, came running towards us carrying a chair in one hand and a whip in the other. He approached the dog shouting, "Misty, back down, NOW!" as he cracked his whip in the air making a very loud snapping sound. The Shepherd ignored him and continued to try and bring me to the ground. Again he snapped his whip, hitting the Shepherd on the back, but the dog was tenacious and seemed oblivious to the pain. Three successive whacks with the whip finally caused the dog to let go of me. Nicky was able to take control of the dog by artfully swishing the whip around the Shepherd's front leg and pulling her into the backyard, using his chair to keep a safe distance from her deadly fangs.

I stood there in the middle of the street frozen with fear. Tears were running down my cheeks and my backside was inflamed with pain. The commotion had brought most of the Bambrey Street residents out of their homes. My mother ran up to me and wrapped her arms around me. She then spun me around and pulled the back of my pants down to inspect the damage inflicted by the Shepherd's teeth. All these people were staring at me – standing in the street with half my butt in full view of everyone. There was blood on my buttocks and my underwear was stained with pee – I had wet myself. A feeling of embarrassment and shame swept over me that was far more powerful than the fear and pain caused by the Shepherd. "Stop mom! Let me go!" I yelled and pulled away from her, frantically pulling up my pants. Mom must have realized my embarrassment and helped me.

A police officer approached us and offered to take Mom and me to the hospital. She accepted and off we went. There was a long wait in the emergency room before a doctor inspected my wounds. He said I was very lucky, since the Shepherd's teeth had not cut too deeply and the bleeding was superficial.

The main concern was rabies. The doctor was waiting for a veterinarian report. He told my mom that I might have to get shots. The police had called the SPCA – the dog catchers – and they took the Shepherd to the pound where blood was drawn and tested for the disease.

As it turned out, the Shepherd was not infected and I went home with a few stitches in my butt and a torn pair of jeans. (I threw my pee-soaked underwear in the trash basket in the hospital room.) We went home and I slept for the rest of the afternoon, waking up only for dinner and then going back to bed.

Trying to keep dogs in our neighborhood rarely worked out because the homes were small and the backyards were simply oversized cages, causing dogs to bark continuously. They became highly agitated, nervous animals. Many of these dogs would escape their backyard cages and roam the streets in packs, creating a serious threat to children. The city sent out dogcatchers who would snatch them up. There were times when we used our slingshots to keep the pack of animals away from us. I never knew what the dogcatchers did with the dogs; some people said they killed them, others said they sent them to a dog farm, which I thought was a myth to make children feel better about the animals' fate.

The next day Nicky Milano came to my house to make sure I was okay. My mother told him it was the fault of the boys for teasing his dog all these years, but that didn't dissuade Nicky from offering an explanation. He said that the Shepherd's behavior was far more aggressive than usual because she recently had had a litter of puppies, and she thought she was protecting them.

"Boys will be boys," he said matter-of-factly with his heavy Italian accent. "I don't blame them. And I don't blame Misty. She was just protecting her puppies. It was nobody's fault. These things

16

just happen. She had six puppies and I want to give one to your boy," he said.

"Please Mom, a real dog of our own. Wow that would be so cool." I was excited by the possibility.

"That's very kind of you Mr. Milano, but we don't have room for a dog, you know how small these yards are." My Mom was right and I knew it, but I still liked the idea of having a dog, so I tried persuading her.

"Come on Mom, we can make it work. Grandma's had her dog ever since I can remember," I pleaded.

"Grandma's dog is a small Springer Spaniel, not a big German Shepherd, which needs a lot more room," she retorted.

"What if the boys in the neighborhood kept her as a mascot? We would feed her and she could take turns sleeping in our homes. Maybe she could live in the clubhouse," I suggested.

"That clubhouse is an abandoned building and it's just a matter of time before it gets torn down. You kids shouldn't be using that building anyway. It's not safe." I knew my mother felt that way about the clubhouse, just like most parents on Bambrey Street did, but they never told us to stop using it.

"I appreciate your offer Mr. Milano, but we just can't have any pets in our home." That was my mother's final word on the matter and I knew I couldn't change her mind.

"Can I at least see the puppies, Mom?"

"After that dog bit you in the buttocks, you want to see her puppies? You must be crazy."

"It wasn't her fault, Mom. Like Mr. Milano said, she was protecting her puppies."

"I can keep the big dog in the house while he looks at the puppies, Mrs. James. He will be safe. I promise." I liked Nicky Milano and thought he was a reasonable guy.

"All right. Go ahead. I'm just surprised you're not afraid," she added.

Nicky took me to his house. The fence had already been fixed. I waited outside while he put Misty in the house. He opened the back gate and let me in. The puppies were inside a very large doghouse. Nicky reached inside and took them out one at a time. They were mostly black with a little tan color beginning to show, except for the last one; it was pure white.

"Wow! An all-white Shepherd, I've never seen one before."

"They are rare and the dog experts don't consider them to be true Shepherd. She is the runt of the litter and I am afraid I won't be able to sell her. This is the one I wanted to give to you."

17

"I have to have her, Nicky. There has to be a way. Could you please not give her to anyone else until I tell you that I absolutely can't take her?" I was determined to get the white Shepherd.

"I will honor your wish, but you have to tell those boys they can't tease my Misty anymore. Agreed?" he asked.

"You betcha!" I had to come up with a way of keeping White Shepherd. As I was walking up Bambrey Street, deep in thought, I bumped into Ranger, my mom's friend.

"Hey, watch where you're going young lad. What are you thinking about so intensely?" I told him about White Shepherd and how I wanted to keep her, and that my Mom wouldn't allow it. I shared my plan about the dog being the neighborhood mascot and all the kids taking care of her.

"That's a good idea except I don't think you can count on those boys and girls being responsible. Besides, animals like to identify one person as their main caretaker and that would have to be you."

"I want it to be me, but Mom won't allow it. She won't let me keep the dog in the clubhouse either, and even if I did keep her in the clubhouse, I can't sleep in there, and White Shepherd wouldn't like being alone. I just don't know what to do."

"What if I kept her in my yard at night? You could build her a doghouse and be the one who feeds her. Every evening you could bring her to my yard. In the mornings you could come over and take her. She'd have to spend all day with you. Lucky school just got out, which means you have the time."

"Ranger, that's a brilliant idea. I don't see any way my mother could keep us from doing this. After all, White Shepherd would be living with you and spending her days with me and the other kids in the neighborhood. It will work. Thank you so much." I gave Ranger a hug, trying to ignore the stench of his dirty body.

"Come on, let's go to Nicky's and get White Shepherd!" I said.

So this was how White Shepherd became our neighborhood mascot. I followed the plan of keeping her in Ranger's backyard, and having her hang out with me all day and late into the evening. Liam helped me build the doghouse; I had a knack for carpentry and so did Liam. We both enjoyed building and making things. During the summer months, as White Shepherd grew from a puppy into a larger dog, almost everyone developed a fondness for her. As it turned out, most of the families on Bambrey Street were willing to allow White Shepherd in their homes. She truly became the neighborhood dog, but I was her closest friend. Whenever I was around, she was by my side. When I rode my scooter or bicycle around the neighborhood, she ran along beside me. And the most fun we had with her was when we played street games, like Werewolf.

Werewolf was only played at night when there was a full moon. The game worked like this: one person was designated the Werewolf and this person had a den - the wide marble steps of the church. White Shepherd was the Werewolf's assistant in finding all the other boys and girls. The kids could hide anywhere around the block, which included 26th Street and Bambrey Street and, of course, the alley in between, including people's backyards. The reason why so much territory was allowed for hiding was because of White Shepherd. She could find anyone, anywhere. Once spotted by the Werewolf, the person was considered caught and had to go to the marble steps; the cage where prisoners were kept for the wolf's food supply. If you were the very first person caught, you became the Werewolf's assistant along with White Shepherd. The second person to get caught became the Keeper of the Den, guarding the marble steps to prevent the releasing of the prisoners. The first person caught would become the new Werewolf when we played a second round of the game. Prisoners could be released if someone was able to run up to the marble steps, touch them with both feet and howl like a Werewolf, without being touched by the Keeper of the Den. Then, they were free to run and hide once again. Sometimes it became necessary to have White Shepherd assist guarding the den, but only if the person being the Keeper of the Den wasn't good as a protector. White Shepherd enjoyed this task. I liked watching her guard the steps. When someone would try a sneak-approach to free the prisoners, she would catch him by the leg pants or shoe, being careful not to slice her teeth into the invader. The way to defeat her was to have two people approach the den from different directions. No more than two people at a time were permitted to attack the den. That would make the game too easy. White Shepherd was amazingly good at playing this game. She was exceptionally smart, and her sense of smell and keen eyesight made it impossible for anyone to hide for too long.

At first, White Shepherd came with me wherever I went. Then, she developed independence. She liked to roam the neighborhood and, since she was known by just about everyone, no one bothered her. In fact, they liked having her around because she was friendly with little children, old people, and all ages in between. Vare playground was her favorite place to hang out because there were always lots of kids willing to play games with her. She was very good at catching and fetching balls, which sometimes became a nuisance during competitive games, but people only had to tell her a few times not to do something and she understood that that activity wasn't for her.

One night there was a three year old girl who went missing at the local carnival held at Bishop Neumann High School. The little girl, Courtney, was with her family, enjoying the rides, games and food stands. The carnival was very crowded on this Saturday night, and the mom was buying cotton candy while the dad was getting tickets for the merry-go-round. Somehow the little girl became separated from her parents and wandered off. The parents went to the priests, and the priests went to the police. Everyone was looking for little Courtney. Finally, they decided to close the carnival, making everyone exit through one gate, making it impossible for Courtney to walk by without being seen. When the carnival was empty, there was still no Courtney. The mother became hysterical, crying and shouting out Courtney's name. Police and priests were everywhere.

I was standing outside the carnival gate and White Shepherd was by my side. Courtney's mom was standing near the fence being comforted by her sister. White Shepherd placed her nose through an opening in the chain link fence and sniffed Courtney's sweater dangling from the mother's hand. White Shepherd looked at me and barked. I understood that she wanted to leave my side. I said, "Go find Courtney, White Shepherd," and off she ran. First, she sniffed all around the fence. I thought she would then go into the carnival and worried that the police would stop her, but she didn't. White Shepherd sniffed around the gate opening and then began moving quickly down 27th Street toward Moore Street. I was impressed by her keen sense of smell because the sidewalks and streets were filled with people leaving the carnival, yet White Shepherd stayed focused and intensely determined. I followed, running to keep her in my sight. She stopped for a moment at the intersection of 27th & Moore and then turned east. Vare playground was on one side of Moore Street and the high school was on the other. She crossed the street, stopped at the playground entrance, sniffed around in circles, picked up the scent again, and entered the playground. She sniffed her way across the concrete-paved basketball court, then over to the red brick building, moving around the side to the ramp that led to the basement and its wide steel doors. White Shepherd disappeared down the ramp and began to bark. Within moments I was down the ramp.

There was Courtney, holding her doll and crying, saying over and over again, "I lost, Mommy, I lost, Mommy …" It was impossible to tell if she was injured because there wasn't any lighting. I told her my name was Oliver and the dog was White Shepherd, that her mom and dad were nearby, and I would take her to them. I asked her if anything hurt on her body, and she said, "I hurt my head and fell down this dark place. I follow the cat, I follow the cat, the cat gone." White Shepherd was softly whimpering as she approached Courtney and licked her forehead. Courtney started laughing, saying, "Doggy tickle, nice doggy." She reached out and touched the fur on White Shepherd's neck. "Soft doggy."

I gently picked her up and carried her light body to the top of the ramp. Courtney held her little arms around my neck, her hands clinging to her doll. At the top of the ramp she looked at White Shepherd. "Pretty white doggy, give me ride, give me ride." I placed her on her feet and she wrapped her arms around White Shepherd's neck. I looked over her body as she hugged White Shepherd. She had a small scrape on her forehead and there were scratches on her left elbow and knee.

"Can white doggy take me to Mommy?"

"Yes Courtney, she will take you to your parents."

"Can I ride on doggy?" she asked. I hesitated because I wasn't sure how White Shepherd would respond to having a child ride on her back; also I was worried about her injuries. As I looked at her with her arms tightly wrapped around White Shepherd I couldn't resist her request.

"Okay Courtney, but you have to make sure you keep your arms wrapped around her neck, but don't squeeze too tight. And if she doesn't like it I will have to take you off right away." I picked up Courtney, who was very light, and placed her on White Shepherd's back, holding on to her as I allowed her weight to transfer gradually to White Shepherd's back. White Shepherd did not mind at all, in fact, she wagged her tail and let out a bark. We began walking back to the carnival. I held one hand on Courtney's back just in case she lost her balance. White Shepherd knew to walk beside me. Within a very short time we were back at the carnival.

"Courtney, my Courtney," the mother cried as she ran to us and lifted Courtney off White Shepherd. The father came to her as well and they were all hugging each other, crying tears of joy. White Shepherd sat beside me wagging her tail. As I looked at the family and back at White Shepherd, I marveled at the dog's intelligence and sensitivity – she seemed more human than humans – a thought that struck me as odd, and yet it felt true.

I knelt beside White Shepherd and stroked her fur. The police and priests were watching the scene. A policeman took a picture of the family, White Shepherd and me. The police officer asked if he could take a picture of Courtney on the back of White Shepherd and so we did. At the time I thought it was strange that a policeman would be taking pictures, but the next day I found out why. The family thanked me and gave White Shepherd several hugs. The family, police, and priests questioned me and I told them where White Shepherd found Courtney and that the girl was simply following a cat she saw at the carnival.

After I told my parents what had happened, they became more accepting of White Shepherd and gave up on their objection to her spending the night in our home. For the first time, White Shepherd slept with me in my bed. Fortunately I had a large bed, because she took up a lot of space.

The next morning my mother woke me up from a crazy dream and said, "Oliver, look at this and read it to me." My mother was holding a copy of the *Philadelphia Inquirer* newspaper and there on the front page was the picture the policeman took of Courtney sitting on the back of White Shepherd. She asked me to read the paper because my mother had never learned to read or write, and neither had my father. They were immigrants from Ireland and because of the economic struggles of their families, they worked when they were children and never went to school. The headline read:

Good White Shepherd and Boy Find Missing Girl

I read the article to my mother. The story was told just as I had reported it to the policeman. The policeman was also the writer of the article. There was a brief biography on him saying that he freelanced as a news reporter and took writing and photography classes at a local college. In the article the writer said that one of the meanings for the word, "shepherd," is to look after the well-being of a group of people, and that is how I viewed White Shepherd from that moment on: our neighborhood animal friend that took care of everyone. She was a good shepherd, and so her true name was revealed to me: *Good White Shepherd.*

White Shepherd was now seven months old, and stunningly beautiful. She had long legs and big paws; her ears stood straight up; and her forehead and snout gave the appearance of gentle strength; her eyes were a rich brown color and they were expressive and shimmered with the light of intelligence; her hips were narrow and her broad chest and muscular rib cage were accentuated by a bushy tail. Every hair on her body was snow white. My mom said she looked like a beautiful and confident teenage girl. White Shepherd required lots of attention and opportunity to burn off her abundant energy, which was no problem in our neighborhood since just about every kid (and adult) wanted to play with her.

The newspaper article made her even more popular. Every person in Philadelphia could read about "Good White Shepherd." The children on Bambrey Street and their families welcomed White Shepherd into their homes, with the exception of a few families that weren't comfortable with dogs. For a while there was a problem with everyone feeding her table scraps, and she liked to get into the compost buckets just like the alley cats. Although people kept feeding her I was able to teach her to avoid garbage cans most of the time.

And there was another problem – the cats. Since we stopped trying to hunt cats, because we knew many of them as Little Panther's offspring, and because we had sworn a sacred oath never to hunt alley cats again, the cats would frequently visit our clubhouse. White Shepherd didn't take that oath, nor would she – it just wasn't in her nature. The cats became less comfortable visiting our clubhouse. White Shepherd enjoyed chasing after them, occasionally getting a razor sharp claw swiped across her nose. Eventually, she learned to respect the cats, but she continued to chase them, and the cats enjoyed tantalizing her, knowing full well they could easily get away from White Shepherd by climbing a fence or telephone pole. On occasion, White Shepherd would manage to get a kitten in her jaws, and although she'd shake it around a little, she was gentle enough not to inflict harm.

The alley cats and White Shepherd worked out their relationship with each other, which amounted to teasing and chasing with occasional scratches and bites, but nothing requiring serious veterinarian attention. The Fire Department became annoyed by the number of times they had to use their ladder trucks to get cats down from the top of telephone poles. White Shepherd would chase cats up the pole, and then the cats, in an extremely fearful state, were

23

paralyzed and simply couldn't climb down the pole. White Shepherd would sit at the base of the pole wagging her tail and barking, while the firemen would raise their ladder to the top and rescue the cat. I think White Shepherd was quite entertained.

One beautiful Saturday morning, my cousin Butch offered to lead a large group of the neighborhood kids to Wissahickon Creek State Park to roam the wooded hills and wide boulder-filled streams. Wissahickon is a beautiful place in northwestern Philadelphia, an 8,700-acre park that encases a spectacular setting with an outdoor recreation area running seven miles along the Wissahickon Creek Gorge. Despite its city location, the park is a remarkable piece of protected land — wild and free from the intrusion of city skylines and traffic sounds. Cathedral forest, broad-flowing Wissahickon Creek, scenic outcrops, historic stone bridges, ruins that date to the 1700s and a battle site from the American Revolution contributed significantly to stimulating our sense of adventure. This was our first time going there. Butch had gone with my uncle several times. He had memorized how to get there by public transportation.

It takes a long time to get to Wissahickon by public transportation. Butch told us we would be going early in the morning. It was supposed to be a beautiful autumn day with trees bursting in colors. We packed lunches and brought $1.50 for transportation and extra money if we wanted to buy snacks. We trusted Butch to get us there, and for most of us it would be our first time in a big forested area with hills, streams and hiking paths. We were excited. Sixteen of us gathered at the 26th and Morris trolley stop at 7:00 am in the morning. This was a large group, many more than our usual adventure-seeking boys.

The trolley car arrived, but was slightly delayed because the tracks had some metal pipes lying across them, and the two long poles on the back of the bus that reached up to the electric wire lines kept slipping off. The driver had to keep re-attaching them. Butch told us that he heard from his father that they were going to do away with all the electric trolleys and replace them with gasoline buses. I liked the electric trolleys because they were quiet and ran on tracks, which reminded me of trains.

One of our favorite pastimes was to pull the cord on the poles that were attached to the back of the trolley so they would come off the elevated electric wires and lose power. (The poles transmitted the energy from the wires to the electric motor.) This stopped the trolley, making the driver get off to re-attach the poles.

Then we would sneak on the trolley and get free rides. We didn't do that on this particular morning because there were simply too many of us to get away with it – we'd take up half the seats.

It cost \$0.15 to ride the Morris–Tasker trolley, which made an east-west loop from Front Street, along the Delaware River, and 36th Street, along the Schuylkill River. Sometimes just for fun we would ride the full loop several times over before getting off. The trolley drivers never seemed to mind us riding the trolleys like that, even if we had sneaked on by pulling the wire. I guess it made their job more interesting, or maybe they had done the same thing when they were kids.

There was one major problem with our transportation: White Shepherd. Dogs weren't allowed to ride the city transit system. The only exception was the seeing-eye dogs for blind people. I decided to pretend I was blind in order to get White Shepherd on the bus. I borrowed my uncle's sunglasses. Well, sort of borrowed. I never actually asked him if I could use them because he wasn't around, but I knew he wouldn't mind, being a lover of Wissahickon himself. I wore a blue bandana around my neck and tied a matching bandana around White Shepherd's neck. Harry, another neighborhood kid, lent me a walking cane from his grandfather's collection to add to the costume. Well, he sort of borrowed it. It was fun pretending to be blind. People were exceptionally courteous. Most people, anyway. A few were rude and looked at me as if they were afraid or disgusted by me, which was an interesting experience. Liam suggested I use a tin can to collect money for being blind. I told him if we got in a jam and needed money that I'd give it a try.

When the trolley that would take us to the subway came, the boys allowed me to get on first. Blind people and their dogs didn't have to pay, but they had to go to a special wide seat at the back of the trolley to keep the dog out of the aisle so people who were afraid of dogs wouldn't avoid getting on the trolley. Broad Street was our first stop; the street with the subway. The subway ran north and south underneath Philadelphia. The thought crossed my mind that the subway would be a great place for a blind person with a dog and a tin cup to collect money. I also thought it would be easy to fall onto the train tracks and be sliced to pieces by the steel wheels; but not if you had a seeing-eye dog looking after you. We paid our \$0.15, got on the train heading north and rode it all the way to the end of the line. Then, we waited over half-an-hour for the trolley that would take us to the Wissahickon State Park entrance.

The park was beautiful. It was a perfect autumn day; sixty-eight degrees, and mostly sunny with big puffy clouds drifting across the sky like giant cotton balls. The trees weren't at the peak of their colors, but they were close. The green, red-orange, brown, and yellow-gold colors were spectacular. Sunlight filtered through the branches of the trees and leaves floated gracefully to the forest floor, blanketing the ground in preparation for the winter freeze soon to come. The Wissahickon Creek water was cold, and we took off our shoes, hopping from rock to rock, resting now and then on big boulders. White Shepherd was in her element. This was her first time outside of the city, and nature suited her quite well. The sights, sounds, and smells awakened her senses in new ways, ways that were intrinsic to her animal nature going back to the wolves from which her genetic heritage could be traced. She loved running in the water, along the paths and into the woods. It was difficult commanding her to stay with us, because she would follow the scent of animals; yet she always found her way back to us, the flock that she, the good shepherd, had the responsibility for looking after.

We decided to play Cowboys and Indians. We made up the game on the spot and chose sides based on who would like to be an Indian or a Cowboy, and eventually we balanced out the numbers so there were eight kids on each side. I chose to be an Indian. Reading my grandfather's western comic books made me like Indians better than cowboys, even though the books referred to them as "savages." I'll never forget the often repeated sentence: "the only good Indian is a dead Indian."

The Indians were so much cooler than the cowboys. They were better hunters and lived in neat houses: tee-pees, wigwams, and longhouses. Indians rode horses on their bare backs, hunted deer and buffalo and made use of every part of the animal for food, clothing, shelter and tools. Just because they used the bow and arrows to hunt, and for self-protection, and dressed in animal skins, and decorated their bodies with paint and wore feathers were not reasons to call them savages. When I read the comic books I would imagine myself being an Indian warrior, protecting my family and tribe from the white men who were stealing our land. Tonto, the Indian friend of the main cowboy character in the famous television show, *The Lone Ranger,* was the one who always did the right thing at the right time to get the Lone Ranger out of danger. Tonto never got credit for his good deeds. He was more of a hero than Lone Ranger, the masked man who rode the white horse, dressed in fancy white cowboy clothes and shot silver bullets. So, I chose to be an Indian. We decided that the ammunition would be mud clay.

Anyone who got hit with mud was considered dead and out of the game. The team with the only survivor(s) would be declared the winners.

There was a lot of land, so it was difficult for us to set clear boundaries. Butch was an Indian like me, and, of course, White Shepherd ran along with Butch and me in the woods. We went way too far from the place where the game started; going up a ridge, and then down and up again. Eventually, Butch and I realized we were lost. We started looking for our way back when Butch tripped and fell. He cried out in pain and reached for his ankle. He had twisted his right ankle. I tried helping him up, but he couldn't put weight on that side. He sat back down and took off his Converse sneakers – low tops. It would have been better if he had worn high-tops like me. Then, he might not have hurt himself. He couldn't wiggle his toes, which meant that his ankle might be broken. No bone was piercing through his skin, but it might be a fracture. Either way, he wasn't going to be able to hike those hills, ravines and streams. We were lost, Butch was hurt, and the sun was getting lower in the sky. We had forgotten how much shorter the days were in autumn, and the temperature was dropping. We had left our light-weight jackets on a boulder in the stream where we started the game. It had been a little chilly early that morning, so most of us wore our customary lightweight yellow blazer jackets – the style of our gang. They were of no use to us now and besides, the cold air was the least of our worries. I had to get Butch back to the stream, and we weren't certain in which direction to walk. Butch was able to put one arm around my neck and hop on one foot, but not for long. His pain was too great. He had to lie still. White Shepherd knew Butch was injured and tried to lick Butch's ankle causing Butch to cry out in pain. White Shepherd whimpered in response.

"Oliver. You need to leave me here and take White Shepherd to get help. Find a Park Ranger and they'll come in and carry me out."

"Okay, but are you sure you're going to be all right?"

"Not if you don't get going and find help."

"But which way do I go?"

"I don't know. Ask White Shepherd." Butch suggested.

"White Shepherd. Take me back to the stream." I commanded several times before she finally understood what I was asking. She began heading in the direction of the sun, running and then stopping to make sure I was following. We went on for what seemed like forever but finally we got to the stream. All of the other kids were there and I told them what had happened to Butch. It didn't take us long to find a Ranger who got on his walkie-talkie and sent for help. Soon, three Rangers appeared on horseback with a folded up stretcher. They asked me to lead them to Butch, but I was so focused on following White Shepherd that I couldn't remember the way back. Besides, I'm a city kid. I can't get lost in the city, but in the woods everything looks the same.

"I don't know the way. I followed White Shepherd."

"Then command your dog to find your friend," the Ranger said.

"White Shepherd. Find Butch," I said several times. She again started trotting off into the woods and the Rangers on horseback followed, instructing us to stay where we were. Forty-five minutes later a Ranger on horseback, trailing the two horses of the other Rangers behind him, returned and told us White Shepherd led them directly to Butch. He told us Butch's ankle was in bad shape – swollen and colored black and blue, but otherwise he would be fine. The other two Rangers were carrying Butch out of the forest on a stretcher.

"That's quite a dog you have there, Red."

"My name's Oliver, and thanks, Sir. She sort of belongs to all of us." I meant what I said, even though I thought of White Shepherd as the neighborhood dog, this was the first time I had actually *felt* that Good White Shepherd belonged to all of us. They returned with Butch just as the last rays of the sun disappeared and the cloak of night had drawn upon us. There was an ambulance waiting to take him to the nearest hospital. Butch asked if White Shepherd and I could ride with him, and the ambulance guys agreed. Butch gave Liam the directions on how to get home, and the guys had no trouble getting back to the neighborhood. Around 10:00 that evening we were all together at the clubhouse. Butch was on crutches with his ankle in a plaster cast; he had fractured it. Butch put his arms around White Shepherd's neck and said repeatedly, "Good Shepherd. Good Shepherd," while White Shepherd licked Butch's face.

Winter was an interesting time in this first year of White Shepherd's life. She loved frolicking in the snow, but for the most part she preferred staying indoors and sleeping a lot. She spent time at the playground, but most of our winter sports activities were in the building, and White Shepherd was not permitted inside. She spent a lot of time curled up on the carpet in my family living room, keeping Mom and Dad company. Some days and nights she would spend in the homes of other neighborhood kids, and I suspected that her choice of where to spend the night depended on what she was fed for dinner. She enjoyed our occasional snowball fights, and she tried helping us build snowmen. As we rolled giant snowballs down the street, she would push with her head and paws. White Shepherd would sometimes attack our snowmen, destroying them.

Spring arrived, and the neighborhood came alive with kids playing in the streets and the outdoor playground. White Shepherd was now full grown and weighed nearly ninety pounds. Aside from appearing a little overweight from too much food and too little exercise during the winter months, she looked majestic and strikingly beautiful. She followed me to school every morning, hung out in the schoolyard for a little while, barking for me to come out and play. The teacher would make me command her to go home. I don't know what she did while the kids were in school, but she definitely knew when school was out, because she was always outside the schoolyard gate waiting for me at 3:10 when the school day was over. She was truly my companion and protector, a very good shepherd.

One day our school let us out early, so White Shepherd wasn't at the gate to walk home with me. I turned the corner off Morris Street and on to Pie Street. There were three boys from Stillman Street stationed across the width of the street from sidewalk to sidewalk. I recognized them because when I was younger I sometimes played with them, but as we grew older, the bad feelings between the black and white people got in the way of our playing, and things got mean. I learned to be afraid of them, and even though they never physically hurt me, they did call me names and tease me about my freckles and red hair. I decided to keep walking up Pie Street in their direction, thinking I would have to tolerate name calling which didn't bother me too much. As I approached them I said, "Hello guys." They ignored my greeting and the biggest one - the leader among them, Mackey, shoved me against the wall, knocking my books from my hands.

"We're gonna kick your ass, Freckles!"

"Leave me alone, guys. I just wanna go home."

"Things have changed, Freckles. Pie Street is our territory from now on. If you want to walk up Pie Street, you have to pay us twenty-five cents." Arnold was the one demanding the money. I actually taught him how to play half-ball once and even thought that we'd always be friends. This was a naïve thought, because I had seen the teenagers in our neighborhood fight the teenage black gangs several times right outside my front door. My mother would sometimes let our neighborhood kids in our home through the back alley when the police came to break up a gang fight. I knew it was a matter of time before gang violence would directly involve me. I would soon be a teen-ager myself and I was having my first encounter with racial fighting. I was no longer an observer.

"I don't have any money, and if I did, why should I pay you so that I can walk down my own street?" Sleepy Joe stepped forward and gave me a hard shove on the shoulder causing my back to hit the wall.

"Like Arnold said, this is our street, so you have to pay," he demanded. At that moment I realized I was in serious trouble and whether I gave them money or not, I was going to get beat up, so I ran. Not thinking clearly, I ran up an alley that was a dead-end. I turned to face the three boys who were grinning with delight at my foolishness.

"Nowhere to run and nowhere to hide, Freckles. Empty your pockets!" demanded Mackey.

"No way, and no how. You're not gettin' anything from me!" Sleepy Joe punched me in the head and my nose started bleeding. I had on a white tee-shirt and blood was pouring all over it. My nose bled easily. In fact, my nose always bled when I was scared or nervous, a punch wasn't necessary to start the bleeding. I was punched on the side of the head, so it must have seemed strange to the Stillman Street boys that my nose was bleeding.

I started swinging my fist wildly, hitting nothing but air. Then I felt a hard knock on the side of my head, knocking me to the redbrick alley floor. They started kicking me. Through my blood-stained eyes I could see the end of the alleyway, and there appeared White Shepherd. She ran down the alley barking ferociously and grabbed Arnold by the leg and ripped into his flesh. Mackey kicked White Shepherd and she let go, only to grab Mackey's shirt sleeve, tearing it right off his arm. Sleepy Joe and Arnold ran out of the alley and disappeared. White Shepherd stood between Mackey and the only way out of the alley, baring her teeth and growling menacingly. The hair stood up on her neck and along her back making her look even larger.

"Get that dog away from me!" he yelled. I got up, and before I could issue a command, White Shepherd attacked Mackey, knocking him to the ground and taking a bite out of his ear. I knew I had to stop her, realizing that she could easily kill Mackey with one bite of his throat.

"White Shepherd, STOP!" I commanded, as I pulled on her blue bandana that was wrapped around her neck. She immediately backed off. Mackey got up on his feet and ran out of the alley holding on to his bloody ear as he yelled: "I'm gonna kill that dog. I'm gonna kill that dog!"

I knelt and wrapped my arms around White Shepherd, saying over and over, "Good White Shepherd. Good White Shepherd," as I was crying, dripping blood on her pretty white fur. She licked the blood off my face. I took off my blood-stained shirt and tossed it down the alley. White Shepherd and I walked to get my books. I went inside the office storefront of the pie factory, put a dollar bill on the counter and asked for a blueberry pie. White Shepherd and I sat on the sidewalk and shared our much deserved treat. We then went home and told my mother what happened.

"I knew it was just a matter of time before something like this would happen. I was worried about you going to Vare Junior High School when you graduated from Anthony Wayne Elementary School. It's outside of our neighborhood and all the boys from the Stillman neighborhood attend there, including those hoodlums that beat you up today." She hugged White Shepherd and was obviously grateful for her having saved me. She wet a towel with warm water and gently washed the blood off White Shepherd's fur.

"From now on White Shepherd and I will walk you to school and pick you up after school. Those boys will always be after you now. Luckily school will soon be out and we won't have to worry about those Stillman Boys for a while."

There were only three more weeks of school left. I was one of only two boys from our neighborhood that didn't go to Catholic schools, because even though I was baptized Catholic, I wasn't raised one, and if you weren't a Catholic, you had to go to the public schools. In fact I didn't have a religion. Anthony Wayne Elementary School went up to the sixth grade. It was where all the non-Catholics went to school, which meant most of the kids were from outside of my Irish-German Catholic neighborhood, and most of them were black folks. Fortunately for me, from Kindergarten through sixth grade, Anthony Wayne was situated in the middle of my neighborhood, and it was across the street from Vare playground, the main hangout for my friends. I was one of the few kids in my neighborhood who felt comfortable around black people because I spent a great deal of time in classes with them and playing games in the schoolyard, we were friendly. This school year - seventh grade - the situation had changed dramatically because seventh and eighth grades were held at Vare Middle School, which was a longer distance to walk. It was in the heart of the Stillman Street Boys' neighborhood, and we were getting older. All of this meant potentially big problems for me. Fortunately, seventh grade was just about over.

My mother and White Shepherd accompanied me to and from school. During the school day, there were name callings and some pushing and shoving between me and the Stillman Boys, but the teachers kept a close eye on the children, so nothing serious happened. The school administration agreed to let me out of school twenty minutes earlier than everyone else. It was my mother who insisted on this special treatment. School was finally over and it was time to enjoy a summer of play – especially with Good White Shepherd.

Good White Shepherd

She Canine Shepherd Mama
Black & Tan & Strong & Mad
Taunting boys invade your land
Sticks & Balls & Pie Street Games
Aggression breaks the cage your in
Now's the time to take revenge

The boys, they scatter running scared
One stands like a statue
Others run like the wind and
Climb drain pipes and fences
To escape your fangs
And the pain therein

Sink your teeth catching flesh
The boy, he cries and can't break free
They beat you hard to break your grip
It takes your master, his chair and whip
To tame your fury and let loose the boy
Who teased you for years and now he's in tears

To protect your young, was your intent
Six pups and one a runt
A white shepherd female
To be given away
To the boy you bit
On that fateful day

White Shepherd he names you
The mascot of the 'hood
Friend of all, old and young
Rescuer of little girl and adventurous boys
To he whom you shared so much joy
You protect from ones who sought to destroy

The enemies of your best human friend
Threatened to kill you, again and again
Oliver will do whatever it takes
To ensure Good White Shepherd
Lives her life with a promising fate

BOW & ARROW

"Yo Oliver, I heard your cousin Jimmy Blair from New Jersey is visiting this weekend and that he's never been to the city before. Let's show him the city boy version of the country," Liam said, apparently eager for another adventure.

"What do you have in mind, Liam?"

"Let's take him up on the 25th street El and teach him how to hop trains. We'll ride out past the lakes and over to where the Public Television Station has its tower. I heard there's a barn with horses. I want to check it out. Are you up for it?"

"Yeah, sure, let's ask some of the guys if they want to go. White Shepherd can't come with us. We might do some train hopping and that's definitely one thing she can't do. I'll ask Ranger to keep her in his yard so she doesn't follow us."

My cousin Jimmy Blair was the same age as my cousin Butch, but he was bigger and very clumsy. He had a head full of curly flaming red hair and a face completely covered with freckles. The size of him would make anyone think twice about getting him mad, but the fact is, he was a gentle soul and was even a little afraid of other people, especially city kids. Along with a few of my other cousins, I had visited Jimmy Blair lots of times in New Jersey, which is in the middle of nowhere; just lots of trees and farm land with houses spread far apart. We had fun though, exploring creeks, climbing trees and helping ourselves to apples and peaches from farmers' orchards. We even threw stones at cows just to make them run. Jimmy Blair had always wanted to visit the city, but his mother would never allow him. She said it was too rough. His father had recently become ill and my Aunt Sis offered to take care of Jimmy Blair for a while. So, here he was, a country boy in the city for the very first time.

Liam and I rounded up the boys and we assembled at the clubhouse. "We'll climb up onto the El through the coal yard. It's easy to get up there by way of the coal chutes. Since it's Saturday the trains shouldn't be making any coal deliveries, and if we're lucky, we'll catch a slow moving train heading out past the lakes." This was Liam at his best: giving instructions and planning out strategies.

34

We walked to 25th and Mifflin Street to the coal yard and climbed the barbed wire fence, being careful not to catch our skin on the razor sharp wire. I took off my sweat shirt and tossed it over a section of the barbed wire, making it a little safer to climb over the top. I got a few tears in my shirt. Most of the other kids did the same. I didn't think to tell Jimmy Blair about this strategy. Jimmy Blair caught his pant leg while trying to make it over the top and made a big tear, barely missing his leg. He fell 6 feet to the ground and was a little scraped up, but luckily nothing was broken. His extra insulation of body fat and muscle made him sort of bounce off the gravel.

"Hey let's play King of the Coal Hill!" cried Liam as he stood on top of a 15 feet mound of coal. Immediately everyone, except for Jimmy Blair and me, began climbing to the top. One by one they shoved each other down the mountain of coal, replacing one king after another until Liam stood unchallenged, pounding his chest like an ape and yelling like Tarzan.

"I'm the King of the Coal Yard," he triumphantly yelled.

"Yeah, and you're as black as the ace of spades. And so are the rest of you," I hollered as Cousin Jim and I laughed at their coal soot black faces and clothing.

"Let's get 'em, boys," yelled Jonathan Sheehan.

The boys chased us around the coal yard. I ran toward one of the coal chutes and began making my way up its slippery slope. The coal chutes are like giant sliding boards and I escaped my pursuers in the nick of time. Jimmy wasn't so lucky. Jonathan tackled him to the ground and everyone began rubbing coal soot into his hair, on his face, and all over his clothes. I made it to the top of the chute and scurried on to the train tracks. The El was an elevated train track held up by giant steel reinforced concrete pillars spread 10 feet apart. The El made a diagonal path through our neighborhood. Since the trains moved through a residential area, they weren't allowed to go faster than five miles per hour, making it possible for boys to hitch a ride, as long as we were careful.

There were two sets of train tracks – one for each of the South and North bound trains. As I looked around the train tracks I saw a long line of boxcars. All of them were enclosed. None of them were the usual open coal cars. I began looking them over, noticing the heavy locks on the huge sliding doors. The rest of the boys made their way up the chute and onto the tracks.

"Look, a big steel bar, let's see if we can break locks off of the boxcars," Jonathan Sheehan said with a tone of determination. Jonathan was the smallest kid in our gang and he was always trying to make up for his size by doing daring and crazy things. He also liked to make other people feel afraid of him. He had three older brothers – the Sheehan clan. They were among the toughest and most athletic kids in the neighborhood, and Jonathan was the exception. So he tried to make up for his lack of physical strength and agility by being daring.

"Hey, there's a boxcar halfway open," said Luke. "Let's see what's inside."

Since there was already a boxcar without a lock and halfway open, everyone ignored Jonathan's suggestion and ran over to the open boxcar.

"I'll keep a lookout on this side," I yelled. "Luke, you keep a lookout on the other side. If anyone comes we'll head down the coal chute."

Jonathan Sheehan and Liam slid open the huge door. "Holy crap! Look at that!" cried Jonathan.

"Fireworks! There must be a hundred crates in there, at least," said Liam.

Leaving our post, Luke and I ran over to the boxcar. I was amazed at what I saw: wooden crates with the words "South Carolina Fireworks Company," and specific names for the kind of fireworks were labeled on each crate: hammer heads, cherry bombs, roman candles, fire crackers, bottle rockets and much more. We were astonished because fireworks were a prized commodity in our neighborhood. There was lots of money to be made and fun to be had. It was obvious someone was here before us; there were several crates broken open and a third of the box car was empty.

"I'll climb in the car and start handing down crates. We need to form a line all the way over to the coal chute. We can send them down the chute and hide them in the yard, and then we can get them after we return from the horse stables," Liam instructed.

"Forget about the horses, let's just unload the whole damn car and take the fireworks to the clubhouse right now," said Jonathan.

That suggestion made sense to Luke and so he expressed approval. "I agree with Jonathan. We can go to the country anytime, but this is a one shot deal. We should go for it."

"Yo, Liam. If you want to go to the horse stables that badly then go ahead, but I'm getting all the fireworks I can," exclaimed Jonathan.

"Oliver. This is stealing," Jimmy Blair said with a slight quiver in his voice.

"Don't worry about it, Jimmy, this is what city kids do for fun. No harm in it. It's similar to taking fruit that had fallen from a farmer's tree – unless we get caught, a risk that makes it all the more exciting. Think of it as taking advantage of an opportunity. The boxcar is already open. We're not going to listen to Jonathan and break any locks. Stay by the coal chute in case a railroad cop comes along, that way you can get away quickly." He didn't appear to be made more at ease by my less than reassuring words.

Not another word was spoken. We began unloading the crates and sending them down the chute. Six crates were sent down when Jimmy Blair shouted to me, "Oliver, someone's coming and he's carrying a big stick and wearing a uniform."

"Railroad cop!" I shouted.

"Quick. Get down the chute," yelled Liam.

We all slid down the chute, our bodies piling up by the fireworks crates. Luke was the second one down, after Jimmy Blair. After we were all safely down the chute, Luke immediately ran under the chute and started shaking its supports. We caught on to what he was trying to do and, to our surprise, we were able to knock loose the main support. The chute came crashing down. Up above was the railroad cop waving his big stick and yelling for us to stay where we were. We started throwing pieces of coal at him, and I think Luke hit him on the shoulder – he backed off and disappeared from sight. We quickly went to work breaking open one of the crates and stuffing fireworks into our clothes. The crates were too heavy to get over the fence.

"Let's take what we can and hide the rest under piles of coal. We'll come back for them later. That railroad cop isn't finished with us. He probably has a walkie-talkie and is calling the police, so let's move fast," cried Liam.

We did as Liam instructed and within ten minutes we were all over the fence, including my big, heavy, clumsy cousin Jimmy Blair, who didn't bother stuffing his clothes with fireworks. He spent the entire time climbing over the fence – this time he used his shirt to cover the wire. We ran most of the way to the clubhouse and spread our cache on to the floor of our meeting room. The feeling of excitement at what we saw lying in front of us was dizzying.

"Let's divide everything equally," Luke said.

"Hey. I want to set some off right now. Who has a match?" said Jonathan.

"Wait! Remember. There will be cops looking out for kids setting off fireworks. We just found a boxcar opened and helped ourselves to fireworks. We don't want to get caught. It's better if we just stash this stuff and let some time pass before using them. And we have to swear a sacred oath right now not to tell anyone. All agree say 'aye'!" Liam commanded.

"Aye!" We all shouted.

Liam made so much sense that not even Jonathan Sheehan opposed him. We had to be smart about this and make sure we didn't get caught. Liam also said that we shouldn't go back to the coal yard for the rest of the fireworks for a few days because the police would probably be staking out the place for our return. This was the hardest thing for us to agree to because we left a lot of fireworks behind. Perhaps we'd get lucky and they'd never uncover our stash under the coal piles.

It was only 10:30 am. We had the whole day ahead of us. "Why don't we go out to the horse stables and bring some of the fireworks with us? We could set them off out by the lakes somewhere," I suggested.

"How do you suppose we're going to get out there without hopping a train or walking on the tracks?" said Bones. This was the first time he had said a word all day. He was a quiet, tall and skinny kid; and he too had a head full of red hair and a face dusted with freckles – fairly common among the Irish Catholics.

"We can walk down to Passyunk Avenue and get on the tracks past where the El ends. That way we'll be beyond the train and coal yards where the railroad cops don't patrol the tracks."

"Great idea, Oliver, it's still a risk, but what the hell. We only live once, right boys?" Liam cheered.

"Right!" we all chimed in.

So we each put a few cherry bombs, hammerheads and firecrackers in our pockets and headed on our way. We were careful to avoid the El so we walked several blocks west but parallel to it, moving in a southerly direction. When we got to Oregon Avenue we went east, then turned south again on 22nd Street. Upon reaching Passyunk Avenue, we headed up an embankment that supported the railroad tracks and we were, well – "back on track." There were no standing trains, and no signs of any coming, so we walked along the tracks. Remembering the result of not instructing Jimmy Blair on how to climb a barbed wire fence, I began to explain to him how to hop a moving train.

"Listen carefully to me Jimmy. When a train comes it won't be moving too fast, but running alongside it will make it seem like it is moving slower than it is, depending on how fast you can run. Are you a fast runner?"

"I guess I do all right. How fast do I need to go?" he nervously asked.

"As fast as you can without losing your footing, 'cause if you fall - well, it's possible you could go under the train and the game is over, but that's never happened to anyone that I know of," I replied.

"Crap! I'm not going to do it!" he said.

"Jimmy. You can do this. It's a lot easier than it sounds, and it's only dangerous if you don't do it right."

"Yeah! That's what I'm afraid of," he stammered.

"All you have to do is pick a boxcar and focus your eyes on the ladder on the back of it. They all have them and they are positioned toward the side of the back end. You run along side the boxcar and as the ladder approaches you grab on to it with both hands and pull yourself on. It's sort of like hopping on a moving merry-go-round in a playground – just a lot scarier and more fun."

"He could always walk the whole way. It's only 8 miles or so. And then again, he might get nabbed by a railroad cop and have the crap kicked out of him," said Liam in a teasing tone.

"There aren't any railroad cops on this part of the tracks, and we're not going to leave him behind. You can do this Jimmy. Trust me. Just watch a few of the other guys go first, and then I'll watch you before I get on." I tried to sound as reassuring as possible. He was looking quite scared.

"Jimmy Blair, you're just a chicken crap country boy with no guts and no heart. We should never have brought you along," said Jonathan Sheehan.

"You stay out of this, Sheehan. I remember that the first time you hopped a train, we practically had to drag you on and you pissed your pants."

"Screw you, James. What makes you think you're such hot crap all of a sudden? Every time you get in a fistfight your nose starts bleeding before anyone throws a punch and the fight is over. I think you just fake it so you won't get your ass kicked."

"You're always trying to start trouble, Jonathan, and nobody stands up to you because they're afraid of your brothers. If it wasn't for them, you wouldn't get away with pushing around the kids in the neighborhood."

Jonathan Sheehan and I did not get along. I was a skinny kid, and he had it in his head that I was one of the boys that he might be able to beat in a fistfight. He might have been right! Although he also knew that I never backed down from a challenge and to push the issue too far would mean a showdown. Then, if he lost a fight with me, his status among the younger kids in the neighborhood would diminish. I was the youngest in our group and most definitely had the least physical strength and my overall physical appearance was non-threatening – but I had a lot of heart. In fact, one of my nicknames was "James-Heart." Truth was I was just as afraid as anyone else.

"I should kick your ass right now," Jonathan yelled angrily.

"Stop this crap," yelled Liam, "If there is any ass kicking to happen around here it's going to be done by me. Quick, get ready, here comes a train."

The train was moving very slow, about 5 miles per hour, which was good for us. We hid from the view of the engineer, positioning ourselves along the slopes leading up to the tracks. We formed a line with Liam in the lead, then Luke, followed by the rest, with me last and Jimmy Blair just in front of me.

"Now watch Liam and everyone else carefully," I told Jimmy.

Liam grabbed onto the boxcar ladder with relative ease, grinning as he looked back toward us. The slow train made it easy for everyone. It was time for Jimmy Blair to go. He was apprehensive, but to my surprise and his, he had no trouble catching the ladder and pulling himself on. His left foot dragged briefly on the ground, scoffing up his sneaker a little. I guess being a country boy, climbing trees and swinging on ropes to splash in the deep pools of creeks had served him well for this adventure. I ran alongside the train and it seemed to be picking up speed. As I grabbed onto the ladder and placed my right foot onto one of the rungs, it slipped on the greasy metal and both of my legs were dangling as I held on tightly with my hands. I looked down and saw the steel wheels and tracks and thought of my legs being sliced in half if I were to fall. This thought caused a rush of adrenaline throughout my body giving me the strength needed to hoist myself securely onto the ladder. Beads of sweat were dripping from my brow – it felt like a close call.

The ride went quickly, and as we approached the TV tower, following Liam's lead, we leaped off the train one by one, some of us keeping our footing while others rolled away from the tracks onto the large rock gravel, causing scrapes and bruises. My cousin Jimmy Blair was one of those who got a little banged up. He would certainly have a few scars as reminders of his city adventures.

The train tracks were set high above the farm-like property nestled in a small valley. It had a house, a small barn, and a horse corral. The property was purchased by the public television station and so there was a high tower for transmissions. We ran down the hill and spread out over the property. Eventually we were all assembled in the barn-corral area, petting horses, and hanging out on the fences. Several kids who were quite a bit older and a lot bigger than our group appeared on the scene and they gave the impression that they were in some way connected with the operation of the property. They did not like us being there and immediately began to threaten us. One boy had an archery bow with a drawn arrow and as he approached us he pointed the arrow directly at Jimmy Blair.

"Hey, big boy! I think I'm going to shoot you through the heart with this arrow. What do you think of that?" The boy spoke with a threatening tone and he had a menacing look in his eyes. From his appearance and manner, there seemed little doubt that he was capable of doing what he said.

"Please don't. I'm not from around here. I didn't do anything wrong. I'm from New Jersey. Please don't hurt me." Jimmy Blair began to cry, tears streaming down his face.

"Ah, look at the big baby. Do you want your mommy?" he said mockingly.

We were shocked. All of the other alien boys were brandishing various weapons: baseball bats, tire irons, large sticks, car aerials, etc. They had us surrounded and they were in a position to severely harm us. Everyone was frozen with fear. I assumed he was picking on Jimmy Blair because he was obviously the oldest and biggest in our group. I had invited my cousin to come with us, since he was visiting my family, and the responsibility for his safety weighed heavily on my shoulders. Suddenly, and without thought, I stepped in front of Jimmy Blair and with the arrow-point leveled a fraction of an inch from my heart, I said, "If you truly think that killing someone is going to accomplish anything other than pain and misery for the rest of your life then go ahead and shoot. But before you do, ask yourself if you want to spend the rest of your life in jail. We only want to go on our way. We're gonna turn away and leave and if you are determined to injure us then you will do so with our backs turned. Come on guys. Let's get out of here."

I turned and walked away and my peers did the same. The gang of boys seemed stunned by our boldness and they just stood there speechless without moving as we walked away. When we reached the base of the hill we started to run up toward the tracks. As we reached near the top of the hill, the barnyard boys came running after us with renewed intention to inflict harm. I realized that there were lots of small and large round stones, perfect for throwing and for slingshots. I also remembered the fire works.

"Let's light the cherry bombs and hammerheads, quickly, and toss them! Get out your slingshots. This is war! I shouted

We were carrying "strike-anywhere" stick matches, which lit easily on the large rocks surrounding us. The fireworks exploded with thunderous sounds, landing quite close to the rival gang. A few even exploded very close to their bodies. The boy with the bow managed to get off an arrow, and it zinged past Bones' ear, missing his head by mere fraction of an inch.

"Pick up rocks and throw them," I yelled, "And watch out for those arrows. Try to hit the boy with the bow." I placed a cherry bomb in my slingshot, lit it, aimed it at the boy with the bow and let it fly. Simultaneously, he shot an arrow in my direction. I hit the ground, dodging the arrow just in time. Luke had a great arm and one of the rocks hit the boy with the bow in his chest just as the cherry bomb exploded near his ear. With the explosion he fell to the ground screaming. It had worked. The rival gang gave up their pursuit and ran back toward the safety of the corral as rocks were raining down on them. The rocks and stones were far more dangerous than the fireworks. We were jubilant. The plan had worked!

"That was awesome," said Luke. "Did you see me hit him with that rock? That son-of-a-bitch must have thought a hand grenade hit him when that cherry bomb exploded at the same time. Nice shooting Oliver! You were freakin' awesome, man. Where the hell did you get the courage to pull that one off? You just took charge of everything, kiddo."

"Yeah, man. Thanks Oliver. That kid would have killed me. This place is nothing like Jersey," Jimmy Blair said, still shaking from the experience.

"You had an arrow pointed at you, while I almost got one through my freakin' head," said Bones, "Now that's freakin' scary!"

"Good thing we had those fireworks. I loved the way we scared those ass-wipes. Too bad we didn't have real hand grenades. It would have been cool to blow those suckers to pieces," Luke said with a menacing tone.

"Luke. It's fortunate for everyone that all we did was scare them. Otherwise we'd be headed for jail. I'm grateful we got away without getting hurt. Sorry, Jimmy, for putting you through this, but it was exciting, wasn't it?" I said.

"Scared shitless is more like it. You city boys are plum crazy," Jimmy Blair replied.

"Yo, this kiddo deserves a little special treatment." Liam signaled for the boys to pick me up and lift me high above their heads and everyone cheered, "Hip, hip, hooray for Oliver!"

Our high spirits gave us the energy to walk the tracks all the way back to Passyunk Avenue, since no trains came along. The walk took us awhile, but the time went by fast as we each told our version of the experience over and over, adding more and more embellishment with each re-telling.

Bow & Arrow

King of the coal hill
The boys did play
Behind forbidden fences
They toss and tumble
Blackening their bodies
From fossils' withered dust

Train tracks lure them
And there they find
Explosive treasures
A boy's gold mine
To take is to steal
This they do not believe
For they learned to live
By a different creed
Finders' keepers
That's their golden rule
And who can blame them
This lesson they learned
From the inner city school

Daring young lads
They run, jump and climb
On the box car ladders they stride
Showing grace & athletic skill
On steel tracks they ride
Risking lives - yes it can kill

Leap while moving
Fly through the air
Stumble and rumble
On rocks they did fall
Stupid behavior
Although to them
They are bold
If they were wiser
This story couldn't be told

Down to the corral
To see horses they can't ride
Admiring their intrinsic beauty
Like the iron maiden, technologies bride
Enemies appear, older - angry young boys,
Pointing bow & arrow at cousin's chest
Scaring the hell out of the rest

44

Oliver, the best in his nature does rise
Stepping in front of his bewildered kin
Protection is his surmise
This is his aim
The tip of the arrow
Has a different claim
Straight through the heart
Wow, this is insane

"Go ahead and shoot me
But this you must retain
The rest of your life you'll
Live in vain"
Oliver turned his back and walked away
His friends they followed up the rocky hill
Heading for the tracks, escaping the kill

Angry boys take up pursuit
Swish flies an arrow
Missing its mark
"Quick, use your sling shots
Toss at them stones
And cherry bombs too"
Scaring them off we continue our route

The boys are jubilant
A military triumph
Praise to Oliver
For his courageous deed
And military tactician
Yes he took the lead

But if one were to read between the lines
These boys were quite foolish
Yes this can't be denied
For in every act
Their lives they did risk
And Lady Luck
Must have held back her fist

GOD'S HOUSE

On a sunny Sunday morning I came upon Liam while walking along the sidewalk of our city block.

"Yo, Oliver. Want to come to mass with me?" Liam asked.

"I'm not a Catholic. They won't let me in," I replied.

"They have no way of knowing you're not a Catholic. Come on. It's really cool, and if we get bored we'll leave," he said convincingly.

The church was a huge granite monolith with ornate statues of the saints perched on both sides of the wide front steps staring at all who entered with stone cold eyes. I wondered if they could see inside each person's mind. There were several slate steps leading up to the huge wooden doors. The structure reminded me of castles I had seen in books and on TV.

"Hey, Liam. God is rich."

"You're not kidding. Wait 'til you see all the money he gets."

As we walked through the doors, Liam dipped his fingers in a bowl that had water in it and made the sign of the cross, touching his forehead, chest, and then each shoulder. He instructed that I do the same.

"Why does everyone do that?" I asked.

"I think I understand it. We're just supposed to. All the Catholics do it. It is the sign of the cross that Jesus died on. I guess it protects us."

"From what?"

"The devil."

"What's the devil doing in God's house?" I asked.

"He's evil and sneaky."

"We're being sneaky," I replied.

"That's different. The devil tries to steal your soul when you're not looking."

"Maybe he already has my soul 'cause I haven't been protected by religion," I said nervously.

"Nah! You're not a Catholic so the devil doesn't want your soul," Liam said, with a touch of pride in his voice.

"Then I am glad I'm not a Catholic," I said resolutely.

46

"Yeah, and that's why you might end up spending eternity in hell."

"Just because I'm not a Catholic doesn't mean I should be treated with meanness. God isn't cruel, is he?"

"No. God is love, but the devil is cruel. Listen. Do everything I do while we're in here," he whispered as he knelt down on one knee and made the sign of the cross again before entering the pew.

Liam and I took a seat in the front row, which was occupied entirely by old people. As I glanced along the pews, I noticed everyone had gray hair and their bodies looked stiff with serious, almost angry expressions. I wondered what they were so mad or worried about. Maybe it was because we were sitting with them and we weren't supposed to be.

As we sat down I looked around God's house. It had vaulted ceilings with ornamental decorations, paintings of Jesus doing this and that. Statues were everywhere with candles and people kneeling before them in prayer, putting coins in little boxes as they lit candles as offerings for loved ones. The pews were made of beautiful oak wood and they were filled with people of all ages; men in suits and women in their Sunday finest, boys with hair carefully parted all slicked down with hair cream and little girls wearing white, pink, or light blue dresses – the girls reminded me of angels. Light was streaming through the large stained glass windows – each one showing Jesus doing all the important things in his life: working in a carpentry shop with his father, teaching children at his feet, feeding and healing the hungry and sick, teaching his apostles, walking on water, carrying a cross, being put to death and then rising up into heaven with angels all around him. The story was clearly laid out for me to see in stained glass; beautifully illustrated with light filtering through and making the multi-colored glass bring the pictures alive with radiance. Two priests were at the altar wearing long flowing robes as they gracefully moved with spiritual authority about the altar, and there were young boys assisting them in every ritual. I wondered if they were all related to God in some special ways because they looked so important.

"Liam, this place is huge."

"Yeah, I guess God likes it that way. It's his house."

"He has a lot of houses. There are Catholic churches everywhere in South Philly. Why does he need so many houses?"

"He has a lot of children and they don't all live in the same neighborhood, so he needs a lot of houses."

"Who's his wife?" I asked, feeling stupid for not knowing what everyone else probably knew.

"He doesn't have one," Liam replied. "Well, since Jesus is his son, I guess it's Jesus' mom, Mary. But she was married to Joseph and they had baby Jesus without doing it."

"Doing what?" I asked.

"Gee, don't you know anything? It's what adults do to make babies." Liam said, his face slightly blushing.

"Oh, yeah, my parents do that every Saturday. They disappear into their bedroom for a long time and make funny noises. So how'd Jesus get made if Mary and Joseph didn't do it?"

"It was a miracle. She was a virgin."

"Do you think God did it with her?" I whispered disbelievingly.

"Man, you have a twisted mind. But come to think of it, maybe He did. It makes sense since God is Jesus' father and Mary is his mother."

"Do you think Joseph got mad at God for doing it with his wife?" I asked. "I don't want anyone doing it with my wife when I get married - God or anyone else," I added.

"God can do whatever He wants, and Joseph and Mary were lucky that He chose them to have His son," Liam replied.

The mass had begun and I couldn't understand a word they were saying. Liam told me they were speaking God's language: Latin, and that only the priest could understand what God was saying. That's why they were priests and that's why we needed them, so they could talk to God for us and ask him for favors and stuff. There was a lot of sitting down, standing up, kneeling and reciting words after the priest said something. The priest held a big silver cup above his head and chanted some important words, and then he drank some. He raised up a round white disc, broke off a piece and put it in his mouth. Then people started getting out of the pews. They walked up to the altar and kneeled before the priest, and he gave each of them a drink from the cup and then placed a very thin smooth round cracker on their tongues.

"Liam," I whispered, "what are they doing?"

"You see that stained glass window with Jesus and all those men eating?" he asked.

"Yeah."

"Well, that was the last time he ate supper with them and he told them to do this to remember him."

"Do what?"

"Drink his blood and eat his body."

"You're kidding. Is that what they're doing? Gross!"

"It's not really his body and blood - well sort of. A priest can turn the wine in the cup into his blood and the wafer into his body."

"Wow, that's powerful magic."

"Yeah, that's why they're priests. No one else can do that."

"Why do people do it?"

"Jesus told them to."

"But why?"

"So we could all remember him and that he died for our sins – you know the stuff we all do that we're not supposed to do. Adam and Eve were the first to sin and they passed it on to us – we're all guilty.

"How come Jesus died for something he didn't do? And what did Adam and Eve do that was so bad that he had to die for them – us?"

"They ate an apple from the Tree of Life after God told them not too."

"Jesus died on a cross because Adam and Eve ate an apple; that sounds stupid to me."

"It was a very special apple that gave them knowledge about being naked. Oliver, stop asking so many questions. It's all a mystery – and don't ask me what a mystery is, just accept it. So you want to try it?"

"You mean eat and drink Jesus?"

"Yeah."

"I'm not a Catholic."

"So? I don't think God will mind, we're just kids, we don't know any better."

"Yes we do. That's why were talking about it," I said sternly.

"Well, then I'll just go to confession and it will all be made better. I'll tell you about confession later," said Liam.

"That's not fair. You have a way out and I don't. You have to tell me about confession right now if I am going through with this," I insisted.

"Okay. When a Catholic sins, he goes into a closet where he is alone with a priest, and the priest can't see who it is because of a curtain between them. The sinner tells the priest what he did wrong, and the priest forgives him and tells him to say some prayers a bunch of times and then God is no longer mad and you won't go to hell."

49

"Can I go to confession?" Liam looked puzzled by my question.

"I guess so; there are just a few sentences you have to learn."

"Wow, what a deal. You get to do something bad and then get off the hook by fessing up without the priest even knowing that it's you and you're safe from hell and the devil."

"You do pick up some things fast. The best part of the deal is your parents don't have to know a thing and your soul is safe," said Liam.

"What's a soul?"

"That's the part of you that either goes to Heaven or hell forever! It's the big prize the devil and God are battling over," said Liam emphatically.

"All right. Sounds crazy but I better play it safe so let's do it!"

I was surprised by my eagerness to do this; it felt naughty and exciting. I was so curious about drinking the blood and eating the body of Jesus that I couldn't resist the temptation. We knelt at the altar and I carefully watched what the other people were doing as the priest approached us holding the large silver cup and a plate with little round white wafers. The priest said, *"The Body and Blood of Christ,"* and then each person mumbled something back as they sipped from the cup and then stuck out their tongues to receive the wafer - Christ's flesh. The priests came to Liam and I observed them from the corner of my eye as I held my hands in the prayer position. Liam took the blood and body of Jesus, saying amen after the priest recited the magic words. I was so nervous my hands were shaking and beads of sweat were forming on my forehead. Thoughts raced through my mind: *What's it going to taste like? Will the priests know that I'm not supposed to do this? What happens if we get caught? Is God watching?* The priest approached and I looked up into his eyes: they were smiling toward me and I immediately felt welcomed – and suddenly it felt surprisingly good to be here in this moment – and he said: *"The Body and Blood of Christ."* I said, *"Amen,"* and calmly sipped the blood, which tasted like really bad grape juice, and I stuck out my tongue and received Jesus' body, which tasted like an unsalted cracker that quickly dissolved. I slowly stood and moved away from the altar with its elegant décor, fancy crosses, and the stained glass window filtering the light as Jesus was ascending into heaven. I was transfixed by the feeling generated by the ceremony and the intensely focused attention of everyone participating as a community in a sacred act. I was bedazzled. A feeling of lightness came over me and I felt as though I was moving in a dream. I then turned and followed behind Liam. I looked around at all the people kneeling in prayer and wondered if they had this same gentle feeling in their hearts – I did not know the words to fully describe this feeling, I just knew that others must be feeling it too.

We took our places in the pews kneeling with our hands in the prayer position. After everyone finished receiving the body and blood of Jesus, they went back to the pews. Soon there were men with long poles and a wicker basket attached on the end, one person for each main aisle. They walked along extending their poles into each pew as people put money and envelopes into them. As the basket passed in front of us Liam but a few coins in; I felt awkward as I had no money and the man stared at me. I blushed and didn't look at him. He moved on. I whispered to Liam, "That's a lot of money. Why are people giving them money?"

"It's for God."

"Why does God need money?"

"He has to pay the priests and nuns and stuff."

"No doubt about it, God is rich!" I was awed by his wealth and power.

The priest stopped talking and everyone began to leave God's house. I followed Liam as he walked through the exit door and we were soon in the morning sunlight. We quickened our pace down the sidewalk and I moved as though I was walking on air, there was a feeling of lightness in my body, a spring in my step.

"So Oliver, how do you feel?" asked Liam with a tone of anticipation in his voice.

"I feel like someone took a wash cloth and cleaned me up from the inside, like giving my mind a bath."

"Yeah, me too, I feel all pure and clean inside!" Liam was excited but the tone of his voice had a distinctive and unusual quality of softness and gentleness.

"So Liam, how does Jesus' body and blood make us feel this way?" I wanted to know everything about it.

"I think that's a great mystery," he said with a far away look in his eye.

"Well then, I have to ask ya. What's a mystery?"

"That's the answer to your question. It's something that no one can explain because it's only for God to know."

"I don't understand, Liam. It doesn't make sense to me."

"God doesn't have to make sense."

"Why?"

"God is the Creator."

"Oh!" I replied, and I thought:

I've never felt this way before, so calm and light. Is this God I am feeling? Did the body and blood of Jesus make me feel this way? Do the priests have special powers? I don't like it that God doesn't have to make sense; my mother gets annoyed with me when I don't make sense. Why can't we see him? Is the devil real or just made up to scare kids into being good? There's a lot I don't understand; too much mystery! God is rich and he has a lot of people working for him. There certainly is a lot to think about, and I feel good and confused at the same time. All in all, I'm glad Liam brought me to God's house!

As we turned the windy corner of Dickinson Street and on to Bambrey Street we saw my mother and her friend Ranger looking underneath a parked car. Mom saw me. "Oliver, come and help Ranger get his turtle, it got out of his house again and ended up under this car."

I crawled on the asphalt, grabbed the box turtle and safely returned it to Ranger. "Thanks Oliver. I don't know how he got out. Your mother is always nice to me."

It's true. My mother was one of the few adults who even spoke to Ranger; and I suspected that he let the turtle out on purpose as an excuse for talking to my mom; this was the second time this week his turtle got out. My mom was very pretty and Ranger liked her. He was an alcoholic. That wasn't unusual, as most adult males in the neighborhood liked their booze; he was also more than a little crazy. Ranger lived with his mother and never knew his father. His sister went nuts and was in a hospital for insane people. His mother never spoke to anyone. She always dressed in black with a veil over her face, and she went to work every day but no one knew where she worked. Before TV became popular, radio was the main entertainment and Ranger, whose real name was Karin, worked as a storyteller for the radio show telling stories about The Lone Ranger – the mysterious masked cowboy who rode a white horse, shot silver bullets, rescued folks from the bad guys and had an Indian named Tonto as his sidekick. Ranger was very good at telling stories and every Saturday night the kids on our street would gather around him on the stoops in front of his house and listen to him.

I liked Ranger because he liked my mom and I could tell he was a gentle, kind man although very sad, and he had lots of animals, including snakes. Once I saw an animal in his window that looked half rabbit and half cat with back feet and a tail like a rabbit with the head and front paws of a cat - very weird. And besides, it was probably his fondness for animals that caused him to let me keep Good White Shepherd in his backyard. Ranger always smelled as if he needed a bath. His clothes were filthy and his hair was greasy and never combed, all the more reason why adults didn't like being around him. Mom said he wasn't always dirty and drunk. It was after he lost his job that he became that way.

Liam and I decided to go in my house for doughnuts and milk and before we finished eating our snack, we heard the sirens of an ambulance. The truck with flashing lights soon came up our street and stopped in front of Mrs. Hines' house. The ambulance guys were inside her house for almost a half hour. Everyone waited outside their houses with concerned looks on their faces. The ambulance guys brought Mrs. Hines out on a stretcher. I pushed through the crowd and looked at her. She was staring right through me with those familiar cold glassy blue eyes set in an angry, wrinkled face. I gasped as I realized she wasn't actually looking at me because she was dead.

"Whoa, can you believe it? Mrs. Cheapo is dead. She must have been over 90. I thought she'd never kick-the-bucket. Now we won't have to run errands to the store for her no more and we don't have to listen to her yelling every time we play kick-the-can in the street." Liam could be chillingly cold.

"Gee, aren't you the sympathetic type." I responded. Liam was right though. Mrs. Hines was legendary for being tight with her money. She was always asking Liam and me in her heavy German accent to buy her stuff at the store – several times a week, and she only gave us a penny tip, if we were lucky. She was mean-spirited and no one liked her, not even my mother who rarely had an unkind word for anyone (except for the police and my father).

"Oliver, let's climb up the tree in her backyard and see if we can open her bedroom window and check out her house."

"What for?" I asked.

"Don't you want to know what it looks like?"

"Why?"

"Because I heard she's rich."

Everyone on Bambrey Street believed Mrs. Hines was rich. I'm not sure why, I guessed it was because she was tight with her money and she wore fancy jewelry and clothes.

"I don't know Liam, isn't it disrespectful to enter the home of a dead person? Besides, it's illegal too."

"Who cares? She's dead and I've never seen anyone visit her. She has no family so no one owns the house. No one will care if we go in her house."

"So why don't we just see if the front door is unlocked and walk right in?" I asked.

"Are you stupid? Everyone will see us."

"If we're not doing anything wrong then so what," I replied.

"We know we're not doing anything wrong, but other people might not see it that way. We should do this now before anyone else gets the same idea." Liam was making sense. He had a way of making doing bad things seem like the right thing to do and I went along with him far too often.

"Okay, let's go." I surprised myself with the enthusiasm in my voice.

We walked around the corner on to Tasker Street and went up the alleyway and climbed into Mrs. Hines' back yard. "Let's try the back door and windows first," I suggested. They were locked, so we climbed the tree, one of only two in the Bambrey Street alleys. The other one was in Liam's back yard, which was how we usually got on to the rooftops. Liam was the first to reach the thick limb that was close to the second floor bedroom window. He discovered it wasn't locked. He slid open the window and into Mrs. Hines bedroom we went.

Her bedroom was fancy by any standard. I had never seen such nice furniture. The bed had a canopy over it and the head board was shaped like a heart with names carved into it:

Albert & Marianne Hines

"So that was the name of her husband. I wonder how long he's been dead and if she has any children," said Liam.

"My mom said her husband died when she was young before she had a chance to have kids. Hey Liam look at this picture." It was their wedding picture. Mrs. Hines was beautiful and her husband was dressed in a military uniform. I looked closely at the picture and was able to read on the lapel of Mr. Hines dress coat:

Captain Albert Hines, U.S. Army

"Wow, he was a captain in the Army. Maybe he died in a war and Mrs. Hines was left with lots of money," I said.

"Well, if she was left with lots of money she sure didn't give us any. I'm going to look around and see if she was an old money bag," Liam started rummaging through a dresser drawer and he hit the jackpot. "Look at this!" He had a fist full of dollars in his hands.

We opened all the drawers and found money in each of them; I felt like a pirate that just found a treasure chest. As I was cleaning out one of the drawers I glanced at the wedding picture and then a feeling of dread and guilt gripped me.

"Liam this is wrong. We shouldn't be doing this," I said with my voice quivering.

"Are you nuts? There's a fortune here. Finder's keeper is what I always say."

"She's dead and the money probably came from her husband's death, so that makes it a double jinx," I said.

"Jinx sminx, money is money and we're rich!" Liam was oblivious to any wrong doing. He moved through the bedroom like a whirling dirt devil finding money everywhere: under the mattress and rugs, inside socks and pillow cases; Mrs. Hines had money stuffed in every nook and cranny.

"Liam this is stealing, plain and simple. We shouldn't be doing this."

"You're worried about getting caught aren't you? Think about it; she has no children and not once has she ever had a visitor. You said yourself that she was completely alone in the world. How many times did you go to the store for her and got no tip or a measly penny?"

"Lots of times."

"Exactly my point; she owes us."

"Yeah, but not this much money. We wouldn't get this much in ten lifetimes worth of tips."

Liam was not slowed down by my expression of guilt. He opened a closet and discovered it was filled with fancy purses and shoes. My eyes just about popped out of my head. I started opening purses and pulling out money and jewelry. There were loads of silver dollars, old coins bigger than any I had ever seen. Our pockets became so stuffed with paper and coin money that my pants fell to my knees from the weight. We began tossing the money on the bed. I too was intoxicated with having my hands on so much money, more money than I had seen in all my lifetime. The only time I saw more money than this was in movies and that wasn't real; this was definitely real.

"We're rich, we're rich, we're ri ..."

"Oliver, not so loud. Someone might hear us." Hearing Liam's words caused me to freeze with fear. "What's the matter with you Oliver? You look like you saw a ghost," said Liam.

"What if we get caught? We could end up in prison for the rest or our lives." My knees began to shake. I felt afraid and guilty at the same time.

"Snap out of it kiddo. This is the pot of gold at the end of the rainbow. No one owns this money and we found it. Who do you suppose would get this money if we didn't find it? The police? The government? Who? As long as we don't tell anyone where it came from no one can take it from us."

"We're going to jail, I know it." I was feeling really scared.

"Oliver listen to me," Liam grabbed me by the shoulders. "If we let the police have this money they'll take it home for their own use. Remember that gangster movie where the police and the hoodlums steal the money from the poor boys home and the priest saves the day with a miracle?"

"Yeah, that was a good movie." James Cagney was in it and what's his name? The little Irish guy …" Liam interrupted me, "That's the one and what I'm saying is this is *our miracle,* a gift from God. Where were we before we came here?"

"Getting a turtle for Ranger."

"No, before that knucklehead."

"We were in God's house! So are you saying this is all okay because we went to God's house, had communion, felt all squeaky clean inside (that feeling was gone), and that makes it okay to steal a dead lady's money. I think you're as nuts as Ranger. Liam, this isn't a miracle, this is just stealing. You're the twisted knucklehead. We should get out of here before the devil takes our souls."

"You're definitely going off the deep edge kiddo. The devil has no part to play in this. In fact, I think angels are responsible for this. Yeah, that has to be it; our guardian angels are rewarding us for going to church today and having communion."

Liam was trying hard to convince me that what we were doing was a good thing. And he did get me thinking: What if the only other place this money ended up was in the hands of crooked police and politicians? Then poor people who could really use the money would never get it. We knew a lot of poor folks. In fact, we were poor folks. Angels or devils, either way this money would do a lot more good in the hands of those who really need it; the perfect parting gift from an old lady who was lonely all her life because she hoarded her wealth and shared it with no one. Our finding the money could be a way for Mrs. Hines' life to have some meaning as well as being our just reward.

"Liam, we can be like Robin Hood. We can share this with those who need it the most."

"Eh, sounds okay to me. How much are you talking about sharing?" he asked.

"All of it! It makes perfect sense. If Mrs. Hines were to stand before God and ask what she needed to do to get into heaven I think the entrance fee would be to give all her money to the needy," I said.

"That reminds me of a bible story a nun told in class about Jesus talking to a rich man, exclaimed Liam. The man wanted to know what it takes to get into heaven. Jesus told him to give away all his money to the poor and to follow him. That's what Mrs. Hines should have done with her wealth, and now she'll probably spend eternity in hell. By us giving her money to the poor we can help her get into heaven. She's not here to do it herself so we'll do it for her. It's written in the bible so it has to be right. It is our religious duty to accept this money. Oliver I think you're right. Let's save Mrs. Hines soul. She won't go before God until she has her funeral so that gives us a few days."

"Perfect! We can be angel helpers. But I don't want to take jewelry, which would be stealing. Poor people don't need fancy jewelry," I reasoned.

"They could sell it for money," replied Liam.

"And who's going to buy it? Everyone in this neighborhood is too poor to buy this stuff."

"How about just feeling pretty wearing something nice? Wouldn't you like to see your mother wearing pearls?"

"Not if she knew they came from a dead woman. I just don't feel right taking jewelry."

"Imagine police wives walking around with fancy bracelets and earrings when it could be the girls in our neighborhood wearing them," argued Liam.

"And you don't think their parents and the police will ask where the jewelry came from? Giving away jewelry might get us caught and if we're going to be successful playing Robin Hood and in saving Mrs. Hines' soul, then we have to be smart and not get caught. Money can be spent and saved and it isn't traceable but jewelry is. Everyone knows Mrs. Hines jewelry; it would be a dead giveaway that we broke into her house," I reasoned.

"All right already. We'll leave the jewelry, but I think it's a mistake." I was glad that Liam gave in. Otherwise, I would have abandoned the whole idea.

Having resolved our moral dilemma we moved through every room gathering only money. We were now on a mission from God and we took it seriously. Liam said he imagined us being Jesus' disciples. When we felt confident that every cent was now on Mrs. Hines' bed we looked around for something to carry it in.

"How about pillow cases," I suggested.

"Perfect, it'll look just like those bank robbers on TV with sacks of gold."

"Liam. We're not thieves, remember?"

"I know, I know, I was just saying, cheese and crackers, lighten up will ya."

We filled two pillow cases with coins and bills (singles, fives, tens, twenties – there weren't any hundred dollar bills; pennies, nickels, dimes, quarters, half-dollar and silver dollar coins) and stood by the bed staring at the sacks of loot.

"Where should we hide it?" asked Liam.

"Not in the clubhouse, and we can't risk hiding it at the playground. In fact, I can't think of a place in the neighborhood where there's a guarantee that a kid won't find it. And most importantly, we can't let anyone else know about this. Robin Hood would have been better off without his band of merry men. He and Little John should have worked alone. He could have avoided all those battles with the evil sheriff. We have to take it somewhere safe and we want easy access so we can give it to anyone who needs it at anytime."

"Robin Hood got into those fights because of a girl, and I agree that we can't tell anyone," said Liam. "I know just the place to hide the money."

"Where?" I questioned.

"I go to a special place whenever I want to be alone."

"Why do you feel like being alone?" I asked.

"Oh you know, like when mom and dad fight or I get the strap for being bad."

"Where's the special place?" I asked.

"Okay you have to promise not to tell anyone. It has to become your special place too, so spit and shake!" We spit into the palm of our hands and shook on it and then Liam told me about his secret hiding place.

"One day I followed the priest who rings the St. Aloysius Church bells and learned where the key to the stairwell door is hidden. Ever since then I go up there to sit and watch the sunset. We just have to be careful not to be there on the hours when they ring the bells."

"Is there a chance the priest will find the money?"

"No. There are rafters that lead to the top of the steeple where there is a small platform. The priests are too big to get up there and besides there is no reason for going there, it's just empty space. I hide everything there."

"Do you mean stuff you steal? Liam, are you stealing things and hiding them in God's house?"

"Here we go again. Let's just say it's my private treasure chest and leave it at that, except now it will be our treasure chest."

"No. It's where we are keeping Mrs. Hines' money so we can help her get into heaven," I reminded him.

"Of course. Come on, let's toss the sacks into the yard and get out of here."

"Bad idea. It's still only morning, Sunday morning in fact, and we can't take the money to the church yet. Let's take it to the roof and when it gets dark we'll take it to the church," I suggested.

"That's a better idea. I'll go out first and you pass them to me," said Liam, "I have a stronger throwing arm to toss the sacks onto the roof."

"We have to clean up our mess before leaving, otherwise the police will know someone was here." I didn't want the police to have any reason to be looking for us.

"Good thinking Oliver. Let's leave it just the way it was, minus the cash," Liam laughed as he started to clean up. He moved very fast and was quite good at cleaning things up which surprised me, having been in his bedroom and never having seen the floor.

It didn't take long to straighten up our mess and get the money on the roof. Once we were safely on the roof we realized there was no way to hide the over stuffed pillow cases. I was worried that if we left the loot someone might discover it, like a neighborhood kid or adult. We decided to spend the day hanging out on the roof; occasionally going into Mrs. Hines to use the bathroom and get a drink of water. The first thing we did was count the money one sack at a time. I had a better mind for math than Liam so he left most of the counting to me. $3,527.11 was the grand total. We were giddy with delight and Liam started rambling on about how he was going to spend the money. I repeatedly reminded him that we were going to give it away to save Mrs. Hines and to help folks in the neighborhood. We shared ideas on who to give the money to. There were lots of candidates to choose from, and the hardest decision would be how much to give and to whom. I realized that we had to do it anonymously or people would start asking questions. At first Liam didn't like the idea of people not knowing who was doing the good deeds until he recalled another saying of Jesus': *"When being of service to others, do not let your right hand know what your left is doing."* I asked him what it meant and he said a nun told him that when he does something good for another person, it is best to keep it a secret and expect nothing in return, that way it has special meaning. I told him that I thought Jesus made a lot of sense. This is how we decided to become the secret saints of the Gray's Ferry neighborhood.

I liked spending time on the rooftop; it gave me a sense of freedom and I enjoyed the view. I particularly liked watching the alley cats walking along the back yard fences and occasionally I'd see one on a distant rooftop. Many of these cats were the offspring of the most famous cat in the neighborhood, Little Panther. We fed her kittens and gave up the practice of hunting alley cats in honor of her untimely death at the hands of a man we knew as Mr. Nasty. Pigeons were everywhere and Liam kept throwing stones at them until he accidentally hit a window, risking our hideout. I walked along the rooftop looking down into back yards. Everyone had a small yard where they kept their trash and garbage cans. Liam noticed several old baby carriages and said he'd like to get a hold of them because he had an idea for using the wheels.

The sunset was quite beautiful from the roof. It sank behind the oil refinery. The smoke coming from the tall stacks looked red, orange and pink; it looked pretty but the smell was awful. I could see numerous Catholic Churches; they were usually the tallest and most ornamental buildings and there wasn't a neighborhood that didn't have one, along with a playground and ten times as many taverns. The thought of churches and taverns made me chuckle when I thought there were so many more places to drink alcohol than to worship God. When it got dark enough we tossed the sacks into Mrs. Hines' back yard, climbed down the tree and made our way through the alley and to the church.

"It's best to enter through the back way; that's how the priests and nuns go in. You'll have to keep watch on the convent doors to make sure no one is looking while I go inside to see if anyone is in the church."

Liam left me standing guard over the sacks of money in a narrow passageway between the church and the convent as he went inside. After a few moments he came out and said all was clear and that he had already unlocked the door to the bell tower. We moved fast and within seconds we were climbing the bell tower's creaky wooden steps with money sacks over our shoulders. When we reached the bells Liam put down his sack and pointed above the bells' ropes to a small wooden platform near the peak of the steeple. He jumped and grabbed on to the edge of the platform and pulled himself up, then he instructed me to hand him the sacks. There wasn't enough room on the platform for the two of us and the money, which was fine by me because I wasn't confident that I could pull myself up like the athletic Liam. As we were leaving Liam suggested we take $10.00 as a reward. I was hungry, not having eaten since our milk and doughnuts got interrupted by the ambulance earlier in the day, and the thought of a Philly cheese steak and vanilla milk shake from Jayne Devlin's made my mouth water, so I agreed.

Jayne Devlin's store was across the street from St. Aloysius Church, so within minutes we were placing our order. I put a nickel in the jukebox and played "Cherish" by the Associations, and then we played pinball while waiting for our food. I noticed two girls sitting in a booth and didn't recognize them. I asked Liam if he knew them. He told me they were from the upscale Italian neighborhood just on the other side of Moore Street and that they went to St. Aloysius. He rarely saw them in our neighborhood except when they were walking to and from school and church.

"Introduce me to them Liam," I insisted.

"Hey Sandy and Chrissie this is my friend Oliver. He wants to meet you," he blurted out across the room. The girls looked at us and smiled. I walked over and asked if we could sit with them.

"Sure, there's plenty of room. I'm Sandy and this is my twin sister Chrissie." I was mesmerized by Sandy's caramel chocolate eyes and long brunette hair. Her cheeks and nose were dusted with freckles and her smile was warm and friendly. Her sister Chrissie looked completely different with blond hair and blue eyes, not like a twin at all and she appeared to be a little shy. I took my place in the booth next to Chrissie and Liam sat next to Sandy. Our food came; it was the best steak and shake I had ever tasted - a nice reward for the good work we accomplished that day. We offered to buy the girls something to eat but they were sipping sodas and politely declined our offer. We didn't talk about much. I mostly told them I went to public school and they were curious about what it was like. They were surprised to hear that I wasn't a Catholic and that I dared to take communion. I asked them if they wanted to meet us again at Vare playground, and they said their mother didn't like them to go to Vare because it was for kids from the other side of the tracks. I asked what that meant and Sandy said people from her mostly Italian neighborhood thought they were better than the people from the Irish community.

After eating we walked home. As we turned off Tasker St. and on to Bambrey we saw three cop cars parked in the street outside Mrs. Hines' house. Several cops were standing on the sidewalk in front of the open door, laughing and smiling, back slapping each other. Liam and I stood still at a safe distance, silently watching them to see if there was any indication that they knew someone was in the house before them. Their good humor told me they didn't know. And then I saw dangling from one cop's pocket a silver and pearl necklace; they were taking the jewelry just like Liam said. Liam stared hard at the policeman as he watched him stuff the dangling necklace deep into his pocket.

"See Oliver, I told you. They're going to take all the jewelry for themselves. We should have taken it while we had the chance," he whispered with a slight hiss in his voice.

"I'm just glad they don't suspect anything and we have the money. Who knows, if we had taken everything, instead of them being happy, they might just be looking for you and me. I'm counting my blessings." I countered.

"I have half a mind to ask them what they plan on doing with Mrs. Hines' things. That should make them nervous." Liam didn't like police, and he couldn't let go of the idea that we should have taken the jewelry.

"Liam this is one of those times when I am going to demand that you keep your mouth shut and do nothing. So far I've gone along with everything you wanted to do since I ran into you on your way to God's house this morning. We are lucky and let's not tempt sister luck or we'll end up in jail. So let's quietly walk past the police and go into our houses."

Liam ignored my little passionate speech. As we walked past the police Liam said to my astonishment, "Good evening officers. Find anything interesting in Mrs. Hines' house?"

"And a good evening to you lads. We're tidying things up in there; such a shame she died a lonely woman. According to government records she has no family," said one of the officer's kind enough to speak to us.

"Anything of value in there?" asked Liam with a sly sounding tone and a smirk on his face.

"Nothing to concern you boys so get on home before your parents start worrying; it's just about past your bedtime I would think."

"We used to go to the store for Mrs. Hines several times each week for groceries and she always wore nice clothes – and jewelry," Liam's tone was now sounding a little more accusatory which the officer picked up on.

"Like I said it doesn't concern you boys. It is a government matter so get on home – NOW!" he commanded.

We turned and briskly walked away. Beads of sweat were forming on my forehead and the palms of my hands were clammy.

"Are you nuts talking to the police like that; we're lucky they didn't whack us with their nightsticks." Nightsticks were weapons all cops carried on their belts that they used to beat criminals. They also carried guns and some of them kept rifles in their cars.

"They can't beat us for asking honest questions," commented Liam.

"Yeah, well your honest questions could have made them think we knew something that they don't want us to know, and if they knew that we know what they are up to, we both know the kind of things they could do to us – like make us disappear or something," I said nervously.

"You're afraid of blue belly blimps aren't you?" Blue-belly-blimp was the name we sometimes used for policemen because their uniforms were blue and most of them had big bellies.

"You better believe I'm frightened and are you telling me you're not?"

"Not as much as you. I just don't like them because I've seen them beat up on drunken people and teenagers, and I know they're thieves," snickered Liam.

"I've also seen them protect people from hoodlums too and don't they make it feel safer to walk down the street at night when you see one on foot patrol?" I added.

"Safer! They walk up and down the streets just looking for a reason to arrest someone. They don't care about you or me. Actually, I think they're afraid of us. Well, not the ones who grew up in South Philly. They're more friendly and relaxed. It's the ones who come from outside the neighborhoods that act mean because they're really afraid of us." I knew Liam was telling the truth. I could always tell when cops were afraid and usually they were the ones that didn't live in inner city Philly. I sometimes had the feeling that they were zoo keepers watching us in our cages.

"Just the same Liam, it's better to play it safe and not draw any attention. What you just did made be real nervous, especially since I asked you not to."

"No harm done. I'll see you tomorrow morning bright and early. We have a lot of good deeds to do. Good night Oliver."

I was glad to be in my bedroom. I laid my head on my pillow and drifted quickly off to a peaceful sleep. That night I dreamed I was Robin Hood. I rescued Sandy from the evil sheriff, who appeared to look like Jonathan Sheehan – a member of our gang, which I found disturbing.

SOUL SAVING THIEVES

Liam's tapping on my bedroom window woke me up from a deep sleep. He was on the shed roof with his face pressed against the window comically distorting his features. I opened the window.

"Liam, it's too early. What do you want?" I whispered.

"The money is waiting for us. Let's get some before the priests serve their early morning mass; we got some disciple work to do for the needy, remember?"

I jumped out of bed, slipped into my jeans and tee shirt and laced up my black high-top Converse sneakers. We exited through the bedroom window onto the cinder block fence and into the alley. We went to the back entrance of the church, which led directly into the area where the priests dressed in their robes before approaching the altar. Upon entering we heard a priest speaking in Latin; mass was in progress. We quickly left before being seen and headed straight for the playground.

"Our timing was off. We'll have to wait an hour or more before going back," said Liam.

"This gives us time to talk about the people we're going to give the money to. I was thinking of Colleen Murphy. She's young and has two little kids. Her husband ran off six months ago, and my mother said she's having a tough time paying rent and feeding her kids. The neighbors have been helping out."

"What about her mother and father? Aren't they helping her out?" asked Liam.

"Mom says they disowned her for marrying Steve. I think that's his name. She said they had to get married because they got in trouble."

"What kind of trouble?" asked Liam.

"I don't know. Maybe Colleen's parents thought he was from the wrong side of the tracks like we are."

"Her parents live on Pierce Street, on the borderline of the Italian neighborhood, and they're just as Irish and poor as we are," replied Liam.

"Well, whatever the reason, her parents won't let her live with them and they aren't giving her help. I think we should give her money," my voice was shaking as I spoke.

"Okay Oliver. She's our first charity case. How much money does she get?"

"I don't know, what do you think?"

"There are a lot of people we haven't talked about yet so we need to spread it around. Then again, since mostly everyone is poor we should focus on just a few special cases." Liam impressed me with his thoughtfulness. With all his mischievous wrongdoing, he had a good heart and sensible brain.

"I agree. Let's take it one case at a time and maybe just one person each day."

"Two hundred dollars will cover her rent for a couple of months and give her food money," Liam suggested.

"How do you know that will cover her rent?"

"My parents pay fifty bucks a month rent. What do your parents pay?"

"My parents bought their house last year for $4,600. It was a big step because no one else in our family besides my grandparents bought their homes. Most people are afraid of being in debt to the banks, but my grandmother talked my mother into it when they found out the owner wanted to sell. If we hadn't bought it we would have had to move. My grandparents and aunts chipped in for a down payment and we borrowed the rest from a bank."

"Wow, your family is on their way to being rich, owning your own house. That's really cool. Maybe my parents can buy our house. I like the tree in the back yard."

"I suppose the angels would go along with that, Liam. We could give your parents down payment money to buy the house, if it's for sale."

"Good idea, we'll have to check into it, but for now how do we get the money to Colleen?"

"Let's just stick it in an envelope with a note saying it's from a secret admirer and put it in her door mail box," I suggested.

"Easy enough. Let's do it."

We went back to the church, and within fifteen minutes we were in and out with the money; $200 for Colleen. Liam took another $10 for our own use, stating that it was to cover expenses for doing good deeds. I didn't argue. Liam dipped his hand into a bowl of holy water and sprinkled it on the money; he said he was blessing it. We bought an envelope for two cents at Jayne Devlin's store. Liam wrote the note because he has good handwriting. Colleen lived on Bambrey Street so we just strolled up the sidewalk, and hung around the front of her house, and when we were certain no one was looking, we slipped the envelope in the mail box slot on her front door.

"I feel great Liam! Mrs. Hines is a step closer on the stairway to heaven and Colleen won't get thrown out of her house. Her kids aren't school age yet so she can't work. Mom said she won't go on welfare because she's afraid they'll take away her kids."

"Let's do something with the $10." Liam seemed to ignore everything I just said as if it didn't matter.

"Don't you feel good about helping Colleen?"

"Yeah, I feel all clean inside. So what about going to Willie Marconi's to shoot pool."

"On a real pool table like professionals?" I asked.

"Definitely! I'm tired of playing on that toy table in your basement. I want to play real pool."

"Marconi's is where the best pool shooters in the city play. They have tournaments. Do they let kids in?" I was excited about the possibility of watching pros play pool.

"Don't know but we're about to find out." Liam began to walk briskly toward Snyder Ave. As we passed the playground we ran into Jonathan Sheehan and Eddy Maloney; Liam invited them along. I didn't like the idea because they might get suspicious about the money and we agreed not to let anyone find out. I couldn't express my disapproval out loud but I gave Liam a severe look. He just smiled at me and shrugged his shoulders.

It took forty minutes to walk to Willie Marconi's. Jonathan Sheehan said he had been there before and had seen Minnesota Fats shooting around some balls for fun; I didn't believe him. He was always bragging about stuff that we often learned was bull crap.

We could see the big letters spelling out the famous name on the front of the stone building. We crossed the street and walked up to the windows and stared inside. There were several rows of pool tables and no one was in there except for a man behind a counter with a cash register. When we entered the pool hall, I was struck by how large the room was when entering the pool hall. The walls were lined with pool sticks and ball racks. The air smelled like cigar smoke and beer.

"Can I help you boys?" asked the man behind the counter with a strong Italian accent.

"We wanna play pool," said Jonathan Sheehan.

"You boys are a little young to be in here. Who has the money?" asked the Italian man.

"ME!" Liam spoke proudly as he stepped up to the counter with a ten dollar bill extended toward the man.

"The big spending Irish boy; whatcha do, knock off an old lady?"

"No, I stole the collection box from the local Catholic Church." The man laughed as he placed a rack of pool balls on the counter and took the ten dollar bill.

"$2.50 an hour for a table; choose your table and sticks and try not to tear the green felt."

"Hey guys let's play on the table over by that window; that's where I watched Minnesota Fats play," Jonathan spoke proudly. The man behind the counter laughed and said, "Fats and the rest of the pros play only on the best tables and those are in the back room. It takes five grand to pass through those curtains." There it was: proof that once again Jonathan's brag was another lie to try and impress us. We shook our heads while trying to avoid looking at Jonathan's embarrassed face. Liam carried the rack of balls to the table and began setting them up.

"Me and Oliver against you and Jonathan," he said while looking Eddy straight in the eyes.

"Perfect! Rack 'em up," said Eddy.

"That creep doesn't know what he's talking about. I watched Minnesota Fats knockin' around balls with Mr. Marconi himself right on this very table," Jonathan's voice sounded slightly whiney.

"Fuggettaboutit! And shoot some pool," said Liam. We all laughed, including Jonathan. While I eyed the table to get ready to break the rack, Liam got some change and bought four bottles of coke from the machine. Then he walked over to the Italian man's counter and bought four Philly's Perfecto cigars. There were no questions asked. He gave each of us a coke and a cigar. We lit up the cigars, guzzled down the cokes, played several games of pool, drank more cokes, choked on cigar smoke while flicking ashes on the floor and acting cool.

"Liam, you stole this money didn't you?" Eddy spoke in a challenging and slightly condemning tone, "probably did take it from the church collection box."

"I just got lucky and found it on the curbside on Morris Street, not far from your house as a matter of fact." Liam smiled at Eddy as he spoke. Liam sure could keep a cool head in the most surprising situations, while at unexpected times he'd blow his top.

We shot pool for two hours and, all in all, had a great time. Jonathan and Eddy proved to be slightly better pool players than I had expected. The 10 bucks ran out so we split the pool hall and headed home.

As we reached McKean Street we heard fire sirens and soon there were fire trucks speeding up 27th Street. I could see smoke rising in the air and without discussion we ran toward the fire scene. It was a house on 28th and McKean. There were people everywhere. I made my way through the crowd and saw a woman and two small children sitting on the ground by an ambulance. The woman was holding her children and crying loudly. The person standing beside me was telling another person what had happened. The father got everyone out except for the infant child and when he went back in for her the building collapsed and they died in the blaze. I was stunned by what I had heard. One moment I'm having fun with friends and suddenly I am standing before a blazing grave with broken lives sitting before me. Then I saw Sandy walk over to the mother and children. She gave them long hugs and sat there with them. I wondered if they were her family or friends. This was Italian land and Sandy's neighborhood so at the very least they were her friends. I tried to get closer but the police started edging people away from the scene, telling us to go home. The woman and the children were placed in the ambulance and Sandy turned away and walked into the crowd. I tried to follow her but there were too many people and lots of confusion and she disappeared. Seeing her giving comfort to that family made me feel something I had never felt before. I imagined that if angels were real, then they must be like Sandy.

"This is really sad," said Liam, "I wonder if they're Sandy's family?"

"I was thinking the same thing. I saw no one else with the mother and children other than Sandy. Maybe she's a friend of theirs. I want to help them Liam, we could give them some of our …" Before I could finish speaking Liam jabbed me in the ribs with his elbow. He didn't want me to say anything about our money. Eddy and Jonathan were standing very close by and could hear me.

"Give them some of your what?" asked Eddy.

"Kindness, prayers and whatever else might help," I replied.

"Since when did you become religious?" asked Jonathan.

"I went to church with Liam yesterday and I know that people pray for people who need help and these people need help. We should give them some of our prayers," I responded, feeling a little guilty about lying only because I was using prayer to do it.

The firemen eventually put the fire out. My lungs were stinging from exposure to the smoke. Fires were fairly common throughout our Philadelphia neighborhood, which is why there is a fire hydrant at one end of every city block. The crowd broke up, with a few of us hanging around for the dead bodies to be uncovered. I asked Liam if he knew where Sandy's house was but he didn't. Our friends left, leaving Liam and me sitting on the curb watching smoldering smoke drift into the late afternoon sky. Finally the firemen uncovered the father's body from beneath a pile of collapsed charred boards. The father was burnt black and the body of the infant was held close to his chest. I puked in the gutter and tears escaped my eyes. A hand touched my shoulder. I looked up, it was Sandy.

"The family is new to the neighborhood. I have been babysitting for them since they moved here three months ago. The father worked in the Navy Yard. He was an immigrant from Italy and barely spoke English. The mother, Maria, was born in America but her parents are Italian and don't speak English. Maria speaks both Italian and English," Sandy started crying. I felt awkward not knowing how to comfort her. I placed my hand in hers.

"Little Sophia was my sweetheart – so innocent and beautiful and now she is gone forever. Life is so cruel. How can there be a God that allows infants to die; and such a horrible death, too?" I had no answers for Sandy, knowing very little about God and religion. It was all mysterious to me.

"Sometimes things just happen because of accidents with no reason at all and no one is to blame, God or humans. It's just the way it is." The words just came out.

"It is so unfair!" she cried and placed her head on my shoulder. I stroked her hair. Liam was silent and his eyes looked as though his thoughts were far away. The three of us sat there for what felt like a very long time, then Sandy said, "I need to get home or my parents will be worried about me. Chrissie is very upset and my parents are with her. I left the house hoping that they might somehow still be alive. I saw the two of you sitting here."

"We'll walk you home," I offered.

"That's okay. I live just around the corner and it's best that my parents don't see me with you guys; you know, being from the wrong side of the tracks and all." She was able to release a slight smile as she walked away.

"Can I see you again soon?" I called to her.

"Tomorrow for lunch at Jayne Devlin's; 12 o'clock sharp and don't be late, Oliver."

Liam looked as though he didn't hear a thing that was said; he just continued staring off into space. I tapped him on the shoulder and we rose from the curb and drearily walked home.

That night my sleep was restless as I kept seeing burned bodies and flames. I heard voices of people screaming and wanted to save them but my body was paralyzed and I felt helpless. I kept waking up covered in sweat and I thought that I must be dreaming of hell.

After many hours of restless, interrupted sleep I finally drifted off into deep, pleasant dreams. Sandy and I were laughing while swinging on swings. I woke up with a smile on my face and then I remembered the burnt bodies as I coughed up remnants of smoke in my lungs. Sadness once again closed in on me. It was already mid-morning which was unusual for me – the first up in the family – the one who caught the early worm, as my mother always said about me. I lay in my bed thinking of the events of the last two days: God's house, Mrs. Hines, Colleen, the fire and Sandy. I thought of how hard it must be for Sandy. She was close to the infant, Sophia, and the entire family. I thought of Sandy's hand in mine and the wetness of her tears on my shoulder. After getting dressed and bidding good morning to my brother and mother I left the house without eating breakfast. I knocked on Liam's door. His sister answered and said he wasn't awake yet. I decided to go to St. Aloysius church to get a few dollars to buy Sandy lunch. I expected Liam to come with me but since he was sleeping and it was 11:30, I thought it was okay to get the money on my own.

The church was empty of nuns and priests, and only a few candle lighters were saying prayers for loved ones. I slipped into the shadows of the giant pillars that held up the vaulted ceiling and made my way quietly to the steeple chase stairwell. I had some difficulty climbing up to the wooden platform above the bells but after several tries I was successful. I took $20 – twice as much as usual – a ten and two fives. On my way out of the church I stopped by the candles and knelt before them. A statue of Jesus' mother, Mary, was towering above me. I stared into her face and saw an expression of gentle sorrow as she appeared to be staring right at me. It felt like she knew what I was feeling. I lit a candle and placed a five dollar bill in the collection box. I didn't pray because I didn't know how. I just thought of the mother and the two children that survived the fire and felt sorry for them. As I stood up to leave I noticed a person coming out of what looked like a closet door, the place where Liam said people went to secretly 'fess up to

71

wrongdoing. I was surprised to see that it was Sandy. She walked out the front doors of the church without seeing me. I wondered what she could have possibly done that caused her to go into the priest's closet. She was so perfect that I couldn't imagine her ever doing anything she wasn't supposed to do. Instead of leaving through the nuns' back entrance, I too walked out the front doors (dipping both hands in the holy water for extra blessings on the money) and crossed the street to Jayne Devlin's store, where Sandy was waiting for me.

"Good afternoon Sandy," I said as cheerfully as I could, even though I felt a strong sense of sadness hanging in the air like thick cigar smoke.

"I'm happy to see you, Oliver. Where is Liam?" she asked.

"Still sleeping. Maybe he'll join us later. What do you want to eat?" I asked.

"I'm not really hungry. I'll have a coke though."

I ordered two fountain cokes and grabbed a package of Butter Scotch Krimpets, deciding to wait for Liam to show up before ordering a hoagie and shake.

"I'm really sorry about your friends." I avoided her eyes as I spoke.

"They are so poor, Oliver, and now they have no place to live and no father to support them. Her parents are old and live in one room with a shared bathroom down a long hallway, and their health is bad so they can't help. Last night Maria stayed in the Bishop Neumann Norbertine Priests' Priory but they can't do that forever."

"Is that where the priests and brothers live who teach at the Catholic High School?" I asked.

"Yes. My mother works in the principal's office and sometimes she works as a cleaning lady in the priory when they need extra help. My older brother is a priest and he lives in the priory."

"Wow, does your brother have those special powers to change wine and bread into the blood and body of Jesus Christ?" I asked.

"He serves mass once in a while but only when the older priests have other things to do. He usually just assists them, but he is ordained. He is used in all the Catholic churches in the Gray's Ferry neighborhoods."

"What's that?"

"What's what?"

"Ordained?"

72

"You're the only person I know who isn't Catholic. I'm not really sure what it means but I do know if you're not ordained you can't say mass. I don't know what to believe anymore. All the praying we do doesn't seem to protect anyone from harm. I prayed every night for the Santora family and now look at them. I spoke this morning with a priest thinking there must have been something wrong with the way I was praying or the fire wouldn't have happened." A tear rolled down her cheek and her lips began trembling. I stared at her lips and they reminded me of rose petals quivering in the wind.

"How can asking God for good things for people bring about bad things? That makes no sense, Sandy."

"The priest told me that it was God's will and that He works in mysterious ways. But I just don't understand why God would do something like that."

"I don't know much about God, priests or mysteries, but I do know that stuff happens with or without God and prayers. I think you and God had nothing to do with the fire. It was probably caused by burnt toast." For some reason that made Sandy laugh and she couldn't stop. Her laughter was contagious and I too laughed until tears streamed freely down our faces.

"I wish there was something I could do for them. I'll continue to baby-sit for Maria's children, but she needs a place to live. I hope the church continues to help her out." Sandy was very worried about the welfare of the Santora family and I, too, wanted to help.

"Maybe we could raise some money and find a place for them to rent or buy," I suggested.

"Good idea but rent is expensive not to mention food and clothing," said Sandy.

"Yeah, I know. It cost us two hundred dollars to help Colleen and her kids and that will only last for a few more months." Suddenly I realized what I had just said.

"You did what for whom?" Sandy's eyes were wide open with surprise.

"You have to promise that you won't tell anyone." I was excited and nervous. I was about to tell Sandy our big secret, which thrilled me, but doing it without Liam's permission made me feel uneasy.

"I don't like making promises blindly. Tell me first. Then I'll consider promises," she said wisely, although it sounded unreasonable to me.

"You have to promise because it doesn't involve just me, and, and … please trust me Sandy." I pleaded.

"Okay, I promise without knowing what I'm promising. You get only one of those." I was taken back by how tough minded she became all of a sudden.

"Liam and I sort of accidentally came across some money and we are using it to help people in need." I spoke real fast as though saying it quickly would make it feel less wrong.

"'Sort of accidentally came across money. How, and how much?" she asked which sounded a little like a command.

"Sandy you're starting to scare me with how you're talking. You sound different."

"Oh, gee, I'm sorry. I guess I'm just all excited about the chance to help my friends and, I am a little suspicious."

"I'll tell you the whole story just like it happened but you can't let Liam know I told you."

"Too late for that!" Liam's voice boomed through the screened window above the booth. "So, Robin Hood, you told her about Mrs. Hines and the money – that's breaking a bond of trust, and now Sandy is our little Miss Marianne. I wonder who the sheriff will be." Liam stared at me with a grin.

"I can explain everything. It's not how it sounds." I replied.

"Relax Oliver, I was going to ask if you wanted to help Sandy with the fire family anyway, but I didn't want to tell her where the money came from." Again Liam had surprised me.

"I didn't plan on telling Sandy about Mrs. Hines' money. It just slipped out."

"This is the first time you gave up a secret – as far as I know. What caused you to make such a big mistake this time?" he asked. I didn't answer him.

"I'm hungry for a hoagie and vanilla milk shake. What about you two? Feeling hungry?" asked Liam. I wondered how he was expecting to pay for the food because we spent the 10 bucks yesterday and there wasn't any change left; but I knew better than to ask in the presence of Sandy.

"I want a pizza steak hoagie and an extra large vanilla milk shake," I called out to Jayne Devlin who just nodded, "how about you Sandy? Whadda ya havin'?"

"And how exactly is this getting paid for?" Sandy asked. "And for your information Liam, Oliver didn't get around to telling me everything about the money - only that you two helped some woman named Colleen get a place to live. You showed up just in time to tell me about Mrs. Hines and her money. She's the German woman who died on your street the other day, isn't she?" I never heard a kid talk the way Sandy did - fast and to the point, and it felt challenging. She caught Liam and me off our guard – something not even adults were able to do.

"We're on a mission to save Mrs. Hines' soul," I blurted out.

"So now you're a priest. Who ordained you?"

"Huh?" was my only response to her quick wit.

"We're going to save her soul by doing good things for people in need by using her money." Liam said proudly.

"And this is something Mrs. Hines asked you to do upon her death? She left you in her will?" asked Sandy.

"That's not how it came about," I said.

"Time for an explanation, boys!" Again she was speaking in that challenging, moralistic tone that was making the both of us feel very uncomfortable.

Liam and I went back and forth telling the story of how we got Mrs. Hines' money, including the total amount, which made Sandy's jaw drop. I put in the part about going to church that morning and how getting the money was possibly directed by angels to save Mrs. Hines' soul and for us to help out people in need. Liam emphasized the part where *he* decided not to take the jewelry and he told her about the scene with the cops.

"You boys are more trouble than a nursery school filled with screaming babies who need their diapers changed. I get the part about helping out the needy, but saving a dead old lady's soul by giving away her money sounds a little like: 'Oh, gee, mom, dad, God made me do it!' A lame excuse if you get caught and it's an aspirin for your guilt." I didn't understand most of what she said, but I did hear she liked the idea of helping the needy.

"So what about us helping out the Santora family; do you think it's a good idea?" I asked.

"I'm not comfortable with how you guys got the money, but if you're certain Mrs. Hines has no family and the government is going to take everything, then count me in."

"Great, so what do we do now? " I asked.

"Not so fast fellows. You still haven't convinced me that she has no family."

"That's easy. We asked the police and they told us the city records show she has no relatives," said Liam.

"Is that right, Oliver?"

"Hey, what are you asking him for? Are you calling me a liar?"

75

"No, I just want to make sure you guys are on the same page."

"What does that mean?" I asked. Sandy was so smart I couldn't keep up with her, yet I enjoyed the challenge. She made me think.

"It means if you two are telling the truth, then you have restored my faith in boys. It means you're not selfish and you do care about others ... and you're not 'really' thieves."

"We are soul-saving thieves," I said proudly.

"Perhaps, but I think it's safe to say that your conscience, Oliver, moved you in a positive direction, turning a bad thing into something potentially, fantastically good."

"All right, then. Sounds like we have Sandy the Italian working with us," said Liam.

"Half & half!"

"What's that?" I asked.

"My mother is Irish and my father is Italian; although my father wants me to marry an Italian to keep the bloodline more Romanesque."

"What are you talking about?" asked Liam. By now I was beginning to follow Sandy's quick wit.

"She's just saying her father prefers Italians over Irish and that she's one of us. Sandy is not so far from the wrong side of the tracks after all."

We spent the rest of the afternoon talking about how we could help the Santora family without anyone knowing where the money came from. We thought about doing the same thing we did for Colleen, but we decided that wouldn't work because a lot more money was involved and we wanted to secure her a home. We couldn't come up with a foolproof plan. We decided to sleep on it, knowing that Maria and her two children had a grace period with the priests in the priory. It was time to pay the lunch bill.

"So which of you hoodlums are payin' for the bill?" asked Jayne Devlin.

"Me" – Liam and I spoke at the same time and then looked at each other with mutual suspicion.

"Go right ahead Oliver. I'll let you cover this one." Liam and I had something to talk about.

We offered to walk Sandy back to the edge of her neighborhood, and as we passed St. Aloysius church, Sandy's priest-brother turned the Taney Street corner and just about bumped into his sister.

"Hello Sandy. Are these guys your friends?" he asked extending his hand to mine then Liam.

"Yes, Angelo. We were just having lunch and they offered to walk me home."

"Fine gentlemen you two are, and handsome Irish lads too. Well, got to be on my way. I was called to say a funeral mass. It's about to start in 10 minutes and the nuns are probably sweating in their 'habits' worrying."

"Excuse me, Father Angelo. Do you mind telling me whose funeral it is?" asked Liam.

"It's for a Mrs. Hines from Bambrey Street. Apparently she has no family. She intended to give her house and everything in it to the church. She didn't have a written will. Father Steinhagen wrote a will for her but she died before signing it. I don't expect there to be many people attending this service. Rumor tells me she wasn't a very nice person and had no friends."

"Can we come?" I asked. Not knowing what made me ask.

"Sure. It's always nice to have young faces in the pews to smile at, and Mrs. Hines would surely appreciate your prayers."

"Well, she sure could use them," replied Liam, "Father, did she have any money or other valuable possessions in the house?" asked Liam.

"No money, stocks or bonds; not even an earring. Although folks say she always wore nice jewelry. I guess she gave it away to some other charity before she died."

Before entering the church I paused for a moment to think. Sandy's brother was a good man - that was easy to tell and it was clear that the church knew nothing about the money, and the cops definitely stole the jewelry. And we were about to attend a funeral service that would hopefully send Mrs. Hines off to heaven. And suddenly a thought hit me like a lightening bolt: WE STOLE GOD'S MONEY!

The three of us were the only people in the church other than a handful of nuns and brothers to assist in the funeral mass of Mrs. Hines. The mass was similar to the one I attended a few days ago with Liam: it was spoken in God's language (Latin), there was communion (we didn't partake), there were some different prayers, and Father Angelo gave a sermon on death as a doorway to another world – heaven. I folded my hands, closed my eyes and concentrated real hard, trying to imagine Mrs. Hines flying up to heaven. And the truth was I felt scared the whole time, and nothing was scarier than going up to Mrs. Hines' coffin to pay our respects.

Liam, Sandy and I went to her casket that was positioned near the altar. We were instructed by a nun to kneel before the coffin and bless ourselves with the sign of the cross. We looked down upon her body dressed in what looked like a wedding gown; all white and lacy. Her hair was silver-blue-gray and her face was painted like a doll – a doll of an old lady with sunken cheeks, tight lips and skin that looked like plastic. She looked gross! And she smelled like cleaning fluid. I couldn't help thinking that God would tell her to take a shower before letting her into heaven. What made me feel even worse was the thought that we weren't helping Mrs. Hines get to heaven, we simply STOLE GOD'S MONEY, and He was probably very angry with us. I didn't have a chance to talk about this with Liam and Sandy, things happened so quickly. I wanted this funeral service to be over so I could get some air and think this through. Sandy placed her hand on Mrs. Hines' hand and closed her eyes. She looked like she was praying. Liam looked slightly amused with not a trace of guilt on his face. I wondered how he did it. How could he know that we stole the money that Mrs. Hines gave to God and that WE STOLE GOD'S MONEY, and be smiling? For me it was like a neon sign going off in my head with sirens and bells. Father Angelo announced that Mrs. Hines was to be buried in a cemetery somewhere in West Philly and all were welcome to attend. We looked at each other simultaneously, shaking our heads side to side. The service finally ended and we quickly left the church.

"We have to get the money to the church right away. It will be easy. It's already in there. All we have to do is stuff it in all the collection boxes. The priest won't kno…" Sandy gently placed her hand over my mouth.

"It's alright Oliver. Everything's going to work out just fine. The church will do what's best for the church and we will do what's best for Mrs. Hines' soul and the needy. I am convinced that you two are working for the angels and I just signed on board."

"I don't get it Sandy. What about Mrs. Hines giving all her possessions to the church? That money belongs to the church or I should say God and WE STOLE GOD'S …"

"Okay Oliver, we get your point. I just need you to hear me out. Father Angelo, my brother, has the inside scoop on the financial workings of the church and I heard him express to my mother on several occasions his discomfort with how they handle things. Father Steinhagen is in the practice of convincing every old person in the parish to sign over their assets to the church. Father Angelo has been trying to get the church to use more of its money for charity in our community, but most of the money ends up going to support schools in the wealthier suburb parishes. He has brought up this injustice many times and he feels he is being punished for his views. Father Steinhagen is a good man but he must do what his superiors tell him to do. Our schools are suffering from a lack of funds so the quality of education in the Philadelphia neighborhoods is far from what it needs to be. And this is also true for the charity needs of the poor, like the Santora family. If we talk to my brother Angelo he just may find a way to help us."

"We can't tell him we took money from Mrs. Hines' house. He's a priest and he would not only make us turn over the money, but we'd end up getting arrested and going to jail." I was feeling very nervous. This situation was getting out of control and all I wanted to do was help Mrs. Hines and poor people.

"I don't think we should do anything," chimed in Liam.

"What do you mean?" I asked.

"No one knows about the money except for us and we should keep it that way. If I heard Sandy correctly, the church is stealing money from the poor and giving it to the rich and I have a hunch that God is pretty pissed off about that. So if we wanna see this Robin Hood thing through and do the right thing, like protecting Mrs. Hines' money and helping the poor, then we have to keep the church out of it and that includes your brother, Sandy." Liam was making a lot of sense but I couldn't help feeling confused.

"How can the church, which belongs to God, be doing bad things?" I asked.

"That confuses me too, Oliver. That's why I think we should talk to my brother."

"I'm starting to feel towards the church the way I feel about the cops. Sounds like the devil made his way into the church," said Liam.

"Well then where is God in all this?" I asked. Liam and Sandy just looked at me with dumbfounded stares. There was a long silence and then Sandy spoke.

"That's why I decided to help you two because knowing what I know from my brother, well, I think God may be asking us for help."

"Then why doesn't He just come right out and say it?" I asked.

"Because God works in mysterious ways, Oliver. I already told you that on Sunday." Liam sounded like he was losing his patience.

"Hey, I'm not the Catholic here. This is your religion and it's looking very strange to me," I replied, "and it looks more and more like we're going to end up in trouble when all we wanted to do was help folks. Now you two want me to help battle the devil inside God's house. Why doesn't God protect his own house?"

"That's what He's using us for. It's the way God does things, working through people," explained Sandy.

"Then why aren't His priests and nuns doing His work? That's what they're paid to do!"

"Because some of them aren't listening to what God wants. They're being tricked like Adam and Eve got tricked in the garden by the snake," said Liam.

"Snake? Garden? Adam and Eve? You're talking crazy. This whole thing is crazy. God sounds crazy. I think I'm going crazy."

"Oliver, it is our religion so just trust us on this. You're right. You're not Catholic, and maybe none of this has to do with being Catholic, but I know the Santora family needs help, and it isn't right for the church to take Mrs. Hines stuff and use it for people who don't really need it. So just think of it like that and forget about all this religious stuff." Sandy was pleading with me and tears began rolling down her cheeks. She really loved the Santora family and I really like Sandy. I placed my hand on her shoulder.

"That's the most sensible thing I heard either of you say. But I agree with Liam that we shouldn't tell your brother about the money. We need to find a way for him to help without giving him too much information. Besides, if he doesn't know about the money then he can't get in trouble if anything goes wrong." I was making sense and my friends knew it.

"I don't think we need the church to help the Santoras," said Liam. "We have enough money to set them up with a house, food and clothing. We can go to Maria Santora and simply give her the money."

"He's right, Sandy. Your brother and the church need not be involved at all." The idea of leaving the church out of it made me feel a whole lot better.

"But what about the church taking Mrs. Hines' house and furniture and using it for some rich neighborhood school?" Sandy reminded us.

"At least they don't have the money," I replied.

"The house is worth as much as the money if not more. Maybe we can get my brother to convince the church to give it to the Santora family, or at the very least let them live there," suggested Sandy.

"Suppose we talk to your brother about the church helping the Santora family. It can't hurt to ask, but remember, we say nothing about Mrs. Hines' money," I suggested.

"I like that idea 'cause there's nothing to lose," said Liam.

"Okay then, let's go talk to my brother and see what he has to say, but before we do that, is it still possible to get into Mrs. Hines' house?" asked Sandy.

"What for?" I asked.

"I'm not sure, maybe there's more money. Did you guys go through any papers? Any additional information we can get may help when we talk to my brother," she explained.

"Let's do it," said Liam. "There might be some money we missed. We never did look in the basement."

"We better do it now before the church gets in there and starts moving things out, if they haven't already," I suggested.

We headed straight for the Bambrey Street alley and into Mrs. Hines backyard. Sandy wasn't comfortable climbing the tree so I went in the house and opened the back doors. Sandy was fascinated by the quality of the wood floors and leather furniture. The living room had a crystal chandelier and fancy lamps, eloquent drapes, paintings and wall mirrors. "This is the richest house I've ever been in," she remarked. Liam went into the basement while Sandy and I began going through drawers and closets looking for anything of interest.

"The police picked this house clean of Mrs. Hines' jewelry," I commented.

"Are you sure the police didn't just take the jewelry to keep it safe from thieves?" Sandy responded.

"Liam and I saw one officer with a necklace dangling from his pocket, and another policeman got angry when Liam questioned them about Mrs. Hines' possessions. I'm convinced they stole the jewelry, although there is a possibility that you're right."

Sandy and I went through every dresser drawer and closet but found nothing of importance. She silently looked at the wedding picture sitting on the main dresser. Then we heard Liam calling us to come to the basement.

"Underneath a pile of old blankets I found this wooden box but it's locked. I wanted you guys here when I open it." It was a plain pine wood box with tarnished brass hinges and a lock that required a skeleton key to open. Liam found a piece of metal used to stoke the coal burning stove and pried the screws right out of the hinges, opening the box easily.

"The box is filled with letters," Sandy remarked. We each grabbed handfuls of envelopes. The stamps looked like they were from Italy. We opened a few letters but couldn't read them because they were written in German.

"We definitely have to involve my brother. He reads and speaks German. It was a part of his education to become a priest along with Latin and French.

"Do we really need to know what they say?" asked Liam.

"You never know. Besides, I'm curious about Mrs. Hines' life. Maybe she has family after all," replied Sandy.

"I agree. If she does have family then they should know about her death and perhaps inherit her property," I said.

"She already gave her possessions to the church, so I'm afraid it's too late for that," added Sandy.

"We won't know anything for certain until we read these letters so let's take them to Father Angelo Caimi," I insisted.

"Did you guys go through everything in the house?" asked Liam.

"Yeah, we went through every inch of the place. No jewelry and nothing else of interest. The police took all the jewelry," I said, rather cynically.

"No surprise there. Philadelphia's finest doing what they do best," Liam remarked matching my own sarcasm.

"Guys, look at this!" Sandy whispered in a reverent tone. She was standing by a wall lined with bare shelves except for a large book on the very top nestled in a dark corner, barely visible yet begging to be noticed. Sandy stood on a wooden milk crate and took hold of the book. It was dusty and moldy and must have been in the basement for decades, possibly forgotten by Mrs. Hines. Sandy sneezed as she sat on the crate and blew on the front cover revealing gold letters spelling the word in calligraphy: *PHOTOGRAPHS.*

She carefully opened the book exposing a faded black and white picture of a young Albert and Marianne Hines smiling and holding hands. The entire book was filled with photos of the couple in a variety of settings, kissing, hugging and laughing.

"They were in love! I wonder why they had no children, and what happened to Albert Hines?" asked Sandy.

"We know he was in the U.S. Army. Maybe he died in a war." I said.

"Hopefully the letters will tell us more," added Liam.

"If we're done here we should take these letters and photos to my brother." Without waiting for us to respond, Sandy began walking up the cellar stairs and we followed her out the back door, into the alley and on our way to see Father Angelo.

We went to the Norbertine Priests' Priory where Father Angelo lived and where the Santora family was temporarily sheltered. We knocked on the huge ornamental oak doors, and a woman servant answered. It was Mrs. Caimi, Sandy's mom.

"Sandy. Hello dear. Why are you here? Is something wrong, honey?"

"No mother. I, ah, we came to see Angelo," Sandy's voice had a slight quiver.

Mrs. Caimi squinted at her daughter then gave the two of us a quick once-over glance.

"Why do you need to see Angelo?" Mrs. Caimi insisted.

"We found some letters in a box that have something to do with the lady he performed mass for, and he needs to see them," Sandy's voice was still quivering but she sounded slightly more courageous.

"I can take the box to him," she offered.

"No, mother. We have to give it to him," Sandy replied pleadingly.

"Why?" the mother sternly asked.

"Because we went to her funeral, and these two boys are friends of mine and they grew up on the same street with her and ran errands for her all their lives, and ... Mother. Please trust me and call Angelo!"

Mrs. Caimi looked deeply into Sandy's eyes for a tense moment and then her face relaxed. "Of course, dear. I'll call your brother at once. I just spoke with him and he told me he was going to his room to do some paperwork. I expect he'll be down shortly." Mrs. Caimi disappeared into the shadows of the hallway.

"What's your mother doing here?" asked Liam.

"I told you she sometimes cleans the priory for extra money," said Sandy with a defensive tone.

As we waited in the vestibule we were silent, each of us meandering in our own thoughts. I was eager to learn what the letters contained and where the information would lead us. I also thought about the Santora family and how Father Angelo could help us without letting him know that we had the church's – God's money. Even though we didn't speak to each other I sensed we were thinking about the same thing: what would Father Angelo's response be to our entering Mrs. Hines' house and taking the letters and photo album? I remembered what Liam told me about confession and how priests forgave people for doing bad things. Perhaps Father Angelo would forgive us, especially since his sister is involved.

Father Angelo entered with a smile and politely asked what he could do for us.

"We have some letters written in German that we'd like you to read," said Sandy.

"Where are these letters from?" Father Angelo asked.

"Germany, we think," said Liam, "at least the writing looks German."

"Let me see them." Father Angelo took the box from Sandy and stared at the letters in the box, and then he picked one up slowly turning it over in his hands. "Where did you get these?" he asked in a soft tone.

"Can we tell you that after you read them Angelo?" Sandy asked.

"If that's the way you want it," he replied, not expecting a response.

Father Angelo began reading the letters silently for a few seconds and then he looked up and said, "It would be too difficult for me to read these out loud and appreciate their content because the translation into English is not so easy. I will read them first then tell you what they're about." He continued reading, one letter after another. After reading more than half of them he took off his glasses, rubbed his somewhat teary eyes and said: "These are very touching and poetic love letters from Albert Hines to his wife Marianne. They were written while he was in Europe fighting for the U.S. against Germany – the country he originally came from. He talks about his emotional struggles with fighting people from his homeland although he acknowledges that he is now an American and feels strongly that the Germans are wrong. Albert loves Marianne very much. This comes through clearly and he speaks of having children when he returns. The letters were sent from Italy, not Germany. His Army regiment was on the front lines fighting the Italian Fascist regime and trying to push the Germans out of Italy. Albert makes reference to his usefulness to Army intelligence because he spoke the language although he doesn't go into much detail about this, probably because of the need for secrecy. He frequently mentions a close friend who also spoke German. They worked together intercepting German communications. Albert said his friend saved his life on two occasions and, sadly, the man took a bullet for him and died." Father Angelo put his reading glasses on and opened another letter. He read it, put it down for a moment and read it a second time. He looked at Liam and me and asked, "Do either of you boys know anyone in your neighborhood with the last name of Dietrich?" The three of us were stunned by his question and didn't respond immediately.

"That's my last name," said Liam.

"Son, the man that saved Albert's life was Frederick Dietrich, are you familiar with that name?" asked Father Angelo.

"Yes. He is my great grandfather, the first one to come to America. He was a first generation German immigrant who married an Irish woman – great grandma. He died in World War II. What's this have to do with that letter?" he asked.

"Your great grandfather was the man who sacrificed his life to save Albert Hines during a battle. A German soldier had suddenly appeared along the road they were patrolling. Albert didn't see him because he was stooped over tying his boot laces. The soldier fired his rifle. Your great grandfather threw his body over Albert to protect him and was killed by the bullet. Another American soldier shot the German."

"Whoa! This is really weird," said Liam. "I knew he was a hero but I had no idea!" He then went silent and stared off into space.

"That's not all," said Father Angelo. "There is a paragraph in this letter that gives explicit instructions to Mrs. Hines. This letter was written while Albert was suffering from a fatal wound and was told by a medic that he was not going to make it. These are his final words in life."

"Read them!" the three of us said in unison.

Father Angelo read the letter with a tone of reverence that came from somewhere deep within his heart. It sounded as though he was reading from the Holy Scriptures.

"My beloved Marianne, please forgive me for not returning to your loving arms, for I am fatally wounded and will not survive. Oh, how I long for your gentle kisses and warm embrace. Surely we will meet again in heaven. I regret that we will not have the children and life we had hoped for. Perhaps this, too, will be granted us in Heaven. If you should find another to love you as I do, you have my blessing to remarry and have the children you always longed for. I have only one request. Frederick Dietrich was my dear friend and sacrificed his life to save mine. His family lives on our very own

street, and not by coincidence my dear, as I do believe God has played a hand in these events. It is my wish to do something for his family. If you do not remarry and since we have no other family, I ask that all my possessions be willed to his next of kin upon your death."

Father Angelo put down the letter and looked directly at Liam and said: "The letter was witnessed by two soldiers who apparently were there when the letter was written. Do you understand what this means, son?"

"I think so. My father has inherited Mrs. Hines' house and everything in it. I can't believe it. This is like being in a movie – it doesn't seem real," said Liam.

"Oh! It's real, Liam, and legal too!" added Father Angelo.

"Wow! This is incredible. After all we went through worrying about the money and stuff and it turns out it all belonged to your family anyway," I blurted out. Liam and Sandy looked at me with blank stares.

"What money?" asked Father Angelo.

"Oh! Ah! His family is having financial troubles and they're worried about how to pay the rent," I said quickly, thinking fast on my feet.

"Yeah," said Liam. "We thought we might end up asking you to let my family stay in the priory for a while," he added.

"I see," responded Father Angelo in a tone that sounded as though he didn't quite believe us, "Well your family won't have to worry about that now. Your parents own a house with nice furniture too, as you three already know. Father Steinhagen isn't going to be happy about this but there isn't a thing he can do about it, because as far as I can determine, this letter is a legally binding document. I will keep these letters and make copies of them, and I will tell Father Steinhagen and make all the legal arrangements to transfer the deed to your parents. I should go to your home with you Liam and tell your parents the good news."

"Let's all go," shouted Sandy.

"Okay then. There's no time like the present to deliver a present. This is about the closest I have come to witnessing a miracle," exclaimed Father Angelo, "and you children have certainly played a part in its unfolding."

"Yeah. God sure does work in mysterious ways," I added, "far more mysterious than I ever thought possible. I'm beginning to believe there just might be something to all this religious stuff after all."

"That He does Oliver, and this is clear proof of that fact!" added Father Angelo.

Liam's family was ecstatic upon hearing the news, and Father Steinhagen was disappointed. It took some time to settle all the legal details before Liam's family moved into their new home; and there were other matters yet to be resolved – like the money we took, which we didn't steal from Mrs. Hines, the church or God. Liam stole the money from his own family, which wasn't really stealing after all. It was just an unusual way of claiming their rightful possession. After long discussions with Sandy and me, Liam decided to hide half the money in another box in the basement. His plan was to have his parents discover the box on their own. The rest of the money was used to move the Santora family into Liam's old house, paying the rent for a full year and giving Maria Santora the remainder of the money. No one knew where the money to help the Santora family came from (except for the three of us) because it was delivered in a large envelope to Father Angelo. It was the three of us who convinced him to rent the old Dietrich house and give the rest of the money to Maria.

I asked Liam if he felt guilty about not giving all of the money to his parents and he said, "Not at all. If we hadn't gone into Mrs. Hines' house in the first place, we would never have found those letters, and who knows how things would have turned out. And I really wanted to help the Santora family, too. Oliver, there's something I never told you: when I was five years old I was visiting cousins in North Philadelphia. There was a fire, and my infant cousin Andrew and my Uncle Lewis died in the fire just like the Santora dad and child. I always thought it should have been me that died and not the little baby. Somehow, helping the Santora family makes me feel better."

"You truly are a good person, Liam, and I'm proud to be your friend. I think we may have played a part in saving souls after all. Mr. Albert Hines got his dying wish and Mrs. Marianne Hines ended up doing something good for your family – a strange twist of fate, I might add. What I don't understand is why she never honored her husband's wish to give the house to your family."

"I asked my father the same question and he told me that Mrs. Hines tried being romantic with my great grandfather's son. Frederick Dietrich was much older than Albert, and he had a son that was just a few years younger than Mrs. Hines. My father said she fell in love with my grandfather Robert, but that my grandfather didn't love her. My father said that my grandfather tried to be nice to her, but she turned mean and never spoke to anyone in our family after that. What remains a mystery is why she never told my grandfather about Frederick saving her husband's life. I guess God is not the only mysterious being in the universe." We both laughed and headed to Jayne Devlin's for a Philly cheese steak and milk shake, paid for with the money Liam reserved for expenses incurred in our soul-saving deeds.

THE SOUL

What is the soul?
A mysterious thing
The physical senses cannot perceive
Yet some believe it is there
For they want it there
Need it here
For hope and meaning
And freedom from despair

Hidden somewhere in the mind
We search for it in order to be saved
From what?
Death
Meaninglessness
Mythological, evil creatures
Such a strange idea
Yet, for some, appealing for its comfort

For the idea of it
Makes what we do matter
Good and bad
Right and wrong
A thing to be kept pure
An idea that we may live on
After the body expires
And this world is no more

So let us save our souls
By learning to love one another
Freeing ourselves from the fear
That our lives do not matter
Deeds of kindness
Acts of charity
Love expressed
Is love made real

Perhaps our love is the soul
Our only eternal entity
An idea
Surely worth saving
For it gives reason to love
And dispels our hate
Opens our hearts
Forever we embrace

Playground

"Oliver. Check out those girls: Barbara, Linda, Deborah, Terry and the twins Sandy and Chrissie. They just went into the locker room. Come on, I want to show you something," Butch said urgently.

"Go where?" I asked.

"Just follow me. You'll see."

Butch went around the backside of the locker room building, climbed the wrought iron fence, grabbed on to the ledge of the flat, tar- covered roof and pulled himself up with ease.

"Come on, Oliver. You can do it," he said encouragingly.

This was no easy physical task for me, being a scrawny lad. The iron fence was eight feet high, and each individual bar came to a sharp point – intended to be a deterrent to entering the pool late at night when there were no playground officials on duty – one which didn't work. I got to the top of the iron bars, balanced on the cross bars, stood up and leaned toward the building and grabbed the metal edge cap. Releasing my feet from the bars, I swung forward and felt strain on my fingers as the metal flange dug into them. I tried hard to lift my body but my arms were not strong enough and I thought I was going to drop to the pavement below. White Shepherd had followed me and was barking loudly as she stood outside the iron fence. The sound of her bark was alarming, and I was worried it would attract unwanted attention.

"Gotcha!" Butch said, as he grabbed my wrists and pulled me straight up onto my feet as if I was weightless.

"Wow. Thanks. No sidewalk scrapes today - at least not yet."

"Come on," said Butch. "Check out the roof vents. Go on, look in," he whispered eagerly.

I crept closer to the wood louver slats designed to ventilate the locker rooms. The building was made of painted cinder block. The locker rooms were separated by gender and we were looking into the girl showers and changing area.

"Oliver, watch for a few moments and you'll see how beautiful they are."

"You've done this before, haven't you?" I said.

"Yeah. I was up here yesterday and man, I gotta tell ya: those girls are something else - especially the twins."

"Cheese and Crackers, Butch, we shouldn't be doing this. They're gonna change into their bathing suits and be naked!" I said a little too loudly, causing one of the girls, Chrissie, to look toward the ceiling.

"Shhhh!" whispered Butch, placing his hand across my mouth.

"You guys get off that roof," shouted Chrissie. She spotted us. The other girls heard her and they started screaming.

"Get the hell off that roof you little rascals!" yelled the security guard interrupting Butch mid-sentence and breaking my concentration. White Shepherd's persistent barking most likely caught the guard's attention. He knew we were up there before the girls started to scream. He was already on the roof and heading towards us.

"Quick! Follow me," said Butch.

He sprang from his kneeling position and with cat-like speed and agility he ran to the opposite end of the roof and leaped to the field 10 feet below, tumbling before rising to his feet. I stood on the roof's edge, paralyzed.

"Jump!" he yelled.

The security guard appeared on the roof, waving his nightstick as he charged toward me. I couldn't bring myself to jump, so I knelt and grabbed on to the metal edge, rolled my body over and hung from the roof, but I couldn't let go.

"Gotcha!" said the guard as he grabbed one of my forearms. I let go with my free hand and punched his arm. He released his grip and down I went hitting the ground directly in a mud puddle, softening the impact. Butch helped me up and we ran.

"Whoa, that was close. You did good, Oliver. For a moment I thought the security guard had you – nice move hitting him in the arm. It would have been better if you just jumped." Butch said as a way of praising and instructing me simultaneously.

"I know, but it looked higher than it actually is when looking down and I didn't know it was soft mud. I thought it was concrete. I have mud splattered all over my white tee shirt and shorts."

We walked down 26th Street past the entrance to the Vare building and turned right on to Moore Street. This was the southeast corner of the playground, the opposite side from the pool area. White Shepherd had found us and was happily walking beside me. The Vare playground, including the building and outdoor area, took up one square city block. The building had two full size indoor basketball courts, a weight room, two ping pong rooms, and there was even a theatre with a huge stage and approximately 200 seats. The building was big and provided the much needed facilities for the social activities of young city kids. The outdoor grounds had two regulation size baseball fields which combined as a 100-yard football field, and there were two concrete-paved basketball courts. There were swing sets, sand boxes, a jungle gym, monkey bars, sliding boards, a huge climbing wall made completely of chains linked together, and several concrete structures shaped like boxes without tops, with a variety of entrances with bars to climb on. We called them cheese houses. This playground was awesome and it was our main hangout – when we weren't in the clubhouse. Building playgrounds in neighborhoods throughout Philadelphia was the smartest move the politicians ever made.

"Oliver, look! A full pack of cigarettes unopened." Butch reached down and snatched them up.

"Pall Malls. That's the brand our grandfather smokes," I said.

"Let's try 'em," Butch suggested.

"I've got some stick matches. Have you ever smoked before?" I asked.

"Yeah, a few times. You have to inhale slowly and not too deeply or else it hurts and you cough your head off and they make you real dizzy." Butch explained.

We opened the pack and each put one in our mouths. They were non-filtered. I struck a match and lit Butch's before lighting mine. I began puffing and blowing out the smoke. Butch began coughing loudly.

"You all right?"

"Ah! These are strong cigarettes. I inhaled deeply. I have to take it slower," he said.

"I'm afraid to inhale." I added.

"I was told it takes a while to get used to it." Butch explained.

"It tastes nasty." I responded.

Even though I didn't inhale, I began to feel dizzy, and so did Butch. We put the cigarettes out.

"Let's try it again later," said Butch, "I'll hide the cigarettes somewhere safe."

"Hey Butch. I wonder how long Vare playground has been around. Do you know?"

"It's been here my entire life – all fourteen years of it. I bet Richard Hendricks would know," he replied. "Isn't that him walking across the baseball field? Let's go ask him."

"Yo, Mr. Hendricks!" Butch yelled.

We ran up to Mr. Hendricks and asked him about the age of the playground. He didn't know, and he wasn't all that interested in our question. He had something else on his mind. Richard Hendricks was a big man, a couple inches over six feet, a large head with thick black wavy hair, round nose and cheeks, thin lips and a double-chin. His huge hands, big feet, and ears that stuck out like a mouse particularly astonished me.

"The city is offering an opportunity for kids from all the playgrounds boys and girls to go to a two-week camp in the Pocono Mountains. Do you kids want to go?" he asked.

"I don't know. What's it like?" Butch asked.

"There are group cabins, a large swimming pool, lakes, woods, campfires, archery, basketball – just about everything." Mr. Hendricks replied.

"Archery!" repeated Butch, "I love archery and never had the chance to really get into it. Do they have a real archery range?" he asked.

"Sure do, and they have competitions after several lessons. They also have canoeing. I don't think I mentioned that."

"What's the cost?" I asked, knowing that whatever the price, my parents wouldn't be able to afford it.

"Nothing. Zip. Not one red cent. The city is paying for everything. They figure it'll keep you guys out of trouble. Speaking of trouble, you guys know anything about a couple of boys peeking in on the girls' locker rooms? A security guard just told me he chased two fellows that look a lot like you two." Mr. Hendricks looked at us with a gleam in his eye suggesting that he knew it was us.

"Parents wouldn't be very happy hearing about their little girls having a couple of human hound dogs looking in on them, now would they?" he said slyly.

"Nope! Don't know a thing about it and neither does Oliver."

"What's the matter Oliver? Cat got your tongue? Can't speak for yourself?"

"I hadn't heard about it until you mentioned it, Mr. Hendricks. It was probably some kids from another neighborhood trying to stir up trouble again," I plausibly replied without a hint that I was lying. Or so I thought.

93

"Okay, then. You boys let me know if you hear something. And I would appreciate you fellows spreading the word about the camp – sure would like to see you two and your friends sign up." Mr. Hendricks looked down at White Shepherd and scratched her behind the ear. "That sure is a nice looking dog you've got there. I don't mind her in the playground, but if I get a complaint from a parent, she won't be allowed on the premises. Hey, there goes the security guard, should I call him over so he can describe the two boys?"

"Nah, we gotta go. It's getting near dinnertime and our mothers will be wondering where we are. See ya later Mr. Hendricks, and no need to worry about our dog, she's a good shepherd," I said as we quickly walked away.

"So I heard. The Good White Shepherd. Kind of reminds me of Lassie, that T.V. dog. No, better yet, Rin-Tin-Tin, the famous German Shepherd police dog on another T.V. show." The security guard walked up to Richard Hendricks and was pointing at the two of us as we were making our way toward the Morris Street exit. Mr. Hendricks just laughed and put a friendly arm around the guard's shoulders and led him toward the building.

As we headed toward our homes on Bambrey Street, we came upon the girls who had been in the locker room; they were standing outside the corner convenience store. White Shepherd wandered off, probably looking for food.

"Hello girls. How you all doin'?" Butch spoke in a sexy tone that sounded to me like he was saying, *"I know what your bodies look like"*

"We're doing just fine Butchy boy – though we just had a little excitement. Someone was on the pool roof peeking in our locker room," Sandy said. "Can you imagine that? Girls would never do anything of the sort." Sandy and her twin sister, Chrissie, were the most physically developed among the girls - a bit more developed than most girls their age.

"I think girls are just as curious about boys," replied Butch.

"You're right," said Terry, "And we can be just as naughty."

"Prove it!" Butch challenged, grinning from ear to ear.

"How?" shot back Terry.

"We'll show you ours if you show us yours," whispered Butch.

"I'm not showing anyone anything," I blurted out. The girls laughed.

"Don't worry. You don't have anything I ain't seen on my brother. It's no big deal," chuckled Barbara.

"Hey. Does that mean you're willing to show us?" Butch began to look like a wolf with his tongue hanging out.

"What do you say girls, should we give them a look?" Sandy's question sounded more like a dare. They nodded.

"All right! Let's go in the playground and down the ramp," commanded Butch.

I was feeling nervous and very unsure about what we were going to do. I wondered how far this thing was going to go. We walked down the ramp where we were hidden from view and it was a little darker.

"You boys go first." Sandy urged.

"OK!" Butch said a little too eagerly.

Butch unbuckled his belt as he looked around at the girls. The top of his underwear was exposed and the girls' eyes were transfixed on him, holding their breath in anticipation.

"I'll show you the same time Sandy takes off her blouse," said Butch.

Sandy didn't even respond in words. She smiled and pulled off her blouse revealing her bathing suit top. She reached her hands up and grabbed the thin shoulder straps and pulled them halfway down her arms – she stopped just at the crucial moment.

"All right Butch, I'm ready."

"What about the other girls?" he said.

"What about you Oliver? Sandy shot back. "I want to see if you have freckles where the sun don't shine."

"We're ready!" said the girls in unison. The girls were standing with their blouses at their feet and their hands positioned on their bathing suit straps, pulled halfway down their arms, following Sandy's example.

"On the count of three. One … two …!" Butch was counting teasingly slow when suddenly the shadow of a big figure was cast over the ramp.

"Who's down there?" the voice boomed.

The girls screamed. Butch quickly buckled his belt, and stood in front of Sandy shielding her from Mr. Richard Hendricks' squinting eyes. The girls quickly put on their blouses. I ran to the top of the ramp. "Hello Mr. Hendricks. Butch and I were on our way home when we ran into the girls and decided to tell them about the camp you want us to go to this summer."

"That's great, but why are you telling them down there? And why are you out of breath?" Mr. Hendricks asked.

95

"It's just where we like to hang out sometimes. It feels private and it's in the shade – it's cooler." I said.

"Whatever. Come on up, you kids. Here, take these pamphlets on the camp. They just came in the mail. Take some home and show your parents."

We took the pamphlets, thanked him and went on our way. Butch walked with Chrissie, and Sandy was walking beside me. I smiled at her and she smiled back. Then we laughed, the both of us feeling silly and delighted. Sandy and I knew each other fairly well because of our awesome adventure together involving soul saving deeds – or at least we liked to think that we saved some souls. We had helped a family displaced by fire to find a home and we had also assisted Liam's family in owning a home.

"Your cousin Butch is so silly. Do you think he really thought we were going to show him anything?"

"I did!"

"Were you disappointed?"

"I don't know. Nervous, really."

"Butch is so full of himself! I had a little side chat with the girls while we were walking to the ramp. I told them to follow along with me but not to reveal anything. We were hoping to make Butch feel embarrassed."

"What about me?"

"You have your own mind Oliver. If you went along with Butch, well that would've been completely up to you."

"I was really nervous about the whole thing. I don't want anyone to see anything, especially you. And you challenged me to go along with Butch, so you were trying to embarrass me too."

"Tell the truth. Did you want to see me?" I blushed and became speechless, which made Sandy laugh.

"You're cute Oliver. I like your strawberry blond hair and blue eyes, and especially your freckles," she said with the sweetest voice I ever heard. Even though we had previously spent time together this was her first expression of this sort of interest in me.

"And you are the most beautiful girl I ever saw," I said, returning the compliment.

"More beautiful than the movie star, Natalie Wood?" she asked.

"You're more beautiful than angels!" I replied as I thought to myself, *"Nothing on earth or heaven is more beautiful than Sandy."*

Camp

The boys and girls from Vare playground, which was commonly known as the 26th and Morris neighborhood, were hanging out in the Kiddies' Land area on a Saturday night. The older boys were dressed in yellow lightweight windbreaker jackets, penny loafer shoes, permanently pressed white cotton slacks with their hair slicked back with Brill Cream. The girls wore casual dresses and light sweaters and the standard black and white imitation patent leather shoes. There was a transistor radio playing the current top pop hits, with Jerry Blavit, the disc jockey, spinning his usual yarn (the geetor with the heater – the boss with the hot sauce). Songs like "Cherish," by the Association, and "You Can't Hurry Love," by the Supremes, filled the air. It was the beginning of the tidal wave of rock and roll and the crest of the soulful Motown surge of hits. The atmosphere was electric with enthusiasm, hope, and romance. The younger boys hung out just a few yards away from the older kids. We were by the swing set area, which was not far from the basketball courts. The court was lit up and some of the boys were shooting hoops. Most of the kids from the neighborhood were present – the ones that were cool – about 20 of us, split evenly between girls and boys. This was the core group of kids that hung out together on a regular basis. We were between the ages of ten and twelve. Butch was a month shy of his fourteenth birthday, a little old for our crowd, but he liked hanging out with us more than with the older kids. Besides, Sandy's twin sister, Chrissie, was there, and she was 11 ¾ - going on 18.

"Oliver. Tell everyone about the Camp," Sandy suggested.

"All right. Listen up everyone. Yo, guys. Stop shooting hoops and come on over," I hollered.

"Richard Hendricks told us about a two week sleep-away camp. All the kids from the playgrounds throughout Philly are being asked to go. So, what do you think?"

"What about those jerks from Fairmount Park, 30th & Tasker, 26th & South, the Wops from 9th &Wolf and those punks from Southwest and North Philly? Are they all invited?" asked Dave Manahan.

"Does it matter? If we all go they won't mess with any of us because were tougher and we stick together. Right boys?"

"Right Oliver!" everyone responded.

"Can the girls go?" asked Jonathan Sheehan.

"Yep! Richard Hendricks gave us brochures and my mom thinks it's a good idea." Sandy's voice was that of a leader. She spoke confidently, and I knew that if she was going, most of the girls were going.

"I don't think it's a good idea having all the playgrounds together in the woods. There could be a lot of ass kicking going on. And what if we don't like it? Can we leave?" Liam was all for adventure, and taking danger into consideration was rare for him.

"Hey, you're not wussin' out on us are you Liam? Afraid the lions and tigers and bears are going to get you?" Luke said teasingly.

"I ain't afraid of nothin', so screw off Luke," Liam responded.

"Don't get all bent out of shape. I've never heard you back down from a challenge, that's all." Luke softened his tone a little, careful to not get Liam riled up. The last time those two had gotten in a fist fight, Liam broke his nose and Luke pulled out a knife. We stepped in and stopped them before someone got seriously hurt. Luke was fond of knives and Liam was fond of kicking his ass.

"Wops, blacks and harps all mixed together sounds like poison to me, and we ain't familiar with the woods either. I'm with Liam on this one." It was unusual for Bones to speak up so boldly.

"I didn't say I wasn't going, Bones. Screw those gangs. Oliver is right. When we stick together nobody can beat us. Remember what we did to those older kids at the horse stables. Count me in!" Liam said, with bravado.

"Girls?"

"I'm in," said Terry.

"Definitely!" Sandy exclaimed, and the rest of the girls followed along.

"The camp starts in one week so we don't have much time to convince our parents to let us go. It shouldn't be difficult since it doesn't cost anything and they'll be getting rid of us for two weeks," I said.

On the days that followed we worked hard at convincing our parents to let us go to camp. Some of us were allowed to go and some weren't – the final numbers weren't determined until the day camp was to begin.

"I got bad news guys. I can't go to camp." Butch sounded sad, a tone in which I never heard him speak before.

"Why?" I asked.

"My family's moving to New Jersey. My mom and dad are splitting up. Mom has a cousin that lives alone on a farm and we're going to move in with him and learn to become farmers. It sucks!" Butch said angrily.

Aunt Helen and Uncle Ike are splitting up? I was shocked but not surprised. Their arguments on Bambrey Street were legendary. They would have screaming matches in the middle of the street – sometimes long after midnight, waking up everyone. My Aunt Helen would often come crying to my mother complaining how much of a jerk Uncle Ike was. I liked my Uncle Ike – he was always nice to me and taught me how to throw and catch a ball with a glove – he was a blood relative. Aunt Helen had married into our family and it never felt as though she fit in with the clan.

"Wow. That's a drag Butch. Can I visit you?" I asked.

"I don't know. They're not telling me much. I don't think they know what's going to happen. We're supposed to move to New Jersey tomorrow," he replied. "My mom is in a big hurry to move out."

That night Butch and I hung out on the front stoop of the clubhouse. We didn't say much. We just sat in silence, feeling the sadness. A big truck came up the street spraying white smoke and creating a misty cloud covering the entire street. This excited the kids and some adults. They followed behind the truck and started dancing around. They looked like ghost shadows moving eerily through the fog. The smoke had a pleasant perfume smell.

"I don't understand why they spray this stuff in our neighborhood every week during the beginning of summer. They say it's to kill the mosquitoes, but we don't have mosquitoes in the city," I commented.

"Maybe we don't have mosquitoes because they spray this stuff," Butch responded.

"What's in it that kills the mosquitoes?" I wondered out loud.

"It's probably the same stuff in the Black Flag roach spray our parents use in the houses to kill them. I hope it doesn't hurt us."

"Nah, something that smells this good can't be bad, plus no one would be stupid enough to spray poison on people," I said.

"You never know Oliver. Adults can do some really stupid things. I read about the Nazis putting millions of Jews in showers and when they turned on the water, gas came out and killed all of them."

"Wow! Millions of people? That must have been a big shower house."

"Not all at once, you goof ball." Butch laughed at my comment and then began coughing from the mosquito-killing smoke that must have got in his lungs.

"There's White Shepherd. She's walking funny. I think she's hurt!" said Butch. We could see White Shepherd moving like a phantom creature through the mosquito fog. We ran to her and we were shocked by what we saw. Her back was covered in black tar, which was still warm to the touch, and we could smell her burnt fur. The usual light in her eyes was gone, her head was hanging low and her tail was tucked between her legs. We knelt beside her, petting her where she wasn't hurt as we looked over her wounds.

"I know who did this. It was the Stillman Boys. They followed up on their threat from the day they beat me up and White Shepherd rescued me by taking a bite out of Mackey's ear." I was angry and hurt at the same time. Liam appeared on the scene.

"Whoa. How did this happen?" He reached down and stroked White Shepherd's nose. "I'm gonna get Nicky. He'll know what to do for her." Liam headed for Nicky Milano's house.

"I'm gonna get some cold water for her, right now." Butch disappeared and returned at the same time as Liam and Nicky.

"Jesus, Mary, and Joseph! Who could do such a cruel thing? Pour that water on her and hold her head steady," Nicky instructed. "Let's take her to my home. I deal with tar burns all the time. I know how to take care of her."

Nicky kept pouring cold water gently over White Shepherd's burnt back. When it appeared as though the pain had decreased, Nicky began cutting the tar laden hair off her back. He told us that as the burnt skin separated from the healthy skin, the tar would peel off. A salve would then have to be applied every day until new skin grew back. He said it was unlikely her hair would return, depending on how deep the burns were.

Liam, Butch and I stayed up most of the night looking after White Shepherd, keeping her company and petting her whenever she groaned in pain.

"They said they would do this, and there's no way to stop them from doing something even worse. She may already be disfigured for life." I said.

"I think we should find those Stillman Boys and kick their asses." Liam said angrily.

"Yeah, we could do that, but it will only make them go after White Shepherd even more. We have to protect her forever." As Butch said that, I realized what had to be done to protect Good White Shepherd.

"Butch, can you take White Shepherd to New Jersey? She'd make a great farm dog, and she would be safe."

"Whoa. Are you serious? That's the perfect solution! There is no way my mother would say "no" to that. She likes White Shepherd and if she says "no," I'll make her feel so guilty that she'll wish she hadn't. I'd love to have her, Oliver. Who wouldn't?"

"Everyone will miss her, but it makes sense. It's the right thing to do," added Liam.

Tears began rolling down my cheeks. White Shepherd was the best friend I ever had, and now I was giving her up, but I knew it was the right thing to do. We couldn't lock her up in a yard. She would go crazy. No. I had to put my sadness aside to save her life. She had to go with Butch. I hugged her all night long as I fell asleep with her in the clubhouse.

Butch had no problem convincing his mother. In fact, she was delighted. Perhaps she thought it would make the change for Butch easier. Saying goodbye to Good White Shepherd was harder than anything I had ever done in my entire life. A big piece of my heart died that day. This was the first time I experienced the suffering of losing someone close to me; and it was two friendships: Butch and White Shepherd. And yet, there was another, deeper feeling of comfort that came from knowing White Shepherd would be safe. Butch came to the clubhouse early the next morning and took White Shepherd with him. I hugged her for the last time, shook Butch's hand but said nothing. A strange silence passed between us as Butch and White Shepherd walked away and out of my life forever.

The day for camp arrived. We were to travel by school bus all the way up to the Pocono Mountains. The list of boys going from our gang was: Luke, Dave Manahan, Jonathan Sheehan, Liam Dietrich, Danny Koontz, Bones, and myself; we dubbed ourselves *The Magnificent Seven.* The girls going were: the Irish-Italian twins, Sandy and Chrissie Caimi, Terry Connelly, Barbara McCormick, Linda Kelley, Beth McBride and Deborah Keane. We were disappointed that Butch wasn't going, but as it turned out, they wouldn't have let him go anyway because he missed the cut off age. He was too old by one month.

The bus ride was a strange mixture of excitement and anxiety. We were thrilled to be going on an adventure outside of the neighborhood, and we were nervous because the bus stopped in various neighborhoods picking up kids we perceived as potential enemies. We had played several of the playgrounds in basketball, and at times there had been fistfights that broke out on the courts. This was a bold experiment the city was performing and we were the guinea pigs.

The ride took several hours. There were a few camp counselors who tried, unsuccessfully, to engage us in camp-like songs: "Michael Row Your Boat Ashore," and "Knick, Knack, Paddy Whack, Give a Dog a Bone." The neighborhood lines were distinctly drawn as each gang chanted their songs of solidarity rather than chiming in with an all group sing-along. The boys in our group began to sing:

We're the boys from 2T6 that you heard so much about
When we strut through your neighborhood, you're bound to scream and shout!
We carry rocks and cherry bombs and powerful slingshots too,
And if you mess with our girls,
We'll split your precious gems in two!

When we arrived at camp the number of kids astonished us. We knew there would be all kinds of competitive games, and during our bus ride we talked about how we would dominate all the other neighborhoods in team sports. What we didn't know was that they intended to split us up into mixed neighborhood groups with the intention of breaking down gang rivalries and causing us to become friends with one another. This did not bode well for anyone.

There were 20 kids to a cabin, and no two kids were from the same neighborhood. There were several Irish kids in each cabin, but from different sections of Philly, and although we shared the same ethnicity, we might as well have been from different planets since our personal gang allegiances were strong - a necessity for personal survival in our hostile city worlds. The cabins were huge and airy with plenty of space - much more than any of us were accustomed to having. There was a junior counselor (JC), who was an older teenager, and a head counselor (HC) who was an adult, for

102

each cabin. The JC for my cabin was a tall, muscular black guy whose face was permanently etched into an angry scowl. I instantly knew that he and I were not going to get along. I felt fear toward him. Irish, Germans, Italians, Blacks and a spattering of Polish, Russian, and other Eastern European kids were thrown together in these cabins. The American melting pot would start boiling rather quickly. Everyone was afraid and angry at these arrangements and several voiced their opinions. I was one of them.

"Yo, Head Counselor man. Why are we being split up?" I demanded to know.

"First. You are to address me as Mr. Brad. Second. You are not in your neighborhood, so be careful about the cocky tough guy attitude, 'cause around here you're likely to get your little Irish ass kicked by someone whose body is bigger than your mouth. Do you understand me Red?"

"My name isn't Red, and screw you. You don't tell me what to do!"

The junior counselor, who was assigned as the assistant to the head counselor, immediately wrapped his arms around my arms and chest and lifted me off the ground. I squirmed and cursed to no avail.

"Put him down!" Mr. Brad, the HC, yelled. "Do not put your hands on any of these kids. Ever! Do you understand me, JC Comanche?"

"Someone needs to teach this little Mick a lesson," bellowed the JC.

"True enough, but it's not going to happen with physical force. Now put him down!" he demanded.

The JC put me down and I immediately took a swing at him and missed. He put his hand on my head as I stood there flailing my arms in an attempt to hit him without success.

"Stop Red!" Mr. Brad yelled.

I stopped and stood there with clenched fists, my face red with anger.

"You have a lot of spunk for such a skinny boy. With some guidance you could actually amount to something good," he said to me with an amused smile on his face.

I liked Mr. Brad's face. It had a kind expression, and there was a gleam in his eyes. He was a big man with impressively muscular arms. He wasn't as tall as the JC, although he stood nearly six feet high.

There was a loud roar of kids yelling curses coming from another cabin. The boys in our cabin ran outside to see what the commotion was about. What I saw appealed to my pride. There was little Dave Manahan standing in the open field in the center of all the cabins. He had a long board gripped in his hands, and he was swinging it wildly at the boys from his cabin surrounding him. They couldn't get near him.

"Stay the hell away from me you creeps! I ain't staying in this damn bug-infested hellhole with you jerks. I want to be with my boys, and where the hell are our girls?" he shouted.

He was right. Where were the girls? I accepted the fact that they would be in separate cabins, but where were their cabins?

Dave was assigned to the Apache group. He was the only Irish kid in a cabin made up of Italians and Blacks, and he was raging mad. Dave Manahan was a smart and courageous kid, and one hell of a fighter. He wasn't tall but he had a strong muscular body and he took crap from no one.

Several of the head counselors gathered together and forced back the group of Apache boys. They tried to persuade Dave that he would be protected and to put down his board.

"No freakin' way I'm going to give up this board – it's my equalizer. Those Wops and Blacks aren't laying a hand on me," he shouted.

"Okay. Hold on to your board, but stop swinging it. No one's going to hurt you," the Apache head counselor commanded in a tone that sounded more like a request.

"You didn't answer my question. Where are our girls?" Dave demanded.

"Yeah! What did you do with our girls?" I stepped beside Dave as I spoke, and out from the crowd the rest of our boys stepped forward. There we were – the 26th & Tasker Magnificent Seven in the center of the field surrounded by all the boys at the camp, making an impressive sight.

"We're standing right here until we get an answer, and we want to be in the same cabin. No one's going to mess with us and get away with it. You have no right to separate us and to take our girls from us," shouted Luke.

I was amazed at the strength and courage of our boys. We felt proud of ourselves for taking a stand against what felt like the whole world. A loud bell rang, which meant we were to gather in the mess hall for lunch and introductions to camp life. We were not moving. The head counselors instructed the JCs to herd the other boys to the mess hall while a few of the HC's stayed with our group.

"Boys!" Mr. Brad began to address us, "I understand why you are all so upset. You aren't used to being apart, but this is the way the camp is run and you will get used to it. Your girls are in another campground area several miles from here."

"Several miles?" responded Jonathan Sheehan. "When do we see them?"

"Well, it's not part of the plan to get together with the girl camp. Your playground director should have told you this before you came up here," the HC Cherokee spoke.

"Screw this crap!" yelled Dave. "We don't get to see our girl friends and you won't let us be in the same cabin. Crap, man. We should go home. Get us a bus right now and take us back and pick up our girls along the way!"

I'd never seen Dave so angry. He was an assertive boy, but this was astonishing behavior even for him. He was expressing what all of us were feeling and he was doing it boldly. A JC was instructed to get the director of the camp. He soon arrived and there was a look of annoyance upon his face.

"What's going on here?" he demanded an answer.

"These boys are upset that we split up the neighborhoods into different cabins and that their girls are in a different campground and they can't see them," Mr. Brad explained.

"Well aren't we particular. You boys have got to stop acting like a group of sissies and get with the program and do what you're told!" he commanded.

"Screw you!" yelled Jonathan Sheehan.

"Yeah. We were invited to come to a camp, not a damn prison," Luke added.

"Can't you just put us in a cabin together? That way we won't have to worry about the other boys ganging up on us. And we want to see the girls to make sure you guys aren't separating them and, they're probably freakin' out because we're not there to protect them." I said.

"Now aren't you boys the romantic types. I'll bet those girls are getting along a lot better than you hoodlums. You're all scared and city girls tend to be a lot braver and more sensible than inner city boys." The director spoke as though his statement was a challenge, but he had a few things to learn about this group of inner city kids.

"Whadda you know, you freakin' upper-crust do-goody suckin'-on-a-silver-spoon jerk?" yelled Liam. "You think you're doin' us a favor and all your doin' is screwing up our lives. We want out of here, right boys?"

"Yeah!" we shouted.

"Nobody talks to me like that. Come here you little twerp!"

The director grabbed Liam by the arm – a big mistake. Liam kicked him in the shin and elbowed him in the eye as the director bent down to grab his leg. Another HC went for Liam. Dave whacked him in the ass with his board. Mr. Brad, the only HC to keep a cool head, shouted: "Cut this stupid crap out right now! You two are acting worst than these kids. We're supposed to be teaching them a better way and here you two are playing their game and that's a game you're not going to win – not this way! You, kid with the board, drop it. NOW!" he commanded, looking directly into Dave's eyes.

"You gotta be kiddin' me mister. This equalizer is the only thing keepin' those overgrown babies from jumpin' my tail," Dave responded.

So there we were, at a standoff. The director was rubbing his leg with fury in his eyes and the other HC was stroking his ass looking puzzled.

I spoke up and broke the tension. "I have a suggestion." They were all ears since they had no idea how to deal with the situation. They understood that trying to overpower us physically wasn't going to work, and they didn't know how to reason with us – they simply couldn't relate to our way of thinking. "Leave us alone for a little while so we can talk over this problem. We need some time together to figure this thing out. Please understand we ain't used to no camp and we've been together all our lives, so we have to talk this thing over and then let you know what we've decided," I proposed.

"No! You boys have to come to the office with us right now. You can't hit adults and get away with it!" the director bellowed.

"Then you have a real problem mister. Just because you're adults don't give you the right to push us around, and don't even think about laying a hand on us 'cause you may be bigger than us, but know this: you have to go to sleep at night, and if you touch one of us again you just may not see morning." Luke was getting furious and impatient.

"Are you threatening me, you little twerp?" said the director.

"Nope! I'm making a promise." Luke was really pissed.

"Everybody calm down. Let's give the boys a chance to talk things over. But keep this in mind boys: we are not going to let you all stay in the same cabin. That wouldn't be fair to everyone else, and we'll check out about giving you guys a chance to talk with your girls. How's that sound?" said Mr. Brad.

"You can't promise them that!" said the director.

"Do you have a better idea? Trust me on this one, Bill. Give these boys a little time to cool off and talk to each other. Meanwhile we can call over to the girls' camp and see if we can arrange for them to get together for a little while." Mr. Brad spoke convincingly and his tone of voice was calming and his words reasonable. He was proposing a sensible way out of the situation.

"All right then, you boys are missing out on lunch and camp introductions. You have a little more than one hour to talk this thing over. Then, we'll get together," the director said.

"And the girls?" I asked.

"We'll call their campground," Mr. Brad said. "Which playground are you boys from?"

"Vare!" we shouted in unison.

The three HC's and camp director walked off toward the mess hall, leaving us alone to work things out.

"Wow! That was intense. Those HC's are either incredibly stupid for leaving us alone or they're really cool." I said.

"Yeah, we showed them ass-wipes," Dave said.

"Yo Dave, what the hell happened in your cabin?" Jonathan Sheehan asked.

"They started picking on me right away because of my size, and I'm the only Mick in the cabin. They started teasing me 'cause I'm small and I'm Irish. They also saw me freakin' out about those daddy-long-leg bugs, and one of them put a bunch in my shoes, so when I went to put them on … well, that really got me goin'. I let them know they can't mess with me!"

"That's an understatement," said Danny Koontz. And we laughed.

"So what do we do now?" asked Jonathan Sheehan.

"I say we get the hell outta here right now," said Luke.

"Crap, man. We don't even know where the hell we are and even if we did, we're hundreds of miles from Philly," Koontz noted.

"Yo, guys. Maybe we should give this place a chance. Let's at least wait and find out if they'll let us talk to the girls," I suggested.

"No freakin' way," said Dave, "I saw that jerk director wink at the HC Apache when he agreed to call the girls' camp. No way are they going to let us do anything we need to do. They are not going to let us cabin together and we gotta free our girls. Man, don't you guys think they're experiencing the same thing we are?" Dave sounded very convincing, and everyone started nodding their heads, including me.

"So what's the plan?" I asked.

"We have to find out where the girls' camp is," said Liam, "I saw a map on the wall of the building where the director's office is. It's framed and covered by glass. I can sneak on over there and take the map while they're in the mess hall, but we better act fast."

"There are a bunch of metal hangers by Mr. Brad's bunk and I noticed the JC has a bicycle. We can take the tube from one of his tires and make sling-shots with the hangers, just in case we run into trouble," I said.

"There have to be trains that run through here. If we can find tracks and figure out which direction we need to go in, then maybe we can hop a train home or at least walk the whole way on the tracks," Luke suggested. "I'll go with Liam to get the map and if it doesn't have enough info, maybe there are more maps in the office," he added.

"Danny Koontz and I will go through the cabins searchin' for food, we're going to need some," said Jonathan.

"Good thing our duffle bags aren't unpacked," stuttered Bones.

"All right then, we got a plan. We need to move fast," said Dave Manahan.

"What are you going to do Dave?" I asked.

"I'm going to get even with every one of those jerks in my cabin. I'm going to put sand under their nice, neatly made blankets so when they go to bed tonight the last thing they're going to think about is me and I'll be long gone," he said slyly.

"When you finish with your revenge, can you help me with the sling-shots?" I asked.

"Sure, but why don't you help me first?" he asked.

"Okay, let's get movin', and we have to be quick 'cause those counselors aren't going to give us too much time. We should make sure we have on the clothes we need to travel, and Bones, forget about taking duffle bags. Can't hop trains carrying those things," I advised.

We got in motion. Luke and Liam had an easy time getting the map we needed, and they didn't have to break the glass. The map slid out from an opening on the side, and it had not only the boys and girls campgrounds, but it also showed the country roads and major highways, as well as the railroad tracks. They came back quickly and immediately helped Dave put sand under the blankets in the Apache cabin bunks, and then we set to making the slingshots. We were good at this, having done it many times in our neighborhood. We were a slingshot-making factory! Dave had a sharp knife and easily cut up the tire inner tube into strips; within 35 minutes, we had seven slingshots. Jonathan Sheehan and Danny Koontz discovered that the junior counselors kept stashes of Snicker candy bars, which was all we needed for fuel. Within less than an hour, we were ready to get going.

"Let's look at the map," I said.

"Not here. We need to get away from this camp before the counselors come back. We need to get far into the woods, out of sight and sound, and then we can look at the map and make our plan." I was impressed with Liam's leadership. He was stepping up big-time, and he was making sense.

We entered the woods walking at a brisk pace. No one bothered to consider which direction we should be walking in - we'd determine that later. After walking for about 20 minutes we came upon a wide path, and there, with his hands on his hips, stood JC Comanche.

"What's this? The little Harps making a get-away. Get your Irish asses marching up this path and to the director's office – MOVE!!" he yelled.

Liam put down his head and ran full speed into the JC's stomach, bouncing right off and falling to the ground. The JC then grabbed him by his hair and punched him in the mouth, knocking out a tooth. Luke took out his knife and said, "I'm going to carve you like a pumpkin, as he circled the JC. The JC picked up a stick that was lying at his feet and whacked Luke on the wrist, knocking the knife from his hand, and then he stepped on the knife with his right foot. Jonathan Sheehan kicked the JC in the knee, causing him to gasp in pain and as he grabbed his knee Danny Koontz threw a stone, hitting the JC on the side of his head. We followed his example and started hitting him with stones with our sling-shots – he ran down the path, cursing and dripping with blood. We hooted and hollered over our victory.

"Quick, we need to get away from here. This wasn't the right direction and we don't have time to stand here scratching our heads over this map. I remember the girls' camp is west of this place. We just need to follow the sun, so let's go!" Liam commanded as he spit blood from his mouth.

We walked on for a long time when we came upon a lake. There were Boy Scouts dressed in their fancy uniforms canoeing.

"Hey, I'm hot. Let's go for a swim," I suggested as I kicked off my Converse sneakers, pulled off my shirt and dove into the lake. There was no disagreement when it came to swimming – we loved to, without exception. The Boy Scouts noticed us splashing around and were looking at us with interest. Danny Koontz and I swam over to one of the canoes.

"Holy crap! It's Patrick O'Malley. Yo! Patrick. What are you doing up here?" I shouted.

"I'm a Boy Scout and this is our camp. It's you guys that are the big surprise. I heard that you guys and some of the girls were going to camp, but I didn't know it was up here," Patrick responded.

"Yeah, it's up here all right and it sucks a big one," said Koontz.

"My father makes me come up here every year. It's all right but I can't stand these army brat types. None of them are from our neighborhood, and they think they're much better than South Philly kids. They're real asses," Patrick O'Malley said.

Patrick O'Malley was an awesome kid with an even more awesome older brother. It was his brother, Avery. He had taught most of the kids in the neighborhood how to swim. He was a lifeguard at Vare pool. Patrick's father had been in the Navy during the Korean War.

"Yo, Patrick. Wanna go for a swim?" Danny Koontz didn't give him a chance to answer. He grabbed the side of the canoe and tipped it over. Patrick plunged into the lake.

"Crap, guys! You got my Boy Scout uniform all wet," Patrick shouted. We laughed and splashed each other. Patrick swam over to the edge of the lake where the other boys were. Everyone was surprised and glad to see him. The Boy Scouts in the other canoes started paddling in our direction, shouting incoherently.

"What are they saying?" I asked.

"I think they think that I am being attacked by you guys, and they're coming to save me," Patrick O'Malley said.

"Patrick, we're running away from camp and we're going to rescue the girls. You want to come?" I asked.

"Sounds like an adventure to me and I'd do anything to get out of this place. Count me in!" he replied.

110

Luke decided to have a little target practice and started slinging stones at the on-coming Boy Scout canoes. The idea caught on and we started shooting stones at them, hitting the sides of their canoes.

"Yo, guys. Don't hit any of them, just scare them away. Don't hurt them," Patrick requested.

"Hear that, guys? Just aim for their canoes. Don't hit the wussies," shouted Luke.

The Boy Scouts started freaking out and turned away.

"Well what do you know? Those guys think I was captured and they're running away leaving me at your mercy. So much for Boy Scout loyalty and courage," Patrick O'Malley said sarcastically. "What do we do now? What's the plan?"

"We have a map and we're going to free the girls then hop a train back to Philly," Dave Manahan answered.

"Let me see the map. I know this area pretty well." Liam opened the big map, spreading it out on the ground. "Here's where we are. See the scout marker? Your camp is over there, just two miles away, and this must be the girls' camp. Wow, that's quite a distance - about fifteen miles. We might make it before dark. Do you have flashlights?" Patrick O'Malley asked.

"No. Didn't think of that," I replied.

"I know where we can get them, but we have to sneak into the Boy Scout camp, which we have to pass anyway," said Patrick.

We followed Patrick O'Malley as he led us to a storage building. It wasn't locked. We went inside. It was filled with sleeping bags, lanterns, flashlights, tarps and tents – all the usual Boy Scout stuff.

"Here, everyone take a flashlight. You guys have water canteens?" Patrick asked.

"No, we didn't think of that either - just thought we'd drink from streams," I said.

"You guys are better suited for city life. You wouldn't last long in the wilderness," Patrick stated with a hint of ridicule and personal pride. "Boy Scout training has its advantages."

"That's what we've got you for," Jonathan Sheehan responded.

"Lucky you ran into me – the luck of the Irish I guess."

"Well lookey here, a rifle," Luke whispered.

"Don't take that," Patrick quickly stated. "They'll surely notice it missing and they'll send the police after us."

"The police are going to be after us anyway. Let's see if it's loaded," Luke said.

111

"Give it to me before you hurt yourself," Patrick said as he swiftly snatched it out of Luke's hands. He released the bolt and with a sigh of relief said, "It's not loaded and they don't keep ammunition in here. In fact, I'm surprised this rifle is even here. It must be broken. Yes, look, the hammer is bent." Patrick said.

"We'll then, there shouldn't be a problem if I take it," said Luke, "It may come in handy to scare some folks if necessary."

"I guess you're right. There's no harm as long as you can't shoot anyone," Patrick said. "Let's get out of here before someone comes."

We left the Boy Scout area and allowed Patrick to take the lead. He had a compass, and, like his brother Avery, he had a good sense of direction. His presence made us feel more confident about succeeding in our quest.

We walked for quite a long distance, and we were feeling thirsty. The canteens were empty, so we kept a look out for a water source. Patrick told us not to drink creek, lake, or stream water because we could get some weird sickness. As we were passing a log cabin, I noticed a red well pump and it was out of view of the cabin, this was important because we could tell there were people inside and we didn't want to attract attention. Dave started pumping the handle as we kneeled with our hands ready for the cold rush of water, then Luke shouted, "Yuck, it's gasoline!"

We shook our hands and wiped them in the dirt. We desperately needed water. I told the guys to hike up the road while Patrick and I took the canteens and snuck around the side of the cabin to where there was an outside spigot. We filled the canteens, and then rushed back to the group. They were more than pleased to have water to wash the fuel smell off their hands.

"Look what I have," said Luke as he held up a glass milk jug filled with gasoline.

"And what do you plan on doing with that, setting a forest fire?" asked Patrick.

"Just another little weapon in our arsenal in case of an emergency," he responded.

"Luke, you're going to get us in some real trouble someday. It takes a lot of work keeping you in check," I said with exasperation.

"Hell, if you don't call this situation we're in trouble, then my parents ain't potato eaters. Besides, it'll make it real easy to start a fire in case we need one."

"You just want to make a Molotov cocktail and blow something up, not roast marshmallows," I responded.

"Stop being paranoid, Oliver James. You're starting to act like a sissy – not the same boy who stood up to that jerk with the bow and arrow."

"Screw you Luke! You're always taking things too far. Pulling a knife on that JC was pretty stupid. We're lucky we're not wanted for murder. Next thing, the government will be after us for burning down the state of Pennsylvania."

"All right you guys, that's enough. You can take the boys out of the city, but you can't take the city out of the boys. We have to get moving," Patrick interjected.

"Here's a cap for the milk bottle Luke." Jonathan Sheehan offered, which didn't give me any comfort because Jonathan was always playing with matches and starting little fires around the playground.

The sun was getting lower in the sky and the mountain air was feeling cooler and a little moist. I was getting tired and hungry. "Koontz and Sheehan, break out those Snickers you snitched from the JC, I'm starving," I suggested.

"Great idea. Dinner time fellows," Danny announced.

We each ate two Snickers and there were still half a dozen left; we decided to save them for later. As we sat there eating, everyone was silent. The sounds of the forest became pronounced: the wind gently moving through the trees, whispering its sweet summer song, birds chirping and the hoot of an owl in the distance. I was aware that the sounds were comforting to me, but not to everyone.

"Man, this place gives me the creeps," Jonathan complained. "Yo, Patrick. Are there bears up here?"

"Yeah, Smokey the Bear lives up here and makes sure people like you don't start any forest fires." Everyone laughed knowing how much Jonathan enjoyed playing with matches. "There are lots of black bears. They sometimes walk right through the campgrounds. One year a Boy Scout had some potato chips in his tent and a baby black bear knocked it over in the middle of the night. The boy screamed and the bear took off. The boy was injured: paw scratches on his thigh. They took him to the hospital. One of the first things they teach you up here is to not have food where bears can get it." Patrick O'Malley replied.

"That's why the JC jerks have their give-a-dog-a-bone candy bar treats stashed in a locked metal box. We're smarter than your average bear though," laughed Koontz.

"Don't laugh too hard. You are the one holding on to the Snicker bars, and they can smell food through just about anything," Patrick warned, "including your body odor."

"Crap. Then let's eat 'em now!" said Jonathan. The rest of the Snicker bars were eaten in seconds flat!

We walked on for a few more hours before coming to a major road. Fortunately there was a three-quarter moon so our path was well lit. We walked on a gravel road rather than a foot path, hoping that it would soon meet up with an asphalt road, then on to the girls' camp. Occasionally a car would come and we'd hide in the woods, concerned that it would be the camp counselors looking for us, or worse yet, the police. Finally, we reached a paved road and there was a marker that said Route 537. We got out the map, found the black line with the same route number and circled the intersection where the gravel road met the asphalt. The map indicated that we needed to head north, so we turned right and continued our journey. It was a lot easier and more comforting walking on black top; high-top Converse basketball sneakers and asphalt are to city boys what bare feet and green grass are to country folks. There were a lot more cars and trucks on this road, though the area was still relatively sparse. We were so comfortable walking on this road that we became careless and stopped hiding each time a car approached. This proved to be a big mistake. A pick-up truck screeched to a halt along side us; it was two head counselors: Mr. Brad and HC Apache. Neither of them got out of the truck. We just stood there, a little shocked and bewildered. Mr. Brad was riding shotgun and was closest to us. He said, "Boys, hop in the back of this truck and we'll forget this incident ever happened."

"No! We're going to rescue our girls and you're not stopping us." I replied.

"Funny thing. We're headed to the girl's camp right now. Hop on in. We'll take you there and we'll have a chat with the girls' camp director. She's a nice lady and if you guys act like gentlemen, she just might let you see your girls."

"When we get there, we're not only going to see our girls, were going to take them with us, so bug off. We ain't making no deals," shouted Dave.

"We haven't notified the police yet, and if you boys don't come along we won't have a choice. I had to convince the director that I'd bring you boys back safely and that we didn't have to bother the town or State Police. Now it's up to you boys. So what's it going to be, us or the police?" Mr. Brad sounded very convincing and I knew that what he was saying was true. They were responsible

114

for us and they had to do the right thing, but I was surprised they hadn't notified the police or park rangers. Perhaps it would be an embarrassment to the camp if they involved the police, so the camp director was willing to give them time to find us. I pulled the guys over to the side for a chat.

"We're in a fix guys. They have no choice but to get the police involved. In fact, I'm surprised they haven't already. I guess they don't want trouble with the town folks. It would be difficult to keep a charity camp for hoodlums like us city boys if they can't control us – it wouldn't be safe up here in the beautiful, pristine, crime-free forest. So let's make a deal. Patrick, how far would you say it is from the girls' camp?" I asked.

"I figured we walked about twelve miles so no more than two or three miles."

I walked over to the pickup truck. "Mr. Brad, what if I come along with you to the girls' camp and talk to Mrs. Director about seeing our girls and let these guys walk the rest of the way?

"Why should I agree to that?" Mr. Brad asked.

"You have no choice. You can't force them to go with you. They're determined to rescue the girls so they will get to the camp, which is not far away. By the time they arrive we can have all of the girls together to greet them. What happens after that, who can say?"

"I'm not going for it," shouted HC Apache as he opened the door and stepped around the truck and walked toward us. He was carrying a large nightstick, like the ones the Philadelphia police use.

"Don't take another step or I'll blow your freakin' head off," commanded Luke as he pointed the rifle directly at HC Apache.

"He has a rifle. The crazy twerp is threatening to shoot us!" he cried.

"That's damn right. Now get in your truck or you won't see another day," Luke shouted.

"Get in the truck, Harry," yelled Mr. Brad to HC Apache, who promptly did as he was told.

"You boys are getting yourself deeper and deeper into trouble. That rifle is a bad thing, son, and this situation is looking more and more like steel bars for all of you," Mr. Brad said with an angry and very concerned voice. "I want you to put that rifle in the back of this truck or this matter is going to be turned over to the police."

"Do it Luke, or we're done for," commanded Patrick.

"As soon as we decide the course of action I'll hand over the rifle but not a moment sooner," Luke responded keeping the rifle pointed at HC Apache.

"Oliver, I'll take your deal. Get in the truck. The rest of you have to meet up with us at the girls' campground. If you don't go along with this, then I have no choice but to go to the police. Do we have a deal?"

"Come on Luke; put the rifle in the truck. Let's get this over and done with." I pleaded.

"Stupid thing doesn't work anyway. Here, take the damn thing!" he said as he tossed it in the back of the pick-up truck. I called the boys over to the side of the road for a huddle.

"When you guys get there, don't let anyone see you just in case this is a trap. We need to meet up with you guys somewhere secret to let you know what's going on in case things don't go well. This way we can stick with the original plan or do something else."

"How about hiding out in the woods east of the entrance gate? You guys can figure out east without the sun can't you?" Patrick grinned as he handed over his compass to Danny, and much to my surprise, Patrick O'Malley hopped in the truck with me.

"You're not going alone," he said. "In case they try to pull a fast one on you, I'll be there to help you out."

"Thanks Patrick." It felt good to have his support and company.

"See ya soon, guys!" I said as the truck sped off down the road.

We were there in a matter of minutes. The campus was quiet. It was slightly past 9:00 pm and the cabin lights were just shut out. The camp director was expecting us. We walked into her office. She had a look of worry upon her face. She was tall and slender with strawberry blond hair and a face of an angel. I fell in love the moment I saw her.

"This is Oliver James and his friend, ah, I'm sorry son, and I don't recall your name or your face for that matter."

"I'm Patrick and I don't belong to the camp. These guys are my buddies from the neighborhood. I am a Boy Scout and they, well, sort of picked me up along the way."

"Damn! That means the Boy Scout camp is out looking for you," Mr. Brad said.

"Probably thought I drowned when my buddies tipped over my canoe." We both started to laugh. The adults in the room didn't catch the humor.

"We'll deal with that situation later. Right now, let's take care of this one," Mr. Brad said.

"My name is Miss Leyland and I am the director of the girls' camp. I understand that you boys planned on rescuing your girlfriends so you can take them home. Is this correct?" she said rather nervously.

"Yes, Miss Director. That's what we want to do. Where are the girls right now?" I asked.

"They're in their cabins and probably asleep by now. It was a long day of travel and camp activities. You boys must be tired."

"We are, but we have to see our girls and if they are not happy, we are not leaving without them." I insisted.

"Fellows, I admire your chivalry, but I can assure you they are very happy here and wouldn't want to leave," she said assuredly.

"We want to hear that from them, not you." I insisted.

"Sorry boys, but we can't go around waking these girls up. They are in different cabins and we'd have to disturb the whole camp to do what you ask."

"Miss Director, can my friend and I step outside for a moment to discuss this situation? The rest of the boys will be here any minute and we're going to have to figure out a way to convince them that we can't talk to the girls tonight."

"Sure, just don't be too long. Mr. Brad and Mr. Harry will have to take you boys back to your cabins as soon as your friends arrive," she said.

Patrick and I stepped outside. "Patrick, no way are the boys going for this. What a crappy deal. We're not going to talk to the girls tonight. They plan on taking us back to camp, and there is no guarantee we'll get to talk to the girls at all. And we will not return to the camp unless they agree to put us on a bus for home. This sucks!"

"Agreed! So this is what we do – split and catch up to the guys before they get to the gate. They probably have a bunch of goons waiting for them. Let's go!"

Patrick and I headed toward the gate. Sure enough there were a bunch of JC jerks from the boys' camp hangin' around the entrance waiting for our guys to show up. So this was a trap after all. I realized they hadn't been there when we drove through – they were probably told to stay out of sight. We went into the woods and moved silently from tree to tree and got past the gate. We ran as fast as we could down the road and soon caught up with our friends.

"Guys, the situation is really screwed! The girls are asleep in different cabins. Miss Director won't wake them up; and they plan on taking us back to the campground tonight and the only thing they're offering us is a big 'maybe' concerning talking to the girls. They must be crazy to think we're going back to that camp, and not letting us talk to the girls – that sucks!" I was excited and exasperated. I honestly didn't know what to do.

"We have flashlights. We'll sneak into the campground and spread out in teams of two. Each pair will go to a cabin and go from bed to bed looking for our girls. When we find one, we'll quietly persuade them to come with us." Liam was talking like he knew exactly what we had to do. He continued, "Luke, that milk bottle of gasoline you have just might come in handy – but only if it is necessary. If we get caught, we're going to need a big diversion to get away. Stick a rag in the bottle and look for a small tree that's far away from any of the buildings or people and make us a bonfire. That will freak everyone out, create a lot of commotion, taking the attention away from us – but do it only if all hell breaks loose, meaning we're about to be caught. And guys load up your pockets with pebbles and have your slingshots handy. Those JC jerks are here for the purpose of rounding us up and there ain't a snowball's chance in hell that's going to happen!"

We were impressed with the clarity of Liam's thinking. It made so much sense that we just simply went along with the plan without question. The truth is, we were in a tough situation and we felt like cornered animals. In fact, we had felt that way since the moment we arrived in camp, and now the cornered animals were about to make their big strike. We paired up: Luke and Jonathan Sheehan, Danny Koontz and Bones, Liam Dietrich and Dave Manahan and I stayed with Patrick O'Malley. There were eight cabins and four pairs so each pair was designated two cabins. We agreed to meet with the girls at the present location where we were making the plans. Once we were free, we would make further plans for our exodus.

"We need to get around the JC jerks. Follow us and be absolutely quiet – don't even breathe. We're going to make a big loop around the backside of the cabins to avoid the main gate and the JC jerks. Once we're on the far side of the cabins, we'll split up and find the girls – let's go!" I commanded.

The moonlight was a mixed blessing. It allowed us to see our way without using flashlights, but it also made us more visible, so as we moved we hid from tree to tree. We successfully circled past the main gate and reached the far side of the cabins. I directed each pair toward their two cabins and instructed them to not use their flashlights unless it was absolutely necessary, then off we went. Patrick and I made it quietly up the wooden steps, past the JC and HC bunks and into the cabin. We went from face to face searching for our girls; he was on one side going from bunk to bunk and I was on the other. There were 20 cots to a cabin and on the third cot I recognized Terry's face. Similar occurrences must have happened in all of the cabins because at the very moment I gently shook Terry and whispered in her ear, she woke up with a scream, having no idea who I was. Screams were heard throughout the entire camp. Every cabin turned into complete pandemonium – girls were screaming at high pitches, the campus lights went on and the boys ran out of the cabins intending to head back to our meeting spot. The plan hadn't worked – it had been stupid to think that it would.

Luke took this confusion as a cue to light the Molotov cocktail. Choosing the only tree that was in the center of the field that the cabins surrounded, he set it on fire with an explosion that frightened everyone. The tree must have been fairly dry because it went up like a tinder box, radiating light in all directions and scaring the hell out of everyone. The diversion worked, but instead of making our way through the woods we ran straight through the camp towards the front gate. We were scared! Patrick O'Malley and I were the first to approach near the gate and there stood two big JC jerks with baseball bats in their hands. We jumped behind trees, unnoticed by our enemies, took out our slingshots and started firing. We were excellent shooters and the JC jerks had no way of knowing where the trajectories were coming from. Zing! Bang! We hit them in the chest, legs and head. They were wildly swinging their bats trying to deflect the stones but quickly gave up and started running toward the cabin area for protection. Meanwhile Liam and Dave were performing a similar task. They were positioned behind a cabin, not able to move because of two patrolling JC jerks. Zap! Whack! Smack! They successfully hit their targets with similar results – the JC jerks' only protection was to run for cover. We escaped and met up at our meeting place.

"Damn, that was super intense!" I cursed.

"That's the understatement of the century. Did you see that tree light up into flames? And the girls were screaming their heads off, and those JC guys didn't know what hit 'em." Luke boasted.

"Are we all here?" asked Liam.

We looked around and sure enough there were nine excited faces. One girl was with us - Sandy.

"Sandy, you're free!" I exclaimed.

"Free, my ass. You guys really screwed up. We had no problem being here. They paired us up with a friend from the

119

neighborhood and remember, guys. It's you boys who get into the fighting thing with kids from other neighborhoods, not us girls. The only saving that needs to be done is your sorry asses." She was angry and we were flabbergasted. She continued, "Your little Irish hides are in a lot of trouble. Where in blazes do you think you're going to escape to where they won't find you? Do you plan on being fugitives, and how long will that last? You guys are just plain stupid!"

We were stunned! The truth of her words shook us to our very core. There was no argument to make against what she had said. We were screwed, clear and simple. Here we were thinking we were brave, smart and courageous, using our inner city smarts to get us out of a tight jam, but the rules of the game we were used to playing simply didn't apply in this setting. Our responses to a situation that we perceived as dangerous to our safety were totally crazy. Now we had to find a way out but we couldn't think clearly. We needed time to get away and rest, or should we turn ourselves in this very moment? They were going to be hot on our trails, and that tree burning stunt would bring the fire department and the police. We were freaking out big time.

"This is one hell of a situation. We either run or give ourselves up. That's our choice," I said.

"No way am I giving myself up. After what we did to those JC jerks, the rifle thing, the burning tree, the sand in the blankets – they're going to do us in real good if we let them get their paws on us. I'm going home!" Dave was scared, and it showed in his voice and his face – it was on all our faces.

"I'm with Dave. Someone may have seen me throw that gasoline bomb at that tree; they can throw my ass in jail for that stunt, and the rifle too – I have to run fellows." Luke was convinced.

"What if we explain everything to them? Maybe they'll understand. Mr. Brad's a pretty cool guy. He'll help convince them," I suggested.

"Convince them of what? That we're really good kids who got a little confused and homesick? So we tried to set one of their camps on fire. Who the hell's going to buy that line?" said Liam.

"Well it's true enough," I responded.

"I wasn't homesick. I just didn't want any ass wipe JC jerks and kids from other gangs beatin' on my hide," Dave said emphatically.

"Patrick O'Malley, what about you?" I asked

"That's easy. I just blame it all on you guys. The hoodlums from South Philly who kidnapped me from the Boy Scouts," he said half-jokingly.

"No way man, that'll bring kidnapping charges on top of everything else. You're not serious are you, Patrick?" asked Bones.

"Relax. I'm just bull crapping. I'm in this thing with you guys all the way."

We could hear fire engine trucks coming down the road. The police were sure to follow. This was crunch time, and we had to decide on a course of action.

"Guys, what if I go in alone and give myself up while you hide out. I'll plead our case with them, explain everything and strike a deal, but we have to be willing to give them something," I suggested.

"Give them what?" asked Liam and Danny simultaneously.

"What if we offer to stay at the camp and follow the program?"

"No freakin' way!" shouted Dave.

"Hear me out. These people are in the business of turning inner city, deprived, bad boys like us into little angels. If we can convince them that we now see the error of our ways and ask for their help to straighten out our screwed up little minds, they might go for it." I was working hard to convince the guys and it didn't appear that I was succeeding.

"He's right!" shouted Sandy, "you guys honestly thought they were hurting your girlfriends, and from what I understand, they screwed up from moment number one by splitting you guys up. They should have at least let a couple of you stay together in the same cabin. It's obvious they don't understand inner city kids. We have to give Oliver's plan a shot. I'll walk in with him and demand to stay by his side. I'll help convince them." Sandy was amazing! She spoke clearly and convincingly, and standing there in her slightly revealing pajamas made it easy for the boys to keep their attention on her.

"Think guys! Would Butch support this plan?" she asked.

Everyone was silent for a moment, and then Patrick O'Malley spoke. "I know where there is a small Boy Scout cabin that's rarely used. They have it equipped with food and other provisions for the scoutmasters when no scouts are up here. It's their personal vacation getaway spot and it's a well-kept secret. My brother Avery showed it to me two years ago when I first came here. He was an Eagle Scout at the time. It was his last year at the camp, and they wanted to convince him to become a Scout camp leader so they took him to the cabin. He took my father and me up there last Thanksgiving on a hunting trip. I can take all of us there to hide out until Oliver and Sandy come and get us. Oliver, I'll draw it on the map so you can find us."

"Sounds like a plan that will at least buy us some time," said Liam.

"I agree," said Luke.

Everyone agreed to go along with the plan.

"Let's get moving boys. We need to get back to the gravel road we came in on. There is an old logging road not far from where that cabin with the gasoline pump is located."

Patrick took out the map and a pen and started drawing lines to the hidden cabin.

"Oliver, just follow these lines. I'll make an arrow mark on trees at important locations for you to follow. Luke, I need your knife." Luke reluctantly handed his knife to Patrick. "Don't let anyone else see this map. I don't know all that you're going to say to those people but make it good, and don't let them know where we are; my father and brother weren't supposed to bring me to the hidden cabin, and I need to protect their right to use it. We're counting on you."

"What about you Patrick? The Boy Scouts are going to be looking for you." I asked.

"I'll figure that out later. The worst of it will be they'll toss me out of the Scouts, which will piss off my father and brother, but I can deal with that," he said a little weakly.

Patrick led the boys off into the woods. "Good thing he's a Scout," I said to Sandy, "if anyone can get them guys through the wilderness at night it's Patrick O'Malley, if he's half the person his brother Avery is." Now it was time for Sandy and me to take action.

"So I guess we just stroll in through the gates and turn ourselves in." I suggested.

"I think it would be better if I changed into more suitable clothes first and then we need to seek out this Mr. Brad guy you mentioned and have a private pow-wow," Sandy replied.

"Good plan. I'll follow you and hide out in the woods by your cabin. Then you come get me and we'll seek out Mr. Brad."

The campus was still in utter chaos. The fire truck was putting out the tree, which wasn't as big a deal as it first appeared – about eight or so feet tall and not very bushy. It was a scraggy cedar and the smoke smelled pretty good, actually. The girls were in their respective cabins, much calmer than earlier now that they knew there was no longer any danger of being snatched up by those mysterious boy marauders. In fact, they were talking rather excitedly about the thrill of it all. Sandy slipped into her cabin without anyone noticing, while I sat by a tree a few yards away. They had done a head count and knew she was missing. The JC gal saw her sitting on her bed.

"Sandy, my god, you're here. We were worried about you. I heard someone say you know those boys and you are one of the girls they came looking for. Is that true?"

"Yes. I know them, and I was just speaking with them. I have to change my clothes and find a guy named Mr. Brad, a counselor from the boys' camp. They want me to speak to him," Sandy explained as she changed into her jeans and tee shirt.

"I'll take you to Miss Leyland. She'll know where he is," she offered.

"No! Go tell Miss Leyland that Oliver and I want to meet alone with Mr. Brad in her office in 20 minutes. Tell them it's important that they tell no one else about this or they'll never find out where the boys are. Tell Mr. Brad the boys want to turn themselves in, but Oliver needs to talk with him first."

"You're a good girl, Sandy; I'll trust you on this. Good thing the HC isn't in here right now or she'd never let me do this. I'll be back as soon as I can. Girls, be quiet and don't tell anyone what you just heard." She quickly left the cabin. Sandy then came to me and told me all that just happened and then she returned to the cabin to wait for the JC gal. She came back quickly.

"It's all set. Mr. Brad said it would be better if you met him over in the Sacagawea campfire circle. That way you'd be far away from the commotion, and there would be less chance of anyone seeing you."

"Good idea. We'll be there in a flash. When did he say to meet us there?" Sandy asked.

"I think he's already there waiting."

Sandy told me the plan and we proceeded to the campfire circle. There was Mr. Brad, all alone smoking a cigarette.

"Want one?" he asked.

"How'd you know I've smoked before?" I asked.

"Don't all city kids by the age of ten?" he responded.

"I guess. Sure, I'll take one."

He handed me a cigarette and offered one to Sandy, but she refused. He flicked his lighter and lit my smoke. I puffed and blew out the smoke without inhaling.

"Don't inhale yet, eh?"

"No. It makes me cough and gets me dizzy."

"Maybe you should quit before you get in too deep."

"If you mean the situation we're here to talk about, then yeah, we want to quit this thing. It got out of hand." I said.

"It sure as hell did, boy, and now the police are involved. Let's see; you're facing charges of running away, stealing, assault and battery, destruction of property, and yes, kidnapping! We heard from the Boy Scout troop about that boy - what's his name, Patrick Mallory or something like that? How'd you get him involved? You two seem pretty chummy."

"That's not what we're here to talk about. We're scared and want to make a deal." I pleaded.

"You're in no position to make deals, son. This has grown into serious business."

I was getting nervous and knew I had to come up with something good, and fast; then it occurred to me.

"From the way I see it, it's the camp and this program that's in big trouble. We're minors - barely teenagers. We are under your care and supervision, and from where I stand, this program is not only in a heap of trouble with the locals and the Philadelphia Department of Recreation, but there could be a few law suits as well from our parents for neglect." I said rather forcefully.

"Well, you're a smart little devil aren't you?' he responded. "What makes you so sure about all this?" He asked.

"You didn't go to the police right away. And your first big mistake, besides splitting us up and not listening to us, was allowing us to be alone to talk things over. You guys don't know city kids at all. And hiring a bunch of tough knuckle-headed, big-bodied JC jerks to keep us in line was another stupid idea. This entire situation was a setup for disaster from the get-go. You have to help us figure a way out of this so no one else gets hurt. Tell the police some bull crap story that you have it under control, and pray they believe you."

"Where the hell do all those thoughts come from? You're just a kid. You're talking like a freaking lawyer." He let out a chuckle. "I got to hand it to you, kid. I think your idea just might work. The planners of this camp are scared that they'll be shut down. There's a lot of money riding on this thing, and believe it or not, these people have good hearts and they want to make a difference for kids like you," he said.

"Well here's their chance to make the biggest difference in the life of these kids that ever was," added Sandy.

"I think you might be right, sweetheart," Mr. Brad agreed.

"Don't call me 'sweetheart'!" Sandy warned.

"Sorry young lady, no offense intended. So where are the rest of the boys?" he asked.

"We'll get to that later. First we have to talk specifics and plan out a strategy for how to present this to everyone." I stated.

"Your little speech worked for me and I can repeat it to the directors. They'll send the police on their way, telling them the tree was an accident and the whole boy invading the camp incident was a kid prank. They'll buy it – they must! The alternative would be too high a price for everyone to pay. And you're right about us being liable; we are your guardians while you're at the camp and we were negligent. The last thing the creators of this program want is an investigation and a bunch of lawsuits. You thought this one out pretty well, Ollie."

"Oliver!"

"What's that?"

"My name is Oliver, not Ollie!"

"Sorry Oliver. So when do the boys come in to camp?"

"After you talk to everyone and then you bring me to them and let me hear their agreement," I demanded.

"Sounds good to me but you may need to hide out until I get them all together. It'll take a little time for them to see the picture you presented, but they'll get it loud and clear. Thanks for coming in, Oliver and Sandy. Where are you going to hide out so I can come and get you when the agreement is made?"

"Don't you know of a place?" Sandy asked.

"Come to think of it, he can sleep in my station wagon. I'll bring you some blankets and leave a few cigarettes with you, and some food and drink. How's that sound?"

"I'll take the drink but forget about the cigs. They make me sick. Where's your station wagon?"

"I drove it over here earlier today looking for you guys before teaming up with Mr. Harry in the pickup. I'll leave it parked here, on the other side of this campfire area, behind those trees. No one will bother you."

"Can you trust him, Oliver?" Sandy asked.

"I have to," I responded, "even though he drove the JC jerks over here in his station wagon to capture us."

"You are clever Oliver. That was a stipulation from the camp director. I didn't have much of a choice. Besides, the way you guys handled JC Comanche convinced everyone that some brute strength in numbers would be necessary."

Mr. Brad got his car while Sandy and I sat waiting for him. We talked about Butch and White Shepherd and our sadness over them moving away. Mr. Brad soon returned with food and water but he wouldn't give me the keys to his car, explaining he couldn't take a chance with having his car used as a getaway vehicle. Then he left to take on the challenge of presenting our plan to the authorities. Later that night, Sandy slipped away from her cabin and kept me company in the station wagon. Sandy and I talked through most of the night then fell asleep next to each other in the back of the station wagon. (In my dreams I saw Sandy standing in front of me with a twinkle in her eyes and her lips were bright red and moist in anticipation of me kissing them.) The next morning, Terry came and woke us up. She and Sandy went back to their cabins while I waited for Mr. Brad's return.

I sat in a huge tree about twenty-five yards away from the car as I waited for Mr. Brad, just in case he came with others. Intuitively I trusted Mr. Brad, but I had no way of knowing if the authorities accepted the plan and if they would demand that he lead them to me, so I waited in the tree. Mr. Brad arrived, but not alone. He had Sandy with him, which was a good sign and a smart move on his part.

"Oliver, where are you?" he called out.

"Over here." I yelled as I climbed out of the tree.

"So, what happened?" I asked.

"The police are out of the picture; they bought the prank line, but they warned us to keep a tighter rein on our kids. The camp directors and counselors want to ship you boys back to Philly as soon as you turn yourselves in, with one exception; I convinced them to let you stay - that is if you want." he reported.

"No way, I'm leaving with my buddies. What about the girls?" I asked.

"They'll be given the choice to stay or go home."

"What about giving us the chance to see them?"

"I didn't talk about that. Let's not push this thing any further. We worked out a good deal. No one is in trouble. The boys get to go home and the girls have a choice – and so do you. The camp is over in two weeks and the girls, if they stay, will be home soon enough. Hasn't Sandy convinced you that they aren't being mistreated?"

"Yes. You're right. Now I have to find the guys and tell them the good news."

"Where are they?"

"I can't tell you. I have to go get them myself."

"Are they far from here? How long will it take you?"

"I'm not sure, but I made a promise to a friend that I wouldn't reveal where they're hiding. I have to go alone."

With a backpack containing food and water, the map, a compass and sheer determination, I set out to find the cabin. It was a long hike but finding my way was made easier by Patrick's tree markings. Three hours later I arrived at the hidden cabin.

"Yo guys, look, it's Oliver!" hollered Liam.

Everyone piled out of the cabin eager to hear what happened. I told them everything as I handed out the sandwiches I brought in the pack – they were starving. The news was well received and all doubts were put aside by the simple fact that I was there feeding them and no one followed me. We gathered up our belongings and started the long walk back to camp.

"Patrick, what are you going to do?" I asked.

"Simple. I'm just going to tell them I got lost in the woods chasing after you jerks and spent the night successfully surviving in the wilderness. That should earn me a merit badge!"

"Good thinking." I responded.

"Not anywhere near as clever as what you pulled off. I guess city street smarts can come in handy in the wilderness after all."

"Well, we wouldn't have needed them if our city kid stupidity and distrust hadn't gotten us into this mess in the first place."

"Yeah, there is that!" Patrick O'Malley replied.

When we got back in camp, the Apache cabin boys came storming out determined to kick Dave's ass for the sand-in-the-bed prank. We gathered around him in a circle threatening to kill anyone who laid a hand on him. The head counselors intervened and safely led us to the bus. Our gear was already on it.

"Sure you don't want to stay, Oliver? All of the girls decided to stay. You'll make a damn good JC someday," Mr. Brad said.

"Nah. I had enough excitement for two days. I don't think I could handle two full weeks. Besides, these are my friends and as you well know, we don't like to be split up."

"That is a lesson I will never forget!" And that was the last I ever saw or heard of Mr. Brad. Our bus ride back to the neighborhood went quickly. We spent the whole time talking excitedly about the short and very intense adventure of our first and only camp experience.

HOT DAMN! SUMMER IN THE CITY

Soon after returning to the neighborhood from our great camp fiasco – or triumph, depending on how one chose to view the experience, the boys got together on the basketball court at Vare playground. We were relieved to learn that Richard Hendricks, the Vare playground director, was on vacation and wouldn't be back until after the 4th of July weekend. This meant that possible expulsion from the playground for our wayward behavior at camp would not occur until his return. We went about our usual summer activities of playing basketball and baseball, or simply hanging out on the street corners, in the clubhouse, or on the front stoops of one another's homes. The 4th of July weekend was approaching and we were excited that the girls would be home on the 3rd. The weather was tenaciously hot and humid and to our disappointment the usual methods of cooling off our overheated bodies were no longer an option.

"Richard Hendricks is going to be really pissed about the camp. I wonder if they told him what went on." Jonathan Sheehan was eager for the start of the summer basketball league, which Mr. Hendricks ran. It was Jonathan's favorite sport, and he was hoping that our camp adventure wouldn't prevent his participation.

"Yeah, I hope he doesn't toss us out of the playground for what we did," added Luke.

"He won't. No matter what he was told by the camp, he'd understand that what they did was wrong." I replied.

The truth is, I wasn't worried about Richard Hendricks. We'd work around him. After all, he might be the playground director, but this was our neighborhood. He might keep us out of Vare during operating hours for a little while, but this was our territory and when the staff wasn't around, we ran the show. The thing that bothered me was with all that trouble we went through, we were without the girls for nearly two weeks. Yeah, we had a victory in that we came home and managed to escape serious consequences for doing some outrageous and stupid stunts, but what else did we gain? The girls were due back soon. I would have only two days to be around Sandy because my family - and I mean all of my family: aunts, uncles, cousins, grandparents and close adult friends - would be heading for Stone Harbor, NJ after the 4th of July weekend, and we'd stay there up to the fourth week of September, even though school started after Labor Day. It was unusual for a poor family from the inner city to vacation for so long in a beautiful seashore town. This was made possible by my grandparents' commitment to encourage the extended family to save a portion of their hard earned money throughout the year. It was the collective effort of our extended family that gave us such a wonderful and unusual opportunity. I loved Stone Harbor. It was like being transported to a different planet, but it also meant being away from the girls for what had already felt like an eternity, and the girls had suddenly become a paramount priority in my life. I couldn't stop thinking about Sandy, and I wanted to see her again in the worst way before leaving for Stone Harbor. I worried that the girls, as well as Richard Hendricks, would punish us for our antics at camp.

"They're closing the pool for plumbing repairs. Can you believe it? Summer just started and they're closing down the pool," Bones complained. He was a tall and lean kid with curly orange hair, on the skinny side, and these physical qualities made this otherwise non-competitive gentle soul a speed demon in the water. He loved to swim and he was one of the many reasons we had one of the best neighborhood swim teams in the city; every summer we'd win a lot of swim meets with other playgrounds.

"Do you know for how long?" I asked.

"My mom said for at least three weeks and maybe the entire summer. They want to replace all the copper pipes and add new showers," Bones replied.

"You can count on the "city of brotherly love" to do something as stupid as pool repairs at the beginning of summer. How the hell do they expect us to keep cool?" Luke complained.

"We'll turn on the fire hydrants like we used to do," Dave said eagerly.

"Good idea except for one very important piece of information: it is no longer legal and the cops will arrest anyone caught with a fire wrench," said Jonathan Sheehan.

"Yeah, the creeps came to my house last summer and took my father's wrench. It used to be that the city put one person in charge of the fire hydrant wrenches for each city block and when they decided it was costing them too much money in water use, they took away the wrenches and changed the hydrants so the old wrenches don't work anyway," complained Liam.

"So the firemen are the only people with wrenches," I stated.

"Them and the police," added Liam.

"Well, looks like we're just going to have to help ourselves to some government property," Luke proposed.

"Not again, Luke. The last time we went along with your crazy ideas a tree went up in a blaze in the middle of the girls' cabins. I'm not keen on your ideas," protested Bones.

"Yo! You have to admit that was one hell of a fire. No one got hurt and we're all here, aren't we? Besides, putting gasoline in the bottle was my idea. The burning of the tree was a military field decision made by Mr. Brilliant Tactician: General Oliver James. As the Nazis would say, 'I was just following orders,' and where's your sense of adventure, Bones?"

"Where are your marbles, Luke?" Bones shot back.

"Cool down guys! It's actually a good idea. It shouldn't be too difficult to get fire wrenches from police and firemen." Dave commented.

"You gotta be joking. I suppose we just waltz right up to a cop car while they're inside Jayne Devlin's store stuffing themselves with doughnuts and coffee and checking out her rear parking gear, and then we swipe the wrench from their car. Are you nuts? That's a crime we'd end up in the juvenile detention center for," Bones protested.

"Gee Bones, that scam just might work. You've got quite a criminal mind for the type that's nervous about performing a little mischief now and then." Luke was serious about liking Bones' unintentional plan and urged us to go along with it. Bones was right. It would be a big risk stealing from cops, a daring feat – more daring, perhaps, than trying to rescue girls who didn't need rescuing.

"Yo, is anyone up for playing stickball in the Anthony Wayne schoolyard?" asked Jonathan.

"Good idea! I'm up for it. We need more players if we're going to play a full game unless we use the gully and have three on a team," commented Liam.

Anthony Wayne was the local public elementary school and it was big: a three-story redbrick school a city block long and a quarter of a city block wide. The schoolyard took up the rest of the square city block, and it was enclosed by a wrought iron fence. The yard was paved in concrete, and there was a baseball diamond painted in yellow where we often played stickball. Bats were made from sawed off broomsticks and the balls were made of rubber filled with air, about the same size as a regular hard baseball. When we didn't have enough kids for nine players on each team, we played in the gully. The gully was a U-shaped cove on the backside of the building that faced the schoolyard. There were no windows, just four one-story high walls and when you hit a ball hard enough you could send it over the roof. We chose teams and were playing for a while when Jonathan hit the second, and our last ball, over the roof. We were bummed out because we had to stop playing and our team didn't get a chance at bat.

"Anyone have any money to buy a few more balls?" Bones asked with a tone of hesitant optimism.

"Nah. Let's go up on the roof. There must be a hundred balls up there." Luke again expressed his wild and dangerous imagination.

"No way! The Green Witch lives up there and if she sees us, we'll be turned to stone." Bones was a superstitious kid and the Green Witch was a myth told by teachers at the school to scare children who misbehaved.

"Don't believe that nonsense, Bones. I went to this school for seven years. I graduated 6th grade the year before last, and all the kids knew it was crap made up to scare us and it never worked past kindergarten. You guys are Catholic schoolboys and the idea of a witch on the gully rooftop is appealing in a freakish kind of way. I guess it's because the nuns got you scared to death over demons, devils and a God that'll punish you for wrongdoing. I think I know of a way to get on the roof."

I don't think I convinced Bones about the witch, because he went on about the witch's pitchfork that was clearly visible when standing a block away. I explained that it was a lightning rod, to no avail. Climbing onto rooftops was one of my specialties; looking out over the neighborhood gave me a sense of freedom similar to what I felt when in Stone Harbor where I had nothing to fear and no one could harm me.

"If we get a rope and tie a rock on the end and swing it around a few times and let it fly, we can hook it on to the fire escape that goes to the fourth floor and pull it down." I explained.

"Great idea, but how do we get up the rest of the way?" asked Luke. "It must be another eight feet or more to the roof line from the platform."

"See that drain pipe? If it's strong enough, the lighter among us - that would be you, Dave - could shimmy up to the roof, take the rope with you and tie it on to something strong enough to hold the heaviest among us – that would be you, Luke – and up we go." I was confident that my plan would work. We just had to get a thick rope.

"My father keeps lots of rope stored in our basement and on his roofing truck. He needs them for his scaffolds and hoist." Dave Manahan's family had a tar roofing business.

All of the redbrick row homes in Philadelphia had flat roofs that had to be resurfaced every few years with hot black pitch-tar for waterproofing. Dave was proud of his family's business, although I always thought it was funny how his father, uncles and older siblings were always covered in tar. I had the urge every time I saw them around the neighborhood to hit 'em with feathered pillows. I told Dave about the tar and feather fantasy and he wanted to punch me in the nose. Liam stopped him.

Dave ran home while we hung out in the gully. He was back in a flash with a humongous thick 30-foot rope slung over his shoulder and dragging behind him. There was dried pitch-tar all over the rope.

"Nice going Dave. That's just what we need. I'm going to tie this rock on the end of the rope, then swing it so it wraps around the railing of the fire escape steps."

The fire escape was made out of iron. It was hinged every four feet and folded up so that it was tucked out of the reach of persons on the ground to keep burglars from gaining entrance into the school. It was suspended at least twelve feet above the ground. It took several tries, each of us taking turns until Liam, who had the strongest arms, was able to swing the heavy rope high and accurately enough for the rock to wrap around the railing. We then pulled on the rope and the fire escape came creaking down. Quickly we ascended the steps, bringing the rope up with us. When we got to the top platform, we looked down.

"Whoa! This is way high up," Dave said as he let out a whistle. He looked a little nervous. "I don't think it's a good idea for me to climb up this drain pipe."

"You're a freakin' wuss, Dave. Always talkin' big with a trash mouth but when it comes to action, you got nothin' to show." Luke had a bad habit of taunting anyone who didn't show courage, or a lack of willingness to risk physical safety as he always was.

"Screw you, Luke. You're so freakin' brave, you climb up." Dave was clearly pissed off.

132

"I would if I had the weight of a fly, like you. You're just scared. Admit it!"

"Wait a minute. It was Dave who stood up to a cabin filled with 18 or so boys from other neighborhoods. He was the first among us to refuse to accept what those ass holes at the camp were trying to do. If not for him we'd still be up there singing happy camper songs." I came to Dave's rescue, not that he needed it; I knew if this bantering didn't stop, one of them was going to start swinging and here we were, six of us bunched together on a small platform suspended four stories above the ground.

"I ain't so light with that rope slung over my shoulder," Dave protested.

"He's right," chimed in Liam, "I can throw the rock with the rope attached over the roof. Hopefully the weight of the rock will keep it from falling down." Liam was clever and a great strategist. He was excellent at stuff like this. He was also the most athletic and daring kid in our gang. He threw the rock and made it on the first try and we held the rope so the weight of it wouldn't let it slip off the roof.

"All right, foul mouth boy, time to see if you got the right stuff," Luke said teasingly.

"Screw-off Luke!" Dave was red in the face and beads of sweat were forming on his head. In fact we were all starting to feel hot as it was getting closer to noon and the air was full of moisture and the temperature was quickly rising. Dave swiftly made his way up the pipe and flipped over the edge of the roof just as the pipe pulled loose from the wall and crashed 40 feet below.

"Hell! That coulda been me," Dave yelled but I could detect a tone of pride in his voice.

"Quit crying and tie the rope around something strong." Luke never gave Dave, or anyone else, a break, relentlessly pushing till he raised the hackles on the back of your neck.

Dave tied the rope securely around a metal vent pipe and one by one we climbed up the knotted rope. Bones refused to climb, claiming that someone was needed on the fire escape platform to keep a lookout, but we knew he was too scared to climb up the rope and that he really was afraid of the Green Witch. I was the last one up the rope, and after I swung my body over the edge I stood up and looked around. The roof was covered with black tar, just like all the flat roofs throughout our neighborhood, and there were ventilation pipes everywhere. The boys were in glee running around picking up balls that had accumulated over years of boys playing in the gully.

There must have been a hundred balls! They began throwing them over the side and into the schoolyard.

"Yo guys, toss the balls into the gully area only. That way we won't have to run all over the schoolyard picking them up," I suggested, and everyone agreed.

I was so captivated by the view of our neighborhood from this elevation that I lost interest in collecting balls. Stretched out before me was a maze of blacktopped roofs, streets lined with cars like one continuous parking lot, concrete sidewalks and narrow alleyways. I could see the entire neighborhood: Vare playground with its large playing field and swimming pool, which was in the process of being emptied, the five-story textile factory that was an entire square block, the Italian, Irish and German Catholic Church steeples and the oil refinery factory with its huge smoke stacks and giant cylindrical containers all situated along the winding Schuylkill River that inexorably dumped its murky chemically tainted waters into the Delaware and out to the Atlantic ocean. The skyscrapers in downtown Philadelphia reached proudly into the sky and reminded me of giant missiles. I could see the statue of William Penn sitting on top of the City Hall building looking over the city like a proud father, and I wondered why he was so important. The view contained a strange mixture of beauty and ugliness, poverty and wealth. The sun was directly overhead, beating down on the black tar surface making us very hot and sweaty.

"No more balls. We got 'em all," boasted Jonathan. "Let's get off this sky-high oven and play some ball!"

"Wow, this is quite a view. Looks like a great spot for a sniper," said Luke.

"Man, you always think of the wackiest things," I replied.

We began our descent, which was easier than going up. Bones had a surprise waiting for us. "The fire escape door isn't locked. I guess they figured no one would be able to get up to it. Do we want to go in and check it out?" Bones asked with a sly grin on his face, knowing full well that we wouldn't pass up the opportunity.

I had attended Anthony Wayne Public Elementary School from Kindergarten through 6th grade, and I had been in Vare Middle School for one year. Next fall I would be in 8th grade. All of my peers attended Catholic school and they had never been inside Anthony Wayne, so they were very curious, especially since the school was closed. We rarely passed on an opportunity to be mischievous.

"Yo, Oliver. You know this school building. Why don't you lead the way?" suggested Liam.

"Sure thing. I've never been in there without teachers and other students. It should be fun."

I pulled open the door, which led into a small hallway and then another door that was locked. "Crap! The door is locked; looks like this little adventure is over," I said disappointedly.

"Not so fast. Move aside!" Liam brushed me aside and kicked the glass in the door and it shattered all over the floor. He reached through the opening and turned the doorknob. We were in! The hallway was relatively dark, with some light filtering through from the classroom doors and from the windows at the ends of the locker-lined hallway. The air was stale and slightly cooler than outside. I had an eerie feeling as we walked down the hall peeking into classrooms. Scenes from my elementary school years flashed through my mind and I could almost hear the laughter of children and the stern voices of teachers. Overall, I had a good experience attending this school and fond memories associated with pleasant feelings rushed through my body – I was enjoying this experience.

"So what classroom were you in, Oliver?" asked Jonathan.

"At one time or another, I was in all of them. The room at the end of the hallway was my 3rd grade homeroom. Let's check it out and see if it's changed since I was here."

The rooms were without locks. My 3rd grade classroom was just as I remembered. It was the world of Mr. Rodeo, a place where I felt safe and appreciated, at least most of the time. I moved over to my desk and lifted up the wooden lid. On the under surface was carved my initials, OJ. I sat in the seat slowly looking around the room. My eyes stopped on a picture of President John F. Kennedy, and my mind called up cinematic images of the day our president was shot and the announcement that Mr. Rodeo made to the classroom:

"Children, I have some very sad news to tell you: President John F. Kennedy has been shot!"

We were stunned. President Kennedy was much loved by all of us. We didn't realize it at the time, but he brought a magical feeling similar to what I had read about the glorious age of Camelot, and I pictured President Kennedy as King Arthur, his wife Jackie as Guinevere, and his brother Robert as Sir Lancelot. I remembered the feeling of optimism he brought to our community, and we were filled with idealism and I dreamed of joining the Peace Corps and saving the world. Upon hearing Mr. Rodeo's announcement, I began to cry uncontrollably. Tears dropped on to my world history textbook and strange sobbing noises escaped from somewhere deep down in my gut.

"Mr. Oliver James!" The fifty-something year old teacher had addressed me. "You are to cease this childish and womanish crying at once!" I could barely see him standing in front of the class through my tear-filled eyes. I couldn't stop crying, so he ordered me to the hallway. I got up and moved through the doorway and then stood against the tiled wall next to the lockers. Mr. Rodeo came to me.

"You are an embarrassment to yourself young man. Baby boys cry, not young men, and this is a time for you to be courageous and master your emotions. Do not cry! Am I making myself clear?"

"Yes, Sir."

"I want you to stand here and think about what it means to be a man. You have to set an example for the girls in this school and be strong for them. Most girls do not have the strength to control their emotions. They are sensitive and need to be, for when they become mothers, but you must be strong. When you feel ready, come back into the classroom and continue completing your history lesson." He turned and walked back into the classroom. I stood there fighting back the tears and wishing that I wasn't such a sissy. How could I allow myself to cry in front of everyone? I made a solemn vow to never let anyone see me cry again – ever!

I wasn't successful in fulfilling that oath, though.

"Yo, Oliver. So what's in the basement?" Liam's voice brought me out of my transfixed reminiscent state of mind. I looked at Liam and saw his eyes gleaming with that familiar look just before he's about to embark on a stealing spree.

"The music room and the atomic fallout shelter," I replied.

"Awesome, I heard about the public schools having those in case the Russians hit us with a ballistic missile," Jonathan commented.

"Yeah. We had drills every week, especially during the Cuban Missile Crisis. Those Commies were trying to take over America, and President Kennedy stood up to them," I said proudly.

"It was the Commies that shot that Oswald guy; I remember seeing him get shot on TV by some guy named Ruby," Bones added his piece of historical knowledge into the mix.

"So show us this shelter, and then I want to see the music room," said Liam.

The bomb shelter was bolted closed and when I convinced them that there really wasn't anything interesting in there, just a room with storage of canned food and water, we turned our attention to the music room. The first music class I had was in 3rd grade when students were introduced to a variety of instruments and then asked to choose one to learn. I chose the flute but since we had to pay a rental fee, my mother wouldn't allow it. She told me that no one in our family was a musician and that I would only be wasting time and money that we didn't have. At the time I believed what she was saying was true. After all she was my mother and I never heard anyone in our family play an instrument. However, throughout my Anthony Wayne school years a fascination with flute music remained along with the sadness that came from believing that I wasn't capable of learning to play music. There were, indeed, very few kids in our neighborhood that played instruments and they were the ones who came from families that were slightly better off financially. Oddly enough, these kids hid the fact from peers that they played instruments because the poorer kids adopted the idea that playing an instrument was for sissies.

We proceeded to the music room, which was locked, so Liam did his kick-in-the-glass routine. The room was large and there were musical instruments neatly arranged around the room. The boys spread out taking hold of whatever instrument that caught their fancy. Luke went for the trumpet and screeched out a sound so loud that everyone protested while he grinned and went at it again, causing Liam to pull it from his hands.

"Whatcha do that for, jerk?" yelled Luke.

"'Cause you're blasting out my ears and the sound is going right through those glass windows, a sure way to get our asses busted." Liam was right, and everyone realized that we couldn't just start playing instruments.

"So what are we going to do, not play around with the instruments?" Bones asked as he balanced a French horn in his hands.

"Well I'm not interested in getting busted for breaking and entering. A little mischief is okay as long as we don't hurt anyone or get caught." I was beginning to feel nervous, and my eyes were fixated on a flute - my favorite instrument, and I never even held one. "Perhaps we can just check them out without playing them, since none of us knows how anyway."

"Crap, man! How hard can it be? Ya just blow in the holes," added Luke.

"Yeah, and bust my eardrums," responded Liam.

"Then let's take 'em outta here," suggested Luke.

"How the hell are we going to explain to our folks where these came from? It's not like we can play them in our clubhouse or on the playground field without attracting attention. No. We gotta just leave them here." My comments convinced everyone with the exception of Luke, who insisted on taking the trumpet with him and he did. Everyone else agreed that we should go back to the gully and pick up our balls. I was the last one to leave the music room. I stared at the flute case and walked over and opened it. It looked beautiful - silver and shiny, but I didn't know how to put the pieces together so I just picked up the head joint and turned it in my hand, then gently put it back. I was tempted to take the case but didn't. It was hard for me not to take one of the flutes, an instrument I wanted to play since 3rd grade. I liked Anthony Wayne School and somehow it just didn't feel right for me to steal anything from there. As we were about to open one of the side doors to leave, Luke impulsively pulled the fire alarm lever and the whole building was filled with the awful sound of alarm bells and flashing lights. We quickly exited through the side doors and ran to the gully. Liam was the last one to come out of the building and he was carrying a small black case. I wasn't surprised that he managed to find something worth stealing.

"We have to get out of this schoolyard and fast!" said Bones. Liam was so angry with Luke that without saying a single word, he punched him in the mouth and knocked him to the concrete pavement. Luke got up and charged at Liam and the two of them hurled to the pavement entangled like alley cats. Liam was the stronger of the two, pinning Luke so that he couldn't move.

"That was really stupid!" Liam yelled into Luke's blood stained face. We intervened and pulled Liam off Luke.

"The cops and firemen will be here any minute; we gotta get outta here, now!" I commanded.

"Not before picking up the balls," demanded Jonathan.

"Are you crazy? We'll end up in jail for certain," Bones exclaimed.

"None of you are thinking of the opportunity this gives us," Luke yelled. His eyes were on fire and his flaming red hair had the appearance of a lion's mane. His face was streaked with blood. "The cops will come, and we can pretend we we're simply playing stick ball in the gully. There's no evidence that we were in the building; we just get rid of the rope and the broken door glass could have happened at anytime. And besides, they don't know there was a burglary. They just think it's a fire, that is unless we spread a rumor that we saw someone on the roof with a rifle and heard gun shots." Luke, in spite of his recent ass whipping, was in full scheming mode. "When the cops and firemen come, we'll keep our eyes open for a chance to steal a fire hydrant wrench."

"Wow, you really are amazing sometimes, Luke. I think your idea just may work. Let's split up. Three of us will collect the balls and three of us will run over to Pierce and Morrison streets to tell people there is a sniper on the roof. Someone will call the cops to tell them." To my surprise, Liam supported Luke's crazy scheme.

Although I wasn't completely comfortable with this plan, I was feeling thrilled by the excitement and filled with anticipation of what was about to unfold. Jonathan, Bones and Dave started gathering the balls, while Liam, Luke and I ran up the streets telling everyone about the sniper and gun shots. There were already lots of people coming out of their houses because of the fire alarms blaring through the narrow redbrick streets. The rumor of a sniper caught on quickly and people began claiming that they had seen him running along the school's rooftop. I was amazed by the tendency for people to see evidence of things that aren't real just because someone tells them it is so, automatically believing in its existence. I was struck by the fact that people are so easily influenced and controlled, and I wondered if that was the reason religion played so central a role in people's lives.

The cops arrived quickly with flashing lights and squealing tires as they sped into the schoolyard. A captain directed the policemen to cover every entrance of the building, although they refrained from entering, saving that for the firemen. The fire trucks soon appeared and they immediately busted through the main doors. One truck hoisted its ladder into position to reach the rooftop and two policemen with protective gear and rifles led the way up the ladder with firemen following. We were mesmerized by all that unfolded before our eyes. It was like watching a three dimensional movie and we were part of it. For several minutes we were so stunned by what we had created that we almost forgot to follow through with our plan.

"Hey Liam. Look at all those cop cars with their doors open and no police near them," I said.

"I know. Quick. Keep yourself low and let's check them out for fire hydrant wrenches," he commanded.

Over a hundred people from the neighborhood flooded the area to see what was going on. The cops were so focused on the school building they didn't remember their unattended cars. It was very easy for Liam and me to find the wrenches. We took five in all and passed them on to the other boys for them to stash in our clubhouse on Bambrey Street. We were successful! Within 45 minutes the firemen and cops realized it was a breaking-and-entering scenario and possibly a ghetto-boy act of mischief. They began to question folks and got nowhere. Most people in the Grays Ferry community weren't fond of the police and resented their accusatory manner of questioning. I heard one adult telling them to screw off. After a few hours the commotion completely died down, and the crowd dissipated. Only two cop cars remained, and they stayed long into the evening. As far as we knew they hadn't noticed the missing wrenches, and they probably wouldn't until they had a need for them. The police carried them primarily to shut off plugs that were turned on by renegades like us and as a backup for the fire department.

That night we got together in our clubhouse and, in the glow of candlelight, went over the events of the day, feeling triumphant and eager to turn on the hydrants. Danny Koontz had joined us and he was mesmerized by our story. It was a hot evening and everyone, with the exception of Liam, wanted to turn on the hydrants. "It would be stupid for us to turn them on so soon after stealing the wrenches. The cops, in case they discovered them missing, would expect us to do just that. I say we do it tomorrow morning when everything is quiet and people are sleeping, like six in the morning," It sounded like Liam had thought this one out quite clearly.

"That's stupid," said Luke, "it's hot as hell right now and in the morning it'll be cool so what's the sense in that idea?"

"Not getting caught by the police," said Bones.

"That's right, Bones. The minute we turn on the plugs the police will be on top of us. They're on patrol all over the neighborhood on Saturday nights, and if we turn 'em on they'll be led directly to us. We won't be able to enjoy the water for long and then they'll be chasing us through the alleys." Liam was making a lot of sense and I supported his position.

"This isn't about playing in the water like the good-ole days. It's about revenge on the city, and if we keep them from catching us maybe we can persuade the pig-headed politicians to let us use the fireplugs again. Or at the very least we'll make a statement," I added in a tone of persuasive passion.

"And what might that statement be?" asked Jonathan. "You're always lookin' for a fight with the people in charge. I say screw it and let's turn 'em on now and flood the streets all at once."

Jonathan's position had some appeal, I had to admit. It would be great to see every plug in the neighborhood gushing with water and all the kids in the streets getting wet and having a good time, but it would be short lived. The police would shut them down soon after we turned them on and there was a strong likelihood that someone would snitch on us and we'd get caught. Liam and I again expressed this to everyone and we finally came up with a plan that everyone agreed to. We decided to get up early the next morning and simultaneously turn on at least five plugs several blocks apart. That way the police would have a difficult time tracking us down. Then, when they turned those off, each person would already be on a different block to turn on another. That would keep them busy. I decided that we should make up flyers to leave by each plug demanding that the city change its fire hydrant use policy to the way it used to be, making it clear that unless they did we would continue to turn on fire hydrants throughout the city. It was an excellent plan. Liam said we should include a complaint about the pool being closed during the summer. The making of flyers was a good idea.

I had a hard time falling asleep that night in anticipation of the next day. I got to the clubhouse at around six in the morning. Davy, Danny and Luke were already there; none of them had parents that cared whether they came home or not, so they spent the night in the clubhouse. Liam, Jonathan Sheehan and Bones arrived together. We had five wrenches among the seven of us.

"I think we should team up. One person as a lookout and the other to turn on the plug," Bone's voice sounded a little shaky.

"I thought we were going to' turn on five plugs at a time. If we team up that'll leave two wrenches outta use -- a freakin' waste," complained Luke.

"It's a great idea Bones; a lot safer and some of those plugs are on pretty tight and it may take extra arms to knock 'em loose. It won't slow us down because the plugs are only a block apart. Besides, just in case we get caught, we'll still have two wrenches stashed away."

Liam had a convincing argument. I only turned on a fire hydrant once and it was really hard. First, you have to take the front cap off before turning the top lug bolt to full open position. With two people, it could go faster and the added advantage of having another set of eyes to look out for cops and anyone who might snitch on us was a big plus. We went along with the idea. The pairs were: Jonathan and Luke, Dave and Bones, Liam and me. Danny Koontz volunteered to be the messenger; running back and forth between the teams making sure everything was going smoothly and to keep a look out for cops.

We went over our plan and I emphasized the importance of not being seen by anyone, especially the police. If a hydrant couldn't be turned on without anyone noticing, then the plan was to leave it alone and move on to the next position. There was one fire hydrant for every city street, so there were plenty to choose from, especially since we planned on extending beyond the boundaries of our neighborhood. We decided to turn on six plugs, with no two plugs closer than two blocks apart. This took a little time to figure out, and Dave's math brain came in handy. He sketched out a grid map on the floor with a piece of charcoal, showing a rectangle three blocks by four blocks, marking where the hydrants were. We discovered that this idea allowed us to cover a very wide area. In fact it took in the entire St. Aloysius Parish, which was our territory. We divided up the streets.

I made up a bunch of flyers the night before:

POLICE BEWARE

WE ARE THE MAGNIFICENT SEVEN FIRE HYDRANT LIBERATORS

If you do not allow us to turn on the fire hydrants to keep ourselves cool during the hot summer months, then we will continue to turn on fire hydrants throughout the city.

PS: It isn't cool to close the pool for fixing up in the summer. Only fools would plan that way!

THE MAGNIFICENT SEVEN FIRE HYDRANT LIBERATORS

"Wow, these flyers look great!" said Liam, "and what a terrific name. Let's do it!"

The air was much cooler than the day before but I could tell it was going to be another hot one. It was Sunday morning, July 3^{rd,} and sometime later in the afternoon the girls were expected to return on the bus. I was thinking of Sandy and how I would impress her with our fire hydrant plan. I imagined her looking at me with admiration and even kissing me on the lips, which made me excited.

"What are you thinking about?" asked Liam as we were strolling toward our first fire hydrant.

"The girls are coming back today and I was wondering what they would think of our plan."

"They'll probably think we're stupid asses. Especially Sandy, she's a smart aleck with a superior attitude." I was surprised by Liam's assessment of Sandy, especially since he experienced saving souls with her and in the process his family now owned a home. I agreed with her being smart but not about the attitude. She was right about not liking our actions at the camp and she sure did come through in helping us get out of the mess.

"Sandy is very smart, but she doesn't act like she's better than anyone. She's just more sensible than most, that's all."

"Whoa. You're a little touchy about Sandy there, freckles! Got some feelings stirring in your heart for her, don't ya?" Liam laughed. My face blushed with embarrassment, and Liam was quick to point out my complexion change and he started chanting, "Sandy, Sandy, come to Oliver 'cause he's got a crush on you." I told him to shut up and get ready to take the wrench from the shirt in which it was wrapped.

"It's a good idea to be teamed up. That way, one of us can keep a look out while the other one turns on the plug," I said.

"Yeah, Bones is quite surprising with his ideas, given that he's so nervous all the time. What's he so nervous about anyway?" asked Liam, not really expecting or needing an answer.

"His father left his mother and little brother, so he feels responsible for taking care of them. His mother's health isn't good; he feels the heat!" I explained.

"Oh, that's a shame. So who's going to turn on the first plug?" Liam asked.

"You, since you're holding the wrench. Go ahead turn it on, there's no one around."

It was easy getting the cap off but Liam had to give the wrench a kick to loosen the huge nut on top of the hydrant, then it turned easily and the water came out slowly at first and then began to gush. We couldn't resist jumping in front and getting soaked before taking off down the alley and on to the next fireplug.

We ran as fast as we could, turning on the next hydrant and leaving a flyer tacked to a nearby telephone pole. The other boys did the same. We were back at the clubhouse within 30 minutes, except for Danny.

"Wow, that went really fast and it was fun. And I see that none of us could resist taking a dunk under the water," Jonathan chuckled as he spoke, looking over our drenched bodies.

"Where's Danny Koontz? Did anyone see him?" Everyone shook their heads back and forth just as Danny showed up in the clubhouse alley entrance drenched and holding a wrench in his hand.

"Wow that was fun! I went all around 'Deigoland' turning on fireplugs: four in all. The streets are flooding!"

"Whoa how'd you get so many so fast? I hope no one saw you." I was worried that he had led police right to our clubhouse.

"No problem. My father and I were in charge of turning on the plug on Garret Street every day each summer, so I got real good at it."

"Let's hope no one saw you, since you didn't have a lookout," chided Liam. "So, that makes ten fire hydrants blasting full force. That should get a lot of attention."

"So what do we do now?" asked Bones.

"Wait and see what the cops do. They'll be searching for *The Magnificent Seven Fire Hydrant Liberators*." I liked the name of our little gang; I got the idea from an old cowboy movie. "We can't let anyone know about any of this. We broke into a building, stole an instrument, caused a false alarm and stole wrenches from police. If we get caught, it's juvenile detention for all of us." I stared each of my six co-conspirators in the eyes then continued. "And we know for certain that we won't get caught because no one snitches, and if anyone did see us we'll just deny it. We are *The Magnificent Seven,* and we shall liberate our fire hydrants and get our pool back!"

Forty-five minutes passed and we could still see the water running down Tasker Street from the second floor window of the clubhouse. We decided to go on the rooftops for a better view. We ran along the roof toward 26th and Tasker Streets. There was so

144

much water running through the streets that the sewers couldn't handle the volume. The streets were flooding.

"Crap! If the police don't shut off these hydrants soon, basements are going to start flooding. We might have to go shut 'em off ourselves," Bones said nervously.

"No freakin' way man. If we go down there with wrenches we're going to get caught. I'm not interested in spending time in a juvenile home." Luke shouted

At first I was surprised by Luke's expression of fear, but then I recalled that he had already spent three months in a detention center. He stabbed his older brother in the shoulder with a pencil to stop him from beating up his mother. His brother was drunk and wanted money. The reason he got so much time in the juvenile correction center was because he had a long police record that included stealing, vandalism, truancy and several acts of violence. The mother wouldn't give his brother the money because she knew he would use it for more liquor. This didn't stop Luke from taking risks with the law. Quite to the contrary, he enjoyed toying with them – but on his terms, which to his own twisted way of thinking meant that he wouldn't get caught. Turning the hydrants off was a risk he would not take. Getting busted for an incident like this would surely send him away for a longer time period.

"You should have thought of that before pulling the fire alarm," said Liam with a hint of anger in his voice.

"I knew what I was doing, thought it through carefully and it turned out just like I expected. This morning's plan wasn't mine and it's not turning out so well."

"Stop arguing. We have to decide what to do. Look at those families getting their shoes soaked crossing the streets on their way to church. It's a mess. We have to do something," I was really concerned for the houses. "We need to call the police and let them know what's going on."

"Are you crazy? Snitching on ourselves?" yelled Luke. "Look at it this way, the church goers are walking on holy water." He then blessed the people below with the sign of the cross.

"Well, Saint Luke. The cops don't have to know who called them," I replied.

"Yo boys, not to worry," Liam said with a wide grin. "The police are headed this way. I just saw a patrol car turn off Dickinson Street." The police screeched to a halt in the middle of the intersection and flung open their doors.

"I think they're looking for their wrench. Crap. They can't find it – oops, wonder why? It looks like they're calling on the police radio for other patrol cars and probably telling them to bring fireplug wrenches. They'll be able to stop the water before the houses get flooded." Liam was right. The police finally turned off all the plugs, and the kids were in the streets playing in the flooded street water. We were happy to see them splashing about! Everyone headed back towards the clubhouse and I took one last look at the scene below. I noticed a policeman reading the flyer that I had tacked on the utility pole. He was a big Italian cop and I could tell that he was in charge of all the other police. He tore it off and looked around and then his head turned toward the rooftops as I got a good look at his face. I ducked down and slipped away, not knowing if he had seen me. The cop was Captain Frank Rizzo, the most popular cop in South Philly because he grew up in one of its Italian neighborhoods.

We hung low for the rest of the day and swore an oath that none of us would tell anyone about what we had done. The police would surely begin an investigation, which meant they would use scare tactics to get someone to snitch. Rarely had anyone in our gang ever ratted-out anyone, and on the few occasions when it did happen, a big price was paid in the form of a major ass whopping. And if the snitch wanted back in the gang, he had to run the ramp and take whacks from our belts. I had witnessed this only once. Phil Riddick ratted me out for spray painting the symbol of our gang, "2T6," on the playground tile walls with green paint on St. Patrick's Day. The Tasker neighborhood boys made him run the ramp, but I refused to participate.

I thought about each one of the six other members of *The Magnificent Seven* and I took comfort in the fact that in all of our adventurous misdeeds, we were completely loyal and trustworthy. I was confident that no one would break under pressure and become a rat.

The neighborhood was buzzing with talk about Anthony Wayne and *The Magnificent Seven* fire hydrant liberation movement. People were wondering if *The Magnificent Seven* had anything to do with the fire alarm and break-in at Anthony Wayne Elementary School. We talked with people with the same tone of curiosity and mystery, although we tended to praise *The Magnificent Seven* as heroes with a just cause and expressed the opinion that the school break-in had nothing to do with them.

Just about everyone agreed that the city should allow the neighborhoods access to the fire hydrants, especially since the adults enjoyed playing in the water as well, even though they rarely swam in the pool. Parents were concerned about the kids having too much idle time on their hands, not being able to swim all day. The heat made everyone irritable. Popular support for *The Magnificent Seven* gained momentum and the word was out that if anyone saw or heard anything about the identity of the gang members, they were not to give the police information. By late afternoon we were strolling around the neighborhood with cocky struts, enjoying our anonymous popularity. We eagerly awaited the arrival of the bus that would deliver the girls into our deserving arms.

We assembled on the wide front steps of the playground building, waiting for the bus to arrive. Shortly after 4:30 in the afternoon it pulled in front of the steps. The bus had arrived an hour early, which is why there were no parents waiting. The sight of their beautiful, tanned bodies and smiling faces mesmerized us; they looked older and I sensed that something about them was very different. They were smiling and obviously happy to be home. I was struck by how healthy they looked - vibrant and self-assured, and why shouldn't they be? They spent two weeks in the Pocono Mountains with girls from other Philly neighborhoods, and they were engaged in activities that they otherwise would have never experienced. I felt sadness in the pit of my stomach, wishing that I had stayed at camp. But that was over and now I was involved with *The Magnificent Seven* and we were popular. I was eager to tell Sandy about everything.

The girls collected their bags from the storage compartment and we ran up offering to help.

"Welcome home girls. It's great to have you all back." I said while staring directly at Sandy.

"I have to admit; as much as I liked being at camp, it's good to be back in the old neighborhood, although everything looks smaller than I remember." Sandy had a wispy tone in her voice and her eyes slowly scanned up and down the sidewalk. She turned her body towards me, opened her arms wide and, stepping forward, embraced me as she lightly brushed her lips on my cheek, causing my body to light up like a candle. She sparked my feelings and I felt light-headed. Sighs of enjoyment escaped from our vocal chords as we hugged each other. In that instant we forgot we were standing in front of our friends.

"Yo love birds, take it to the clubhouse before you embarrass yourselves in front of the entire neighborhood." Liam broke our reverie with those words and we both looked around us, noticing that everyone was staring in silence at the two of us, including the bus driver.

"I'll carry your bags, Sandy, if you ..." Before I finished speaking, cop cars converged upon us from both ends of 26th Street, sealing off any route of escape.

"What the hell is going on here?" exclaimed Sandy.

"I'll explain later. Hey guys don't crack under pressure. They have no evidence of any wrongdoing. Let's just let this thing play out."

"Oliver, what did you do this time?" asked Sandy.

"Trust me on this; it is for a good cause."

"Yeah, like rescuing us from the evil camp! I better not end up in a jail cell because of your brilliant ideas!" I couldn't tell if Sandy was angry, surprised, or intrigued by what was happening.

The events that followed unfolded very quickly as the cops had apparently pre-planned every move. Explaining nothing and commanding us to keep our mouths shut or we'd be whacked with their nightsticks, they lined us up along the iron bar fence with the clear intention of searching us. They were looking for any evidence that would link us to *The Magnificent Seven*. I suddenly remembered that I had a flyer folded in my pocket. I intended to show it to Sandy, anticipating that she would be impressed by our radical behavior. This piece of paper now threatened to expose my role in the fire hydrant liberation movement. I had to come up with something fast to divert the cops attention long enough for me to dispose of the flyer. At the moment that all of this was flashing through my mind, I caught Liam's eyes glancing at the pockets in the back of my jeans; the flyer was sticking out. He looked at me with fire in his eyes and then he turned and yelled, "What the hell do you pigs think you're doing? This is a violation of our rights – you can't ..." A cop quickly came over to him and as he did, Liam started to run and all police attention went towards him. I quickly turned my body, slipped out the flyer, crumbled it and dropped it through the playground bars. The police caught Liam and whacked him on the calves of his legs with nightsticks. He cried out in pain as he fell to the concrete. Liam had saved me, again!

The police put us in a 'meat wagon," the name we gave to the vans they used to carry large numbers of 'criminals.' They had squeezed in all 15 of us, *The Magnificent Seven* and the eight girls that just arrived from camp. They left the girls' camp gear on the sidewalk.

"Oliver, you owe me an explanation." Sandy demanded. I looked at her and then I addressed everyone, knowing full well that the police in the front cab were listening.

"There is no explanation. I heard a rumor that some kids stole fire hydrant wrenches and they're making demands on the city. No one knows who these kids are, but they go by the name of *The Magnificent Seven* and their identity is a mystery. Everyone in the neighborhood is talking about them. They're heroes because they are demanding that the fire hydrant ban be lifted because the pool is closed and people have no way of keeping cool. It's not just the pool in our playground that's closed for plumbing repairs, but all the pools throughout the city. I placed a finger over my lips as I looked around at each of *The Magnificent Seven*, warning them with a hushed whisper to keep silent. I especially looked into Sandy's eyes hoping that she would get the message not to ask any more questions. She nodded her head and then started shaking it from side to side as if to say, "*You did it again, didn't you?*"

Liam was moaning as he rubbed his now black and blue calves. He looked and me and whispered, "You owe me, big time!"

It took only fifteen minutes to get to the police station. They put us in a big room and one by one took our names, addresses, names of parents and phone numbers, before putting us in jail cells – the girls were in a separate area, once again. *The Magnificent Seven* and their completely innocent girlfriends were behind bars.

One by one they took us out for interrogation. Liam was the first to go, probably because he ran and so they figured he had something to hide. He protested as they led him in handcuffs to the interrogation room. "This is against the law. We have done nothing and you have no just cause for arresting us. We were simply greeting our girlfriends as they got off the bus. You cops are breaking the law!"

"Shut your trap before I shut it for you, you dirty little Mick."

"Screw you, blue-belly blimp!" In a flash the big fat Italian policeman slapped Liam in the mouth. A trickle of blood oozed from the corner of his lips. Liam was having a rough time, to say the least. We protested, yelling "Police brutality! Our parents are going to sue your asses!"

Twenty minutes later they brought Liam back to the cell. His face was red with anger and the blood had dried on his chin.

"What happened, Liam?" I asked.

"A lot of questions and they want us to confess to being *The Magnificent Seven* and to all their crimes. I didn't tell them a thing."

"Did they hit you again?"

"No. There was a social worker there from the juvenile detention center so I suppose they were careful. Although the social worker kept warning me that we could all end up in juvenile jail if I didn't tell the truth."

"Well this is where the teaching that states, '*the truth shall set you free,*' does not apply." I sarcastically added.

"Yeah, you got that right. At least not the truth as the cops see it."

None of us cracked during the interrogations. They basically hurled the same threats at each of us, with the promise that the one who told the truth would get let off easy for cooperating. They also interrogated the girls; they truly knew nothing except for us filling them in on the generalities while in the meat wagon, so there was no danger of them slipping and mixing up stories. It was my mother who was the first of the parents to arrive, and she was angry. As the police were escorting me in handcuffs to the interrogation room my mother saw me and she began to yell:

"What the hell are you doing to my son and our kids? There are robberies and rapes going on all over the city and here you are wasting time harassing children who were doing nothing but greeting friends as they came off the bus from camp. You all ought to be ashamed of yourselves! That's my boy you have there – release him, now!" She briskly walked over to me and pulled me away from the policeman, demanding the cuffs be removed as she quickly examined my body for injuries.

"Calm down Mrs.," said the policeman. His badge said, Captain Frank Rizzo. "These kids were loitering on the playground steps."

"Loitering on the steps built for children to play on. Now that makes a hell of a lot of sense. What's wrong with you people? First you take away our right to use the fire hydrants; then you close our pool for repairs during the summer, and now you arrest our children for hanging out on the steps of their own playground building." My mother was furious and when it came to protecting her children, as she often had to do, there was no fear in her.

"It's a Sunday afternoon and the playground building is closed," said Rizzo.

"Funny. I'm not aware of any locked gates in front of the playground steps, or any signs that say you can't be on the steps on Sundays!" my mother retorted. "You cops are clearly breaking the law. Release these children at once!"

I noticed two men standing in the corner dressed in cheap suits and narrow brimmed hats that were slightly pulled over their eyes. One had a small notebook in his hand and was feverishly writing, while the other was concealing something in a cloth bag. I thought they were spies whose job was to record everything as part of investigating *The Magnificent Seven.* I worried that somehow my mother would become implicated in all of this. A policeman approached Captain Rizzo and whispered something to him as he nodded in the direction of the two men. As I looked at the men, the one with the bag took out a camera, a bright flash bulb lit up the room as he took a picture of the scene before him. Just then, Sandy & Chrissie's mother walked in accompanied by some other man. An officer yelled at the two men who took the picture to get out of the police station. The men flashed identification cards showing they were reporters from the *Philadelphia Inquirer.* Rizzo threw his hands up in desperation. Things were getting more interesting by the moment.

"Captain Rizzo, I am the mother of Sandy and Chrissie Caimi, and this is my lawyer."

"Mr. Rizzo, on what charges are these children being held?" asked the lawyer.

"Loitering on city property." He replied. "There's no need for lawyers or news reporters in my station. Joe, get those reporters out of here!" boomed the now very angry Captain.

"Reporters have a right to be here and so do I. The question is, do you have the right to detain these children?" the lawyer insisted.

"It is a Sunday and the playground is closed. There have been incidences of thievery and vandalism in that neighborhood and we have reason to believe that these gang members are responsible."

"Based on what evidence?" asked the lawyer.

"Well, these hoodlums are from the neighborhood where the school was broken into, fire wrenches were stolen from my police cars, and they vandalized the neighborhood by flooding the streets, all of which is breaking the law!" Rizzo was a big man with a loud voice and a very intimidating presence.

"And what evidence do you have that links these children to the stated crimes? I may add that they are not 'hoodlums' or 'gang members'!" The lawyer was clearly not intimidated by Rizzo.

151

"I've had enough of this freakin' bull crap. Joe! Release these hoodlums to the custody of this woman and clear my station of this lawyer and those reporter vermin. NOW!" This was an admission that he had no evidence, much to my relief, and we were free to go.

Outside the police station, we were chatting to each other excitedly, clearly ecstatic that we were free. I hugged my mother as the reporters approached us.

"Hello. My name is John Henry and I work for the *Philadelphia Inquirer*. We took your picture in there and we need your written permission to print it if our editor chooses to use this story." He handed my mother a piece of paper and she willingly signed it. The reporter then took our names and asked permission to interview me. My mother said, "Yes."

I told him what I had heard about *The Magnificent Seven* and their cause, emphasizing that they were very popular in the neighborhood - downright folk heroes, I told him. The reporter was fishing for more details as to the identity and ages of *The Magnificent Seven*. I gave them nothing that would incriminate anyone. However, I was adamant about the injustice of the fire hydrant ordinance and the city-wide closing of the swimming pools.

We took the subway and trolley cars back to the neighborhood; Mrs. Caimi gave us the money for the fares. She took Sandy with her in the lawyer's car. He turned out to be Mrs. Caimi's brother and Sandy's uncle.

It was late afternoon when we got back to the neighborhood. The girls were tired from their long day of travel and then getting arrested, so they went home with their luggage, which was thoroughly searched by the police; we surmised they were looking for fire hydrant wrenches. Their clothes were strewn all over the sidewalk. It was dinnertime and the boys went home. The clubhouse was on Bambrey Street where Liam I lived, so at the very least I thought that Liam and I would have a chance to talk over the day's events and plan our next move. As for the other boys and girls, well, it was doubtful their parents would let them outside that evening, given the mood of the local police.

As it turned out, my mother wouldn't let me outside after dinner and neither would Liam's. Besides, he later told me his legs were so sore that it hurt to walk. I was mostly responsible for his battle wounds. I was up bright and early on the Fourth of July and decided to hang out with some of the boys who delivered the

Philadelphia Inquirer newspaper. The headquarters for the newsboys was on Taney Street, a few blocks from my home. As I approached the headquarters, I saw a group of boys gathered around the boss; they were listening to him read an article. "Yo, Oliver. Take a look at this!" The boss, Mr. Murphy, held up the front page of the newspaper, and there underneath bold headlines was the picture of me in handcuffs with my mother pulling me away from the clutches of Police Captain Frank Rizzo. The headlines read:

Hot Damn! Summer in the City!

Rizzo Rounds Up Suspects in the Fire Hydrant Liberation

Movement: Mother Courageously Takes on Captain, Children

Released - No Charges!

I couldn't believe my eyes. There I was on the front page of the most widely read newspaper in Philadelphia and under the picture, which took up a quarter of the front page, positioned directly in the center, were our names along with Captain Frank Rizzo's. The article went on to directly quote my objection to the fire hydrant ordinance, and it gave a historical account of the political process that led to the city council's adoption of the now infamous ordinance. The article also mentioned the Anthony Wayne break-in, the stealing of fire hydrant wrenches, and the Sunday morning flood that sloshed the shoes of early morning churchgoers. There was even a printing of the flyer at the end of the article on the back page. I was pleased to read that the article was slanted in favor of the suspects, stating that we were wrongfully apprehended and that when no evidence was forthcoming, we were released. It also gave an account of the scene in the police station where my mother, along with Mrs. Caimi and her lawyer, boldly confronted Rizzo. The article revealed to me a very important piece of information that must have been known to every adult in the city but went completely unnoticed by me. Captain Frank Rizzo was a very popular person and he was running on the Democratic ticket for Police Commissioner in the upcoming elections. There was a side article about the city council and its various positions on key city issues along with Rizzo's positions. It pointed out that the public did not know Rizzo's stance on the fire hydrant ordinance. The news reporter suggested that Captain Rizzo make his opinion about the ordinance clear since it was quickly becoming an important political issue.

Throughout the rest of that morning and into the early afternoon the neighborhood was buzzing with the news. It was being aired on several television and radio stations. The entire city was discussing the fire hydrant ordinance and its effect on the neighborhoods. One radio talk show host suggested there might be a link between the extreme heat of the summer and increased citywide crime. There was talk of the long-standing tradition of fire hydrant use by citizens during the hot summer months and that city government was going too far in its restrictions. The effects of this issue were staggering for another reason: the heat on this Fourth of July had reached a record high 97 degrees with 75% humidity by mid afternoon. The city was sweltering and rival gang tensions were on the rise with several violent outbursts throughout the neighborhoods. The issue was becoming a political liability to the city council members, many of whom were Democrats running for re-election, hoping to ride the popular support of Captain Frank Rizzo in the upcoming November elections.

The biggest surprise of the day came on the 6 o'clock news. Police Captain Frank Rizzo announced that after discussions with the majority of city council members, it was decided to lift the ban on fire hydrant use for the Fourth of July celebrations, and when the council reconvened after the holiday the issue would be placed on the agenda for immediate reconsideration. *The Magnificent Seven* had won after all; it only took civil disobedience and getting arrested to make it all come about, especially because the news reporters happened to be present in the police station at the right moment.

By 7:00 that evening policemen were going around the neighborhoods turning on fire hydrants and equipping them with sprinklers. People of all ages were literally dancing in the streets and cooling off in the spray of the fire hydrants. *The Magnificent Seven* converged on 26th and Tasker Streets, where the fireplug was not turned on. We retrieved one of our wrenches and turned it on. There was no sprinkler – just water gushing out at full force. The girls assembled as well and we had a water party complete with Fourth of July fireworks (from our own cache, of course).

"Oliver, take this with you to Stone Harbor!" Liam shoved a black case towards me.

"So you did take something from Anthony Wayne. I knew you couldn't resist, and why a flute? Don't you want it?" I said in complete disbelief.

"I took it because I knew you wouldn't, and I know how much you want to play the flute. Consider it an early birthday present. I thought about selling it to you, but after today, I figure you earned it."

"Wow! Thanks!" Liam was full of surprises.

Sandy approached and Liam winked before slipping away. There we were standing side by side on the front steps of Jayne Devlin's store appreciating the scene of happy people playing in the water filled streets before us. I turned to her and asked: "So, how did your mom get to the police station so quickly along with that lawyer?"

"I demanded that I be allowed to call my mother and to my surprise the female officer let me. But I didn't call my mom, not directly that is. I called the *Philadelphia Inquirer* and told them what happened and that there might be a good story because Captain Frank Rizzo was behind the round up. And, I asked if they would call my mother to let her know what was going on. The lawyer is my mom's brother – my uncle."

"Oh my God! It's because of you that all of this turned out the way it did. I can't believe it! Sandy Mary Caimi, you not only saved Oliver James's hide twice in less than two weeks, you also rescued the whole city of Philadelphia from the oppressive fire hydrant ordinance. You truly are my guardian angel." Sandy stepped forward, placed her hand in mine and, looking directly into my eyes, she smiled and said: "It's because of your mischievous nature – and your quest for justice - that all of this happened. I just have a special interest in your welfare." And then she kissed me!!!

Blossom or Wither

Daring young lads & lassies from an inner city world
Mischievous behavior or simply a form of play
They believe their actions are warranted with little –
And sometimes much conscious thought
Even though to steal is breaking a universal rule
Perhaps the directive is justifiably different in this concrete jungle school

Human nature is at play
In their exclusive social world
Territorial imperative
Gee, those are fancy words
Evolutionary scientist they believe
Is nature's survival decree
So they develop a tribal mentality
Protecting their neighborhood from perceived enemies
Creatively using available resources
Overcoming limitations however they can
For adaptability is survival's demand
So they do what they must to set themselves free
No matter the social chains their world may wrap them in

Morals and ethics
Lessons to learn
Nature's handiwork
The potter's wheel of life, it turns
In the lives of these children
In this modern day playground
For some a garden – for some a wasteland

Yet the seeds of their potential
Sprout in this desecrated soil
Taking unusual twists and turns
With wounds that run deep
Creating soul searing scars
Thorns in their psyche
To teach them or defeat them
From this they cannot hide
For they are the children – the offspring

Of the ghetto, it's just the way it is – a phrase from the wise
To blossom or to wither, this is their struggle
These Ghetto Flowers must do what they can
No matter the trouble

Freedom from cultural deprivation
Is possible to achieve
And many of them do
For there are cracks in the pavement
That's how the light gets through - and flowers bloom
That's why I am here
Telling these stories to you

STONE HARBOR

A few days after I was born, my mother, assisted by my Grandma Ann Moss, who was taking care of my one and a half year old brother, left the hospital carrying me in her arms wrapped snug in a blanket. She walked across the street to a bus depot and bought tickets to Stone Harbor, New Jersey, where all of my extended family were vacationing. The families collectively saved money throughout the year and rented a large house on a cove along Stone Harbor's bay. They did this every year throughout my childhood. The women and children of the families stayed at the seashore for the entire vacation, while the men rotated visits, based on their hard-earned annual vacations and on weekends, if they could afford the bus fare and weren't working overtime. The bus we boarded left Philadelphia sometime before midnight (bus tickets were cheaper at that late hour) and made multiple stops in towns throughout South Jersey before arriving in Stone Harbor shortly before sunrise. My mother walked the one-half block trek to the ocean and just as the sun was rising from the sea, she lifted me into the air and whispered a blessing in thanks for my creation. She told this story to me many times; reminding me that it was one of the most joyful moments of her life.

The most nurturing times of my youth were during summer vacations in Stone Harbor. Children were free to roam the sand dunes, building castles several feet high, playing chasing games, collecting shells, burying each other in the sand and, of course, swimming - morning, noon, and night. We learned to fish in the bay, catching dozens of sea bass, flounder, blowfish, sea robins, croakers, blues and kingfish. We explored the salty marshes while catching bushels of crabs for the dinner table. The women spent their days on the beach as well, relaxing and engaging in idle chatter about their lives. It was a time for them to spend every day together, sharing the responsibilities of child rearing and preparing food. The cove of the bay is where the children learned to swim, for it was a sanctuary of calm waters. And the men - they were all amateur fisherman - spent their days and nights primarily engaged in three activities: fishing, drinking beer, and playing cards. For the most part, everyone was happy and this is how it was every summer throughout my early childhood.

"Jimmy K., when the men come back from fishing this afternoon, let's ask Grandpa if we can take out the boat. We can crab, swim and explore the back marshland of the bay."

"Great idea! We can save the heads from the fish they catch and use them for crab bait," he replied with enthusiasm.

The powerful and compassionate personality of my grandfather was the central male force in our extended family. He was the strong silent type, a man of few words whose communication was his charismatic presence. His spirit kept our family close and guided us every year to Stone Harbor. My grandfather was a fisherman and he taught all of his grandchildren how to fish and made sure we became strong swimmers as well. He loved and respected the ocean and desired to share this passion with his offspring. He had "Popeye" arms, complete with tattoos, powerful muscles and protruding elbows. He had a clipper ship tattooed on his chest and an angel on each shoulder blade. He always ran the motor and steered our little fishing boat. In like manner, he was the captain of our family. Whenever there was a fraternal dispute it was my grandfather, if necessary, who settled the issue. He was incredibly compassionate and had a reputation throughout the community for his generosity toward the less fortunate. The number of homeless people he took into his home during the years of the Great Depression is legendary. We truly loved our grandfather, and it was his ability to win our affection and admiration that made him the family leader.

I shared with Jimmy Kilpatrick, my younger cousin, a love for crabbing and exploring the bay. We knew every channel, cove, bridge and basin in the intra-coastal waterway of Seven-Mile Island extending southward from Townsend's Inlet where Avalon begins to the tip of Stone Harbor and across Hereford Inlet where the Wildwood Boardwalk and its amusement piers with Ferris wheels, roller coasters and a myriad of stomach-churning rides drew lines on the southern horizon.

"Grandpa, can we use the boat, please?" asked J.K. as he ran his fingers through his short sandy-blonde hair. Grandpa was fond of Jimmy K. They shared a strong personality and physical resemblance, as if they were genetic replicas – noticeable even though Jimmy Kilpatrick was nine years old and skinny as a rail, the shape of his chest and the knobby elbows were uncannily similar. It was obvious to the rest of us that J.K. was Grandpa's favorite among his fifteen grandchildren.

"Depends!" said Grandpa in his low baritone voice. "When the men come in with their catch, you boys can clean the fish and use the boat after dinner – but you need to bring back a bushel of crabs for our evening snack and be sure to keep the boat clean."

"Thanks, Grandpa!" we said simultaneously. Crabbing after dinner, just a few hours before sunset, would be perfect because the tide would be at its highest flow. The men liked to fish as the tide comes in because the advance of the ocean brings lots of fish into the bay.

"Let's not forget the nets and an extra bushel basket in case we get lucky. We should take along the minnow box and cast out a few lines for fish." I was excited! This was the first time since September of the previous summer that I'd been out on the bay and I was hungry for it. Grandpa had taught me how to use the motor, observe the tides, steer clear of sailboats – of which there were often too many - and most importantly, he taught me the art of crabbing.

The men returned earlier then expected. We offered to clean their fish, which was a big chore: sea bass, flounder and a few blowfish, adding up to twenty-three in all. It took some time to gut them, cut off their heads, and filet. We had more than enough fish heads for crabbing. After we finished, J.K. and I spent the rest of the afternoon swimming around Pirate Cove, one of seven basins along Stone Harbor's bay where houses were set at the edge of the bulkheads and boats were moored at the docks. Pirate Cove, what we liked to call the 86th Street basin, is where we learned to swim. All the kids knew how to swim and fish, but J.K. and I were the masters at the art of crabbing.

Dinner was usually around six and we were eager to get going so we decided to skip eating and told our mothers not to expect us back until slightly after sunset. This would give us plenty of time for crabbing and exploring the bay. We stocked the boat with everything we needed and shoved off. The boat was twelve feet long and about three and a half feet wide at the center and came equipped with oars and a 25 horsepower Johnson outboard motor. Uncle Joe was the mechanic of the family, and he made sure the motor was in top running condition. It never failed any of the fishermen – it ran smoothly and had just enough power for our purpose. J.K. had not yet learned to operate the motor, which suited me just fine. I pulled the cord on the top of the engine and she fired up with a roar that far exceeded its speed. We went through the mouth of Pirate Cove and out into the open bay.

The Great Channel of the bay was wide and deep and there were large creosoted poles strategically placed as channel markers so bigger boats could avoid shallow waters. There was a maze of narrow channels flowing through the marshlands. Most were too shallow for the larger boats but posed no problems for lighter craft. Our favorite spot to crab was underneath the 96th Street Bridge. The huge lattice of columns and crossbeams was an attractive gathering place for crabs, providing them with lots of marine plants and smaller animals to feed upon, as well as something to cling to as the tidal force made its twice-daily advance and retreat. I steered the boat toward one of the trusses and cut the engine about thirty feet away, allowing us to drift slowly toward one of the huge poles. J.K. grabbed a pole and looped a rope around it, securing our position.

There were those who used the most recently popular metal cage crab traps, which worked quite well, but to use them instead of the traditional method was like an artist painting by numbers instead of relying on his own sense of beauty and talent. We used strong string, a stick to wrap it around, and a four-ounce sinker tied to the end of the string, which we inserted through the mouth and gills of a fish head. We lowered the first line into the water until the vibration of the sinker hitting the murky bottom was felt and then we attached the stick firmly to the side of the boat by wrapping it around a stationary object - like an oarlock. J.K. and I proceeded to put six lines out and then we sat patiently, allowing time for the crabs to 'smell' the fish head and begin feeding.

There was no magic to knowing how long to wait before slowly pulling in the lines. It was by sensing the crabs clawing at the fish head through a slight vibration on the line that we determined when to check the bait. When ready, the line was drawn up very smoothly and very slowly so as not to alarm the crabs of danger – they are not very smart but they are fearful and extremely defensive in nature. One only has to take a quick glance to realize that their anatomy is designed for self-protection: an oblong hard green shell with pointy spines on the edges, two claws with sharp pincers, multiple legs for scurrying from side to side like a boxer dancing to and fro and eyes that appear to dangle and bob in all directions. They are built for defense and it was essential to stay out of the reach of their jagged pliers-like claws – they hurt and drew blood!

As J.K. pulled up the first line, I stood ready with the crab net to scoop up our unsuspecting prey. It was important to pull the line even slower as the fish head came within a few feet of the surface. The key was to net the crabs before they realized that they were near the water's surface, otherwise they would let go of the fish and glide away into the dark green water.

There they were: several crabs dangling on the fish head and a few attached to each other, waiting for their chance to pinch away a piece of flesh. I carefully lowered the net into the water a few feet to the side of the unsuspecting crabs and gradually slid it underneath them. Then, with a quick even motion I scooped up our first catch of the day – seven crabs and I tossed them into the basket. Two were pregnant females with their bulging orange underside filled with eggs; we threw them back. The rest were over 5½ inches and definite keepers. We proceeded from line to line, scooping up crabs, and in the first hour we had a full bushel and soon filled the second. We could have caught twice as many if we had had more baskets to hold them. There was still more than an hour before the sun would set over the bay. J.K. and I discussed what we wanted to do with the remainder of our time.

"We could go back and head down to the beach for a swim in the ocean. The lifeguards are off duty so we don't have to deal with them calling us in all the time. That means we could catch the big waves and body surf them all the way to the beach." J.K. was a pro body surfer, the best among all the cousins - even better than his older brother Johnny Boy, who was the best swimmer and all around athlete.

"By the time we clean out the boat and bring the crabs into the kitchen for Grandma to cook, we'll only have around half an hour to swim and that's hardly worth the rush," I replied.

"So, we'll swim in the dark." J.K. said with a little dare in his voice.

"We're not allowed to swim in the ocean at night – only the bay - Grandpa says it's too dangerous," I said sternly.

"He doesn't have to know." This was new coming from J.K. He was not the mischievous type, and certainly not one to go against Grandpa's rules.

"So what makes you so daring all of a sudden?" I asked.

"Well, you're always having cool adventures back home and I never seem to get the chance to do any of the stuff you do," he replied.

"It's different here, Jimmy K. We can have all the fun we want and never get into any trouble, while in the neighborhood it seems that trouble is what we do for fun."

"It's what you and your friends do for fun, not me. My father keeps me in the house all the time reading and doing homework."

"That's because your father is smart – and so are you. Hell, you'll probably even graduate from high school – that'll be a first in our family."

"Nah. My brother Johnny will be the first in the family to graduate, unless my sister Marge or our cousin Butch decides to stay in school. And besides, if my father is so smart, why the hell is he drunk all the time?" Jim sounded more like he was wondering out loud with his thoughts than asking a question.

"Whose father isn't drunk most of the time? And don't talk about Butch. Its better to not think about him since we're likely never to see him again." I was still hurting from Butch's sudden disappearance when Aunt Helen decided to divorce Uncle Ike. Thinking of Butch reminded me of White Shepherd, my beautiful canine friend that I gave to Butch when his family moved to New Jersey to keep her safe from rival gang kids who were intent on harming my protector. The loss of her caused a sting in my heart. If Butch had gone to the Pocono camp this past spring with my peer group things would have turned out differently. We might even have stayed there the whole time and avoided causing so much trouble and being sent home early, although what happened was exciting even though it was somewhat stupid!

"Hey J.K., let's bait the fishing hooks and try our luck, maybe we'll catch a flounder or two." He agreed and we began putting tackle on the fishing lines.

"Oliver, the lid to the minnow box is off. Look! The minnows are gone. Grandpa won't like that; he may not let us use the boat again. We forgot to bring the minnow box out of the water and into the boat when we left the dock and headed out of Pirate Cove. It's our fault."

"I guess we'll just have to restock the box. There are a lot of minnows in the marsh channels, especially along the sandy edges when the tide goes out. Let's check it out."

This wasn't the first time we went searching for minnows. We did it last year and learned the best areas to catch them, and we developed a method that worked rather well. Using a fine meshed net would have been best but we never did buy one and besides, we had fun doing it our own way. I started the motor and headed for the marshland channels.

"Over there, I see a white line of sand at the edge of those reeds. That'll be a good spot for catching minnows when to tide gets lower."

"Good eyes J.K. We can toss over the anchor and go swimming while we wait for the tide to go down more."

The marshland grasses were tall this time of year and swayed in a wave-like motion as the summer breeze moved across the bay. The air carried the familiar smell of salt and marsh gases, and seagulls and snowy white egrets glided along the air currents in search of food. The sun was getting lower, and the scattered wispy feather-like clouds reflected red, orange and pink pastel colors in a background of changing hues of blue light. Sun beams danced on ripples across the water as we slowed our boat, stopped the engine and tossed the anchor overboard. Barefoot and shirtless, dressed only in our cut off jeans, we dove into the warm July water, taking with us the minnow box. We pretended we were pirates looking for treasure as we swam in the channel, keeping our eyes open for schools of minnows. We swam to the sandy edge, a rarity in the otherwise black muck that supported the reeds. Along the water's edge we could see groups of minnows swimming about. Our strategy was to splash the water up onto the sand, causing minnows to flop about on the shore. Then, we quickly picked the minnows up and deposited them in the wooden box. It didn't take long to fill the box with fat, relatively large minnows. We reattached the box to the side of the boat and continued to swim about.

J.K. noticed a boat drifting in our direction. There was a boy with an oar unsuccessfully attempting to control the movement of the boat. As his boat approached our location, he called out, "Help! Our motor isn't working. We lost one of our oars, and we don't have an anchor – we can't get home," he shouted in desperation.

"We'll help. Just try to use your oar to push your boat toward the marsh grasses," I called back. There were two boys in the boat and they looked similar in age to J.K. and me. We swam to our boat and pulled ourselves on board. They were not successful in beaching themselves in the marsh grasses, so we started the motor and in a jiffy we were alongside them.

"Catch this rope!" J.K. commanded as he tossed our rope to their boat. The smaller boy caught the looped end. Jimmy K pulled their boat next to ours. The two boys looked relieved.

"Thanks guys, that was scary. The tide's going out and we thought we might end up in the ocean. I'm Kevin and this is Frederick, we're brothers." We introduced ourselves and asked them what happened.

"Our motor just quit running and I tried to use the oars to get us back to our dock, but one of the oarlocks broke and we lost the oar," Kevin explained. Frederick was quiet and had a nervous look in his eyes. He was obviously the younger of the two.

"Tell us where you need to go and we'll tow you there." I offered.

"Our dock is at the 86th Street Basin," piped Kevin.

"You boys live in Pirate Cove! So do we," said J.K. "How come we never saw you before?"

"This is our first time to Stone Harbor since we were babies, and we just arrived this afternoon. Our mother and father bought a house on 86th Street. Mom grew up here along with her younger sister and father." Frederick finally spoke. I was impressed with the clarity and tone of his voice, which didn't match his nervous out-of-place facial expression.

"Do your grandparents still live here?" I asked.

"Just our grandfather. Everyone calls him Captain Tom. Do you know him?" asked Kevin.

"Yes! He's a friend of our family. He owns the only remaining open space on Pirate Cove, right next to the house we rent. Captain Tom allows us to keep our boat on his land. He lives across the street. I wonder why he never built a house on his land." J.K. was very fond of Captain Tom and was excited to hear that these boys were his grandchildren.

"Welcome to Stone Harbor and Pirate Cove. Let's get going before it gets dark. The sun has set and neither of us have lights on our boats." I was eager to get home and eat crabs.

We attached our anchor to their boat's bow, let the line out six feet or more and started towing. It didn't take long to get to the cove. Kevin pointed out the house and we guided the boat safely to the dock. They got out of their boat and invited us to meet their parents. We agreed and followed them up the dock to the house. The parents and other family members came out on the patio to greet us. Kevin and Frederick immediately launched into telling the rescue story. The parents were very friendly and lavished praise on us, thanking us again and again. Another woman entered the patio from the house and introduced herself as Ellen Sullivan, Frederick and Kevin's aunt. I immediately recognized her.

"You're Ellen, the one that taught me to swim when I was seven years old, right here in Pirate Cove." I was very excited because I hadn't seen Ellen since that summer when she taught me how to swim and dive.

"Well, haven't you grown into a handsome young lad and you added a few more freckles. How's your swimming coming along, Oliver?" I loved the sound of her voice. She was even more beautiful than I remembered, and she remembered my name.

"I competed in city tournaments and claimed third place in the medley race last year." I spoke excitedly and a little too fast. I was mesmerized by Ellen's beauty. I had had a crush on her since the time we first met, and I had even entertained the fantasy that one day we would marry and live in Stone Harbor. Ellen had short brunette hair with glistening red highlights, emerald green eyes, skin bronzed by the sun and her dainty nose and cheeks were dusted lightly with freckles. She was tall with long shapely legs and a figure that was so perfect I imagined that God had taken a paintbrush and drew her right into existence. "The neighborhood pool is closed for repairs this summer, though. I never swim for our team in the summer because most of the time our family is living in Stone Harbor."

"As I recall, your family stays well into September. Is that going to happen this year?" she asked.

"Yeah. We're going to stay for almost three weeks after Labor Day."

"Well, I hope it doesn't hurt your academic career missing all that school." She chuckled and then told me she received her teaching license, had moved to Stone Harbor year round and would begin teaching in the local elementary school.

It was time for us to get home so we shook hands with the brothers and promised to meet up soon. As our boat headed across the basin to our house, I felt giddy with delight at having seen Ellen again. I guessed that she was almost twice my age, and here I was having romantic feelings. Then I thought of Sandy and a pang of guilt hit my gut. I felt confused.

That night we feasted on crabs. Grandma cooked them in a very large pot of scalding hot water seasoned with Old Bay. It was a form of entertainment to allow a few crabs to escape while being dumped in the pot, falling to the floor and scurrying about the children's bare feet. After eating crabs the men played penny ante poker and drank beer while the kids watched and learned, and the women sat on the back porch and looked out over the moonlit basin. I went outside to sit on the bulkhead on Captain Tom's property and gaze at the night sky. As I was sitting there I heard the sound of a flute. Beautiful music drifted across the bay as if each note was a star twinkling upon the water. I could see a silhouette of a person playing the flute on Kevin and Frederick's patio. It was too far away to make out who it was. I thought of the flute Liam had given me just a few days before and realized that I had not assembled it, let alone tried to play it. Liam, along with our peer group, had broken into the neighborhood public elementary school and stole musical instruments. He knew I was fond of the flute and gave it to me the day I left for Stone Harbor. Everything had happened so fast since the Philadelphia Fourth of July celebration when the break-in occurred that I didn't even think about it until now. After the person stopped playing I went inside to my bedroom and took out the flute and after a few tries, I figured out the proper way of putting the three pieces together. I blew in the hole and only a high-pitched screech came out, causing my mother to investigate the sound source. She came into my room, saw the flute and asked where I got it. I told her it was a gift from Liam. She sarcastically said that it was probably stolen and if she heard of a missing flute she would return it. She told me not to play it around the house, especially at night, at least until I learned how to play it properly.

I was eager to play, so I took it outside. I looked around and decided that since I couldn't get a single note to play clearly, it wasn't a good idea to play where the sound could disturb the people who lived around the Pirate Cove basin. I decided to take it to the beach, just a few blocks away. The lifeguard stand looked like a good place to perch myself and to try playing the flute. I climbed the stand, assembled the flute and began blowing away. The sound was horrible but I didn't care – I just kept blowing until I was dizzy, took a break and tried again. I imagined that the sound of the ocean waves crashing and the gentle blowing breeze were nature's orchestra and I was playing the flute part. The imagery didn't help my playing much, though. Eventually I was able to play a single clear note. I had no idea what note it was and I didn't care. I just kept playing the same note over and over again, and then I was able to play a second note clearly. These two notes and the various sound patterns that I created became my signature melody contribution to nature's orchestra. I experienced my first "high" from producing music. I went home and decided to put a cot on the back screened-in porch. I fell asleep to the sound of the water lapping against the bulkhead and dreamed of music – and the beautiful Ellen.

For the next several days we settled into our Stone Harbor routine: swimming in the bay and ocean, crabbing and fishing, both from our boat and in the ocean surf. We ran along the multiple paths in the sand dunes of Avalon and used our imaginations while playing a variety of games as well as building sandcastles and digging tunnels and small caverns in the dunes. We did whatever our hearts desired – we were truly free without fear for safety. There was no curfew and we showed up for meals as we wished. Our parents never concerned themselves with where we were or what activities we were engaged in.

One afternoon upon arriving at the beach, I was surprised and pleased to see Ellen on the lifeguard stand. She explained that she was recently hired as a guard on the Stone Harbor Beach Patrol and that she was on the waiting list since the beginning of summer. When someone had to leave early she got the job. Ellen was the first female lifeguard in the history of Stone Harbor. I told her that I came out to the beach every night to sit on the stand and play the flute.

"I can't believe you play the flute, Oliver. That's my instrument too." She went on to tell me that she had been playing since she was 5 years old and that she played in a quartet throughout college. She told me that she received her graduate degree in education from Indiana University that spring and that Indiana has a very reputable music school so she also studied music.

"Would you like to take flute lessons from me, Oliver?"

"Yes! When can we begin?"

"Tonight?"

"Definitely!" Wow, taking lessons from Ellen, a real life goddess. I was thrilled.

And so it came to pass that the person who taught me how to swim became my music teacher as well. She advised me not to play on the beach when it was windy because it interferes with the quality of sound and that sand could get into the delicate key mechanisms. Ellen taught me to play long tones as well as the proper fingering for each note. After I was able to develop a good embouchure, she began teaching me scales and how to read music. We practiced in Captain Tom's garage almost every night; the only exception was when she was on a date with another lifeguard, which made me very jealous. On the nights when I wasn't taking lessons from Ellen and if the wind wasn't blowing strongly, I took my flute to the beach pavilion on 88th street, where there was protection from blowing sand and continued playing notes to the sound of the wind and surf, creating melodies that I imagined helped the stars dance their cosmic circles through the night.

One evening I went to Ellen's house to see if she was available to give me a flute lesson. I knocked on the door and Captain Tom, Ellen's father, answered.

"Hello, Captain Tom, you're back! It's good to see you again. It seems like forever." This was the first time I had seen the Captain this summer. I learned that he had attended a conference on physics in California. Captain Tom was a physicist.

"Well, it's the red-headed, freckle-speckled Irish lad from Philadelphia. I haven't seen you since last September. You've grown a few inches. Come on in. What can I do for you, lad?" Captain Tom was in his early 60's; a big man, tall and robust with long white hair and a beard to match – the only man I knew who had long hair, which I thought was really cool. He wore a sailor cap with a "captain" insignia in the front.

"Is Ellen home?" I asked.

"Afraid she's out with the crowd, chasing the boys away like gnats in June, I suspect. Come on in and sit for a spell. I heard about you and Jim Kilpatrick rescuing my grandchildren. That was mighty thoughtful and courageous. Thank you kindly!"

"You're welcome, Captain."

"Ellen says you're coming along quite nicely with the flute."

"She's a good teacher. I am very lucky."

"That you are, and so am I. Both my daughters have moved back to Stone Harbor. It's where they belong."

"Captain, how did you come to live in Stone Harbor?"

"Well, to answer that question properly, you need a history lesson on the origins of Stone Harbor, my boy. Tomorrow morning, before sunrise, I'll be taking Old Betsy on the ocean to sail – row – motor – drift my way along the Seven Mile Beach while hauling in some stripped bass and blues and whatever else sister luck will bring. It's been a while since I salted my beard with sea spray. You and your cousin Jim Kilpatrick are welcome to come along – my way of saying "thanks" for rescuing my grandsons. So, my young mate, think you're up for an adventure?"

"It'd be a dream come true Captain!"

Captain Tom told me to be at his boat by 5:30am. There were no alarm clocks in the house and I was worried that J.K. and I would oversleep. I remembered that Grandpa got up before 5:00 religiously. I asked and he agreed to wake us, especially when I told him why. He liked Captain Tom. J.K. and I slept on our cots on the back porch, which was becoming our permanent sleeping space.

"Oliver, J.K., get up! There's donuts and milk waitin' for ya's. Captain Tom and I loaded his boat with the fishin' gear. We're headin' out to sea shortly, so ya's gotta get movin'."

We hopped off our cots and slipped on our shoes – didn't need to dress 'cause we slept in our clothes. We quickly ate breakfast. Grandpa made a boat snack for us.

"Captain Tom came over to the house last night and told me about your ocean fishin' trip and invited me to come along. Haven't been fishin' on the open sea for a few years. It'll feel good gettin' out where I can see the sky meet the sea and get a view of the seven mile stretch, and maybe we'll catch some fish." Grandpa rarely expressed enthusiasm.

"Have you ever fished with the Captain, Grandpa?" asked J.K.

"A few times over the years. Let's get goin'. The Captain is waitin' on us down at the boat."

It was still dark as we headed out of Pirate Cove. The stars were bright and there was a hint of light in the eastern sky. Captain Tom's boat was much bigger than ours - 22ft bow to stern, with a steering wheel, a big motor and a mast for setting sail when the wind was right. J.K. and I had never been on Old Betsy before.

"Captain, why did you name your boat Old Betsy?" I asked.

"It was my mother's name. This boat was given to me by my father. Not many boats like 'er, either. She's all wood and I take better care of 'er than I do my house. My pa spent a lot of time on this boat – took me fishin' just about every day when I was a young lad, when the weather was right – even in the winter. Speaking of weather, there's a storm advisory warning for late tonight. A hurricane is movin' along the coast of North Carolina and we're supposed to get the tail end of 'er. They're calling 'er Hurricane Eleanor and she's a whopper! Won't affect us much though - perhaps a little choppy early in the afternoon, but the sea's looking calm at the moment, and I plan on being back by noontime."

We passed under the 96th Street Bridge. The bridge had to open because the boat's mast was too high to pass under. This was my first experience having the bridge open for a boat I was on. We were approaching the open ocean. I could see the edge where the waters of the bay and the ocean merge. The waves were a little choppy as the more forceful motion of the tides and wind in the open sea clashed with the calmer bay waters of Stone Harbor. The eastern horizon was becoming increasingly bright with color – orange, red and gold, and there were only a few stars still visible high above the horizon, overhead and in the western sky. There was a light breeze blowing, and I deeply inhaled the sea salt air. Seagulls trailed along the boat, hoping for scraps of bait or fish heads, tails and guts. I liked watching them, hearing their cries, a familiar sound. All the sounds of the seashore were imprinted in my soul like an ancient song stirring feelings of comfort, like being home. I loved the sea and Stone Harbor – everything about it resonated with the very core of my being – I felt free and safe and adventurous.

"We're going off shore about 500 yards where the water is deep and there are plenty of nutrients and prey from the bay to attract schools of fish. If we're lucky we'll catch striped bass, flounder, blue fish and maybe a kingfish or two. The hurricane is pushing the Gulf Stream closer to the Continental Shelf, and that means the fish that are running are going to move with it."

As I listened to Captain Tom and Grandpa talk about the fish we might catch, my eyes scanned the eastern horizon. Rays of golden light appeared as the sun rose out of the sea like a giant golden egg. I was mesmerized and speechless as I stood up and pointed – everyone turned their heads and a worshipful silence fell upon the boat as we watched the sun quickly emerge, majestically crowning the earth. Captain Tom whispered, "Let there be light and the firmament of heaven opened and darkness dispelled – and bring on the fish!" He let out a hearty laugh as the boat rose and fell with a thunderous splash and we all got soaked.

We caught lots of fish that morning, far more than we could eat or freeze for future use. Captain Tom told J.K. and me that we could make a hefty profit by selling them to local restaurants. He suggested that we keep what we couldn't eat or use for bait, but that we had to sell them that afternoon while they were still fresh. We sailed along the seven mile stretch of coast that connected Avalon and Stone Harbor and Jim and I enjoyed watching the people along the beach. They looked quite small from out at sea but the Captain pointed out 86th street and the lifeguard stand on which Ellen was sitting. The Captain gave J.K. and me some responsibility with hoisting and lowering the sails as needed and taught us how to tie a few rope knots. Our Grandpa was mostly silent with a slight smile and a twinkle in his eyes as he contentedly fished and looked at the panorama of sea, sky and shoreline.

"Well, lads. I promised a history lesson and bit of folklore. Whether fact or fish tale, I leave that up to your own sensibilities." So, as we sailed along Seven Mile Beach and made our way back to Pirate Cove, Captain Tom told us this story:

Sometime in the early 19th century, the merchant ship, Sea Crest, sailed by Englishmen Captain Jonathan Stone, was commissioned by the US Government to chase down and capture pirates that were preying on ships sailing in and out of the Delaware River. Philadelphia was a major seaport, and the growing nation didn't have much of a navy at the time, so merchant ships were easy targets for pirates. Captain Stone had once sailed for the British Navy, but personal circumstances caused him to accept an offer from a small shipping company out of Philadelphia to sail goods from the young nation to markets in Europe. The pirate problem was hurting industry, and since Captain Stone had battle experience, he accepted the challenge offered to him by the U.S. government to hunt pirates. His ship was outfitted with cannons and some strong young men from Philadelphia. This was a strange position for the Captain, mind you, having been an officer in the Royal Navy and now commanding a ship manned by Americans, but he managed to get along quite well thanks to the help of his first mate, William Bristow, a young Philadelphian whose family came from England. He was born in the states and was just in his teens at the time.

William was a strong lad and an excellent sailor, and he proved to be popular among the men; he had masculine charisma, a good sense of humor and he was the best boxer and swordsman on the ship. When the first conflict between the hotheaded English hating sailors and the Captain erupted, William stepped in on the Captain's behalf and challenged the mutinous ringleader to a boxing match. The leader, whose name escaped the annals of time, weighed 50 pounds more than William, was very muscular and several inches taller. This was no problem for young William because he had lightning quick feet, strong hands and a keen intellect to match; and his arms were strong with a punch like a sledgehammer. The fight was over in 30 seconds and order was restored. William was made first mate.

Captain Stone and his crew were successful in protecting merchant ships from pirates. They engaged in cannon fire exchanges with pirate ships, scaring them off, but never captured any nor were they ever involved in an all out sea battle; the pirate ships always fled quickly out to sea, except on one occasion. It was a misty October morning and there were rumors of a pirate ship sailing along the coast heading north toward the Delaware Bay. The ship was spotted off Cape Henlopen, Delaware by the lighthouse keeper, who sent warning to the Cape May lighthouse keeper through a series of light flashes, and Captain Stone received the message. The fog made it dangerous for ships not familiar with the Delaware and Jersey coastline. The pirate ship was looking for a safe harbor to wait out the coming storm. The sea was getting angry and the Pirates were desperately seeking refuge. Captain Stone spotted the pirate ship and moved quickly towards her in hopes of firing his cannons. The winds were strong and so the pirate ship was able to move quickly out toward sea and the chase went on. The Captain of the pirate ship was clever and used the fog and winds to his advantage. He sailed due east into the winds, tacking as he went along. The pirate ship was lighter and swifter than the Sea Crest, so Captain Stone soon lost sight of her and gave up the chase, for he did not want to get caught in the storm. What he didn't know was that the pirate ship turned northward and then back west toward the coast, once again in search of a safe harbor to wait out the storm. The pirate captain entered Hereford Inlet and before his ship slipped safely out of sight of the ocean coastline, first mate William Bristow spotted it from his spyglass and shouted a warning to Captain Stone, who immediately took pursuit.

The Sea Crest was as far North as Sea Isle City, so they were several miles from the pirates, and it was a fortuitous break in the fog that allowed William Bristow to spot the pirates from such a distance. The Sea Crest entered Hereford Inlet just as the big storm hit the coast hard with heavy rains driven by sixty-mile per hour winds. Luckily they made it safely into the harbor. Captain Stone was uncertain where, when or if he would come upon the pirates. There are seven basins in the Stone Harbor bay, but big ships had explored none, and there were few people living along this stretch of the Jersey Shore, except for Wildwood, Cape May and the fledgling whaling fleets. The Captain was nervous about sailing too far into the bay, so he laid anchor at what is now 110th street in the Great Channel, not very far in from the open ocean, but far enough for protection from the high wind and waves of the raging storm. He figured if the pirate captain had indeed committed himself to holding up in Stone Harbor bay, he would meet with the cannons of the Sea Crest, for the Captain had positioned his boat broadside to the channel, ready to blast the pirate ship and send her down to Davy Jones' locker.

The strong winds of the storm had died down after six hours although the rain continued. William Bristow suggested to the Captain that he take a small boat and explore the inlet for the pirates, thereby gaining further advantage. The Captain at first was hesitant to allow William Bristow and four of his sailors to go, but William assured him that he would be careful not to be caught by the pirates and that he could gain valuable information on their position. William Bristow also reminded the Captain that the inlet had an outlet at the northern end of seven-mile island, and that the depth of the waters of these inlets had never been measured. Perhaps it would be possible for the pirates to escape northward. The Captain relented and so William Bristow and his men rowed deeper into the inlet. They rowed into what is currently the 101st Street Basin, and saw no signs of pirates. You need to know lads that back then this land was covered with virgin trees, not as tall as the virgin forest inland, but tall enough to hide most of the mast of a ship, especially since the rain made it difficult to see and it was nighttime. Then, William Bristow continued rowing in the Great Channel, exploring each basin, eventually reaching the currently named 86th Street Basin, and there he saw the pirate ship laid on its side and taking in water. She had run aground, for the basin was too shallow for her bulk. The pirates had two choices: escape to land or drown. William was in no hurry to feel the sting of pirate bullets or to clash steel with men known to be ruthless fighters. Besides, his mission was only to spot their location and this he did, so he returned to the Sea Crest.

The storm had passed and Captain Stone, William Bristow and the men of Sea Crest boarded small boats; two were positioned as a block at the entrance of the basin and the others went on land both north and south of the basin. William Bristow led the group from the north while the captain approached from the south. What they found surprised them: a small group of women and children – three women and five children. The pirates had fled in the night, certain of their capture had they remained with their broken ship. Several fled in small boats escaping through the inner coastal waterway while others went by foot northward and into the Pine Barrens. It is said that the descendents of these pirates live in the Jersey Pine Barrens to this day. William Bristow and Captain Stone brought the women and children safely to the Sea Crest and learned that they had been taken during a pirate raid from a small village called Cedar Island, along the coast of Maryland. The men were all killed and what the pirates wanted with the women and their children was not made known to them; other than the killing of their men, they were unharmed. Perhaps they were to be sold into slavery. William Bristow took particular interest in a young woman and her infant child. Her name was Ann Moss and she was still in her teens, young to have a child and to have lost her husband.

William took Ann Moss and her son to Philadelphia and there they married and settled. Ann renamed her child William but she had him keep the last name Moss, in honor of his true father. She took the name Bristow upon marrying William. The basin became known as Pirate Cove, and this barrier island was called Stone Harbor. My ancestry can be traced back to Captain Stone; his offspring settled the area, and this is why I make Stone Harbor my home, and why your family comes here every summer.

I was stunned by what I had just heard and could only stare at Captain Tom with a stupid expression of awe on my face. J.K. was less gullible.

"No disrespect Captain, but do you mean to say that our Grandpa here is a descendant of William Bristow and Anne Moss?" J.K.'s response surprised me and shook me out of my shock. Before Captain Tom could speak, Grandpa spoke.

"It's all true. Our ancestry goes back to Ann Moss and William Bristow. Ann Moss's son, who was renamed William, kept the last name Moss, as his mother insisted, in honor of her killed husband, and William Bristow gave no objection to this. I don't know how many generations that is, but I am a direct descendant of William Moss." My grandfather rarely spoke more than a sentence fragment at a time, let alone spilling out an explanation like that. J.K. and I were now both staring at our grandfather with a look of awe and reverence, even though a twinge of disbelief still lingered in the back of J.K.'s mind.

"Grandpa, how come no one ever told us this story before? We've been coming to Stone Harbor all our lives and you've been coming here all your life. That's a long time and who knows how far back it goes; it's an incredible story, too incredible for us to have never heard and to believe." The words rushed out of J.K. like water from a fire hose. Grandpa smiled and simply said, "No one ever asked." As I listened to Grandpa say those words my eyes were focused upon his chest.

"Of course! It makes sense: the clipper ship tattooed on your chest, that's the Sea Crest isn't it?" Grandpa didn't say a word. He just smiled and nodded his head.

Suddenly, Captain Tom gave us orders to grab the lines and prepare to slip them over the moorings as we approached his dock. We were so captivated by the story that we hadn't noticed we had entered the cove. We unloaded the fish and, just as he had promised, Captain Tom gave us what couldn't be frozen or eaten to sell to local restaurants. For the rest of the afternoon we used our bicycles to go from Stone Harbor all the way up to the bridge that stretched across Townsend's Inlet leading to Sea Isle City, selling our fish to restaurants and small stores, and even to people on the street. When we exhausted those possibilities, we walked along the beach and sold the remaining few. In all, we earned $72.00.

"Oliver, do you believe that story or are they pulling our leg?"

"Well, if they are pulling our leg, that's one hell of a conspiracy, and if not, wow! Our roots run far deeper into Stone Harbor than anyone else living today, with the possible exception of Captain Tom and his family," I replied.

"Yeah, that means our ancestors were among the first people to set foot on Stone Harbor and Pirate Cove. And here we are way over a century later and Stone Harbor and Pirate Cove are our summer playground." J.K. shook his head in disbelief.

"Oliver, do you think we should talk to the rest of the family about this story?"

"Of course! It's too cool not to share. I can't get over the fact that we never heard it before. That alone tips me off that Captain Tom and Grandpa made it up last night while we were sleeping. And it seems a bit too coincidental that Grandpa's name is William Moss, and Grandma's name is Ann. Not to mention that awesome tattoo on his chest that we admired all our lives. It's kind of freaky."

"Well, I'd rather believe it than not believe it."

"Yeah, me too, Jim, and if it's not true, you have to admit it's an incredible fish tale." I laughed. J.K. joined in and we didn't stop for what seemed like five minutes.

That night a big storm blew in and woke us up from our sleep. The lightening flashes lit up Pirate Cove for split seconds and the thunder shook our house. J.K. and I were sleeping on the back porch, and rain was pouring in through the screens.

"Wow! It must be raining sideways." I yelled above the sound of the rain. My father came out on to the porch yelling, "Kids, come with me. The ropes keeping the boats moored along the cove need to be checked to keep the wind and high tide from pulling them loose. Quick."

I wondered how my dad got here but I didn't have time to ask. I figured he must have come in late last night by bus. J.K. and I followed my father's instructions as we walked along the bulkhead that lined the entire cove in a distorted U shape, checking the lines that secured the boats. I wondered where the owners of these boats were, and then I remembered it was mid week and most of the people who owned these homes were what we called weekend sailors. It was fortunate that we were there providing this service, because at least half of the boats were not properly secured. One had broken free and was smashing up against the huge creosote pilings, and had it not been retrieved it may have been lost. We were able to secure it before it was completely destroyed. The lightning flashed and I saw the silhouettes of Grandpa and Captain Tom on the other side of the cove securing boats and checking lines. There were a few residents staying in their vacation homes during the mid-week, so they secured their own lines and then proceeded to help us. They expressed gratitude for our work, saying it made them feel safer knowing my family was there looking out for their property.

We went to bed, feeling exhausted and exhilarated from our adventurous good deed. I felt proud of my father for taking the initiative and enlisting my help. The storm had passed during the night as we slept. J.K. and I slept-in later than usual. We were awakened by the sound of my mother's voice: "Help! Help! Lenny is sinking in the sand! Dad, Joe, everyone, help! We got up and ran outside and there we saw a very strange sight: my father was waste deep in sand and gravel. A sink hole had formed at the end of 86th Street where the street dead-ended into a bulkhead that serves as a barrier to the bay. Apparently my father was fishing from the bulkhead when the ground began to sink. Grandpa called to Uncle Joe to pull up his 1956 Chevrolet Bel Air station wagon, and so he did. Grandpa then tied a rope to the bumper, all the while calling out to my father to stop screaming and not to move, or else he would sink faster. He made a loop on the other end of the rope and tossed it to my father, instructing him to tie it around his waist and to hold on tight. He then told Uncle Joe to slowly inch the Chevy forward. The strategy was successful; my father was pulled from the apparent quicksand, which was really a sinkhole that formed from all the water brought up by the storm surge.

I hugged my father as my mother anxiously brushed the sand off his body.

"Hey, look, there's an old bottle in the center of the sand hole." J.K. shouted.

I walked to the edge of the hole and there lying a few feet down was an old bottle. I then ran to the boat and grabbed the crab net and quickly brought it to the sinkhole. I carefully extended the net and scooped up the bottle. Jim Kilpatrick took it from the net.

"Whoa, Jamaican rum – it's a bottle of Jamaican rum." J.K.'s eyes were bulging out of his head. There was no label, just a clear glass bottle with *Jamaican Rum* spelled out in raised glass. I took the bottle from Jim and turned it over in my hands, along the bottom in smaller letters it read: *West Indies Trading Company, England 1789.*

"1809! England! How did it get here?" I thought out loud. "Pirates!" J.K. and I shouted in unison. Our excitement was shared by everyone in the family. We took the bottle inside the house, and everyone forgot about my father's near brush with death. The family sat around the kitchen table staring at the bottle.

"Let's open it," said J.K.'s dad, known to me as Uncle John.

"No way, it's a relic, a real piece of history. It has to be worth a lot of money," J.K. nervously responded to his father.

"History won't mind if I take a good long swig of that stuff. I bet they made some potent rum back then," responded Uncle John.

"It just might kill you too. No one touches the rum." Grandpa decreed. Grandpa took the bottle away after allowing everyone to hold it carefully.

Captain Tom tried convincing Grandpa to donate the bottle to the Stone Harbor Chamber of Commerce. Grandpa said he'd take it under advisement. Because there was a possibility that the bottle came from the pirate ship that once held Ann Moss captive, I knew there wasn't a snow ball's chance in hell that Grandpa would ever let that bottle out of his possession.

We ate a hearty breakfast, and then went to the beach. The evening storm had brought the ocean over the dunes and into the streets, but by morning the water had receded. It was low tide when we arrived, but the water level was where it usually is during high tide. There was only a light breeze blowing so the ocean looked fairly calm except for the waves breaking on the shore; they were huge. The energy from the storm was still moving through the sea, which made for perfect body surfing conditions, and we were a family of body surfers. It was still early morning and the lifeguards were just coming on duty. We spent all day swimming and riding waves. I hung around Ellen's lifeguard stand when not in the water. I told the story of our good deed in the middle of the night and the rescue of my father and the finding of the bottle of rum. She simply smiled and nodded her head as I chatted away, careful to keep her eyes on the swimmers, occasionally blowing her whistle to signal a swimmer to come closer to shore. In addition to the high waves, the storm must have brought in fish because we saw more dolphins in one day than I had seen in my entire lifetime. We were even able to swim within twenty feet of them; we could have gotten closer if the lifeguards hadn't kept calling us in. It was a great day at the beach, and we stayed until sunset because Aunt Sis, J.K.'s mom, had brought us a lunch basket so we didn't need to go home for food and water. We explored the dunes of Avalon and found an entire set of beach furniture that the storm had carried up the beach. Later that day we found the owners, and they rewarded us with an ice cream treat at Springer's Ice Cream Parlor on 96th Street. My favorite flavor combination is vanilla and black raspberry. The store is family owned and they make the ice cream right on the premises.

The rest of the summer went by quickly, but Labor Day came and went and 90% of the vacationers went home, our family remained for another three weeks. This was a special treat for the children because we missed the hoopla of the first weeks of school, and the entire barrier island was ours to explore. There weren't even lifeguards on the beach, so we swam whenever and wherever we wanted. We were safe of course, and our grandfather warned us to watch for rip tides and never to go out too far. He also instructed us on how to swim out of a rip current. Fortunately, there was never a swimming accident. Ellen and Captain Tom would occasionally join us for a sunset swim. Ellen was used to swimming without lifeguard protection and was well aware of the risk involved and she never tired of warning us to exercise caution and never to swim alone.

Ellen began teaching school. She invited me to visit her classroom and prepared me to play a flute duet of the tune, *Simple Gifts,* the first melody she taught me to play. Her 3rd grade class lavished appreciation upon us with loud applause. I was very nervous and didn't get enough air to make the notes come out clearly but at least I got through the song.

The last night in Stone Harbor before returning to Philadelphia I had my final flute lesson with Ellen. We met in Captain Tom's garage and she had me practice playing the notes slowly and carefully, emphasizing obtaining the clearest sound possible. She told me to begin each day's practice session in this manner, explaining that it would teach me to make the flute sing like the voice of an angel. During our lessons throughout the summer vacation she had taught me how to play every note over three octaves, although I continued to struggle with playing the highest and lowest notes clearly. After our practice session she asked if I would like to take a walk on the beach, which made my heart pound rapidly with excitement. The night sky was moonless with billions of stars scattered like diamonds in patterns that Ellen recognized with ease.

"Over there is Orion, and there's the Big Dipper. If you follow the two stars off the end of the dipper it will lead you directly to the North Star."

"The North Star isn't very bright," I added showing interest and trying to hide my sense of feeling overwhelmed – not by the enormity of the night sky, but by being with Ellen. The tide was still coming in and it was almost at its highest flow. We walked along the waters edge, allowing the water to wash over our feet; then I noticed a trail of green light as we swished through the water.

"That's bioluminescence," explained Ellen, "living light produced by very tiny jelly fish or other organisms as our feet touches them. Step over here on the sand and we should be able to see our footprints glow." As we walked along we could see the impression of our feet glow bright green for a second and then disappear.

"How do you know so much?" I asked, truly fascinated by her knowledge.

"Well, I guess most of what I know I picked up along the path of life from lots of people and of course from school. What is your school like, Oliver?" I thought about her question for a very long moment because it brought back to my awareness that this was my last night in Stone Harbor and I hadn't thought much about my friends back in the neighborhood, let alone school.

"School is okay as long as I can keep from getting beat up." I replied.

"Beat up? That sounds horrible! Are their lots of bullies in your school?" she was obviously surprised.

"I guess you could call them bullies, but really it's the kids from different neighborhoods that give me trouble. There's only one other kid in my school from my neighborhood and he's Italian and he's not a Catholic either."

"Oliver, it must be really difficult going to a school outside of your neighborhood and away from your friends. I have visited city neighborhoods but I really don't know much about what life is like for the people living in them. I grew up in Stone Harbor and went to college in a small university town in Indiana. Tell me what it's like for you in Philadelphia."

No one had ever asked me anything about my life in Philly; not even the people who lived there; not even my family or my friends, so I had to think for a really long time before answering.

"I have to walk ten blocks to get to Vare middle school; it only has 7th and 8th grades; I'm going into the eighth grade this year. School started several weeks ago but my family stays in Stone Harbor longer because we get a special deal on the rent since it's off season."

"Won't you fall behind in your studies starting school so late?" she asked.

"Not really. The classes are pretty easy since most of the kids don't do their homework and the teachers have to go over the material several times. I get bored a lot!"

"That's too bad. I know you're a smart kid; you learn quickly and you speak well for your age, although I have heard you use curse words and I find your South Philly accent unique and interesting. Tell me more about your school and friends."

"The school is big with lots of kids in each class. The work is easy. Like I said the hard part is to keep from getting beat up."

"Who tries beating you up?" she asked with a tone of alarm.

"The kids from the other neighborhoods are enemies to me and my friends. They can't walk in our neighborhood, and we can't walk in theirs. We are mostly Irish with some Germans and Italians, and our neighborhood is bordered on two sides by black neighborhoods with Italians on the other sides."

"Do the kids in your neighborhood fight with them?" she asked.

"Yeah. Ever since I was a little kid I watched gang fights. It's mostly the older kids who fight and the younger ones help out. Since I've just turned thirteen I'm going to have to fight more often. The older kids try to keep us away from the fights until we become teenagers; then we, too, have to protect the neighborhood." Ellen stared at me with a look of concern. I could tell she was puzzled and worried. "It's just the way it is, Ellen. We can't let the black people move into our neighborhood because it makes people want to move out and that's not good. Just this spring I was beat up by a group of boys I've known all my life. I went to school with them since kindergarten, but now that we're teenagers we've become enemies."

"Racism, aggression and competition for territory are universal diseases, Oliver. People have been fighting wars and enslaving each other because of skin color, religious differences, land and its wealth and politics for hundreds of thousands of years. But it is my personal belief that these social diseases are brought about by the human species' innate animal fear associated with the quest for basic survival. The moral and ethical consciousness of our species has not kept pace with our technology, so human beings have become super killers. We need to become super lovers!"

"I think I understand some of what you just said. I just know that because I have white skin, red hair, freckles and come from an Irish-German neighborhood, the blacks and sometimes the Italians want to beat me up."

"Do you know what a tribe is, Oliver?"

"Yeah, like the Comanche Indians. I went to a camp this past spring and was in the Comanche cabin. It didn't work out."

"The kids in your neighborhoods behave like they are tribes in separate villages protecting their territory. It reminds me of my studies in cultural anthropology at Indiana University."

"Cool. I'm a member of a tribe." Ellen laughed at my comment.

"How does your family feel about you going to an unsafe school?"

"My father doesn't really care if I go to school but the law makes me go, and my mother wants to see me graduate from high school. No one in my family ever graduated from high school." Again, Ellen looked at me with an expression of disbelief.

"Didn't your parents go to school?' she asked.

"My father was the eleventh and youngest child in his family, and his parents had a hard time keeping them all fed and clothed. Education wasn't that important, so my father never learned to read or write."

"Were your father's parents immigrants?"

"They came from Ireland when they were young, and most of their children were born in America. The entire family lived in a small house with just two bedrooms."

"I think I understand. Simply having a roof over their heads and food to eat was the priority. Education took a back seat," she said thoughtfully. "And what about your mother?"

"It was a little different for her. She finished third grade and then she just stopped going. I'm not sure why, but I know back then the government didn't make people go to school. My mom can sign her name and she pays the bills."

"How well do you read?"

"I do okay I guess."

"You picked up reading music quickly. What novels have you read?"

"I read one novel, *The Adventures of Huckleberry Finn*; I found it on the sidewalk in downtown Philadelphia when I was shopping with my mom. I liked the book a lot but I didn't understand all of it. Mostly I read the assignments in the textbooks they give us at school, but that's boring stuff. I like to read my grandfather's cowboy comic books, and I buy my own comic books. I especially like *Archie* and *Spiderman.*"

"They don't require you to read novels in your school?"

"No. The kids don't take good care of books, so we aren't allowed to take them home. Everything we read is read in class. I had English classes where teachers tried reading novels in class out loud with each student taking a turn to read, but too many students were absent on any given day and lots of kids can't read very well. Some can't read at all. Teachers just give up even though I can tell that some of them really do care."

"Why don't you use the library in your community?"

"Are you kidding? A library in my neighborhood? That sounds funny. All we have is churches, bars and corner convenience stores, and the stores mostly sell newspapers, magazines and comic books."

"Isn't there a library somewhere near your neighborhood?"

"Yeah, there is one downtown. I guess I can find out how to use it. I tried taking books out of the school library, but they will only let us use them in school. Too many books didn't return so they had to stop lending them. Most of the textbooks we use have to be shared in classes and they won't let us take them home either. The teachers complain that there aren't enough textbooks for all the students and the ones we have are outdated."

"Your school is very poor. Most schools are funded by property taxes, and you live in a poor area. The government should spend more money on education and less on the art of war. That's the only way to stop the cycle of poverty and bring peace into the world." Ellen sounded very serious, almost angry. We left the water's edge and walked up to the dunes and sat down among the dune grasses. I looked around and noticed lots of small violet-colored flowers.

"These flowers are very pretty. How can flowers grow in sand?" I asked.

"Flowers can grow just about anywhere, Oliver; even in the ghetto. These flowers open only at night because it is too hot during the day. Life has amazing versatility and takes on whatever form necessary to survive, this is especially true for human beings, the most adaptable animal on the planet." Ellen continued to speak in a serious tone, and her face wore an expression of concern.

"What's a ghetto?" I asked.

"A ghetto is what people call areas of cities where the conditions are overcrowded, the people are poor, the schools are not very good and the people lack education and proper health care. And it is where most of the poor immigrants from Europe live when they first come to America. Hundreds of thousands of black people left the South looking for work in the industries of the big northern cities – but they are not immigrants, they were brought here against there will as slaves, which is one of the causes for inner city racial troubles and poverty. Immigrants provide the cheap labor needed for many industries, and the ethnic groups compete with each other for jobs. Usually, after a generation or two, families are able to improve their lives. It is just a matter of time before your family will live somewhere else. From what I've heard you say, most of the German immigrants have left South Philadelphia already, and many of the Irish and Italians have moved out and will continue to do so as their economic situation improves – or the conditions in your neighborhood worsen. I believe trying to keep the black people from moving into your neighborhood will eventually fail because of economics."

Again, I only understood part of what Ellen was saying. She used big words and expressed even bigger ideas. "Hey, maybe we could move to Stone Harbor! Has your father told you that my family goes all the way back to the founding of Stone Harbor?"

"I vaguely remember hearing my father tell a story about my family origins when I was a little girl. My father claims to be a direct descended of Captain Jonathan Stone, but there's no evidence to support his claim to fame. But at the very least, it is a fascinating legend."

"You should ask him to tell you the story again. It is very interesting, and we found an old bottle of rum that proves the story is true. I live in a ghetto don't I, Ellen. Is that a bad thing?" I asked.

"Yes, you do, Oliver, and that doesn't make you good or bad. It's just the circumstances of your life. It is a good idea for you to get an education and improve your life. Every child should have the opportunity to develop their potential, especially someone with your smarts. I wish there was a way I could help." She continued to sound increasingly more serious.

"I'm okay Ellen. I like my neighborhood."

"Do you feel safe there?" she asked.

"Most of the time. I'm usually scared when I'm in school, though. As long as I stay in the boundaries of the neighborhood I am safe, but there are places that are dangerous for me to walk, and that includes walking to school."

"That's exactly what I'm talking about. Fear prevents people from learning and cripples the mind and I don't want that to happen to you, Oliver!"

"I'm okay, Ellen. Really. You don't have to worry about me. I'm not crippled at all. I like my family and friends."

"Do you ever feel like you're different than other people?" she asked. I thought for a long time and strange feelings began to stir inside of me rising up from somewhere deep in my gut, and then I began speaking without fully realizing all that I was saying. The words simply gushed out of my mouth like a sudden rainstorm.

"I have lots of friends, but most of the time, deep down inside, I feel scared and alone and that no one really knows me, not even my parents. Liam is my best friend. He gave me my flute - actually he stole it from my old elementary school music room, which I feel bad about. My brother can't read or write just like my father. His teachers put him in some kind of special learning classes called the OB classes, and everyone thinks that means "out-of-brains" and that he can't learn anything. I guess they didn't know how to teach him so he didn't learn. Ever since we were kids my brother got teased because he is different, and I always got in fights protecting him even though he's older than me. When I see people get beat up or when kids are chasing me I get really scared, and sometimes people get seriously hurt. My friends are okay, I guess, but they, too, are always acting tough, and so I act tough too, even though deep down inside I don't feel tough. It's just the way I have to be sometimes to protect myself and to keep my friends. They tease my brother and so he chooses not to hang out with us, and I feel ashamed of myself for spending more time with my friends than with my brother. My mother has been ill with severe arthritis since she was in her early twenties. Her hands and feet are swollen and twisted and I hear her cry out in pain every night. I try to help her by lifting the iron frying pans when she cooks because it is too painful for her to hold them. She has trouble in lots of other ways and I do my best to help her, but it is so hard. My father drinks too much and is often drunk, especially on the weekends. He isn't a bad man. He just enjoys drinking beer. My parents argue a lot and sometimes I'm afraid my father is going to hurt my mother. I often think it would be better if they weren't married, and I feel guilty for having those thoughts." I began to cry really hard and loud. Ellen put her arms around me and pulled me close to her. She felt warm and my body felt tingly all over and began to relax. I cried for a long time and then I began to feel better. "I'm sorry I cried. It's embarrassing."

"Oliver. Tears are the healing waters of the soul and flowers bloom in the ghetto too. Shedding your tears will help you to grow. You are my young Ghetto Flower and I know that one day you will blossom into a wonderful young man. You have love in your heart and you are very sensitive and intelligent. Love is the universal nutrient for all life and the more you give to others, the more you give to yourself. Don't let the toughness of your neighborhood destroy that. Try your best to get a good education and to stay out of trouble." She wiped the tears from my cheeks and kissed me on the forehead.

"I'll do my best Ellen. I promise!" During our walk home we were mostly silent. She held my hand all the way back to 86th Street, right up to the front door of my porch.

"What time do you leave tomorrow?" she asked.

"Some of my family left today. The rest of them will take buses that leave at different times tomorrow. My mom likes to get up early and my father and brother would rather take a later bus. My mom and I are taking the earliest bus, which is about an hour after the sun rises. She likes to avoid the confusion of our family and all the equipment we take back with us." I replied.

"Tomorrow is Sunday and my father and I plan on watching the sunrise on the beach as we worship. Would you and your mom like to join us?"

"My mother and I always watch the sunrise on the day we leave Stone Harbor, it will be nice to see you there. Do you mean worship like they do in the Catholic Church?" I asked.

"I guess you could say that, but we do it very differently. My father and I are Quakers. We worship God in silence and we only speak when the Spirit moves us."

"I don't understand what that means. My mother and I like to watch the sunrise. I'll ask her and maybe we'll meet you and Captain Tom on the beach tomorrow. Good night Ellen, and thanks for listening to me. I didn't know I had so many feelings and no one has ever asked me about my life before."

"You're very welcome, Oliver, and I do hope to see you and your mom tomorrow."

The time had arrived for our return home to South Philadelphia. Another season of freedom in Stone Harbor had come to an end. The morning of our family's mass exodus I walked with my mother to the ocean to watch the sunrise, a ritual she and I followed every year as a way to say goodbye to this wonderful place. On the beach were Captain Tom and Ellen sitting quietly looking out at sea. We approached them and they motioned for us to sit beside them. Captain Tom then said that he and Ellen were there to worship in silence in the manner of Friends (Quakers), this being their religious tradition, and that we were invited to participate with them. The only things I knew about Quakers was the man on the oatmeal box with the black hat and white hair and the TV advertisement that had the Quaker on the box saying, *Nothing is better for thee than me.* And there's the giant statue of William Penn on the top of city hall because he was the original owner of all of Pennsylvania. He was a Quaker and he started the city of Philadelphia, and it was known as the *City of Brotherly Love.* It was supposed to be a holy experiment, whatever that meant. I learned about William Penn and the origins of Philadelphia in school.

We sat in silence as the sun rose from the sea, forming a crown made of light rays on the horizon, adorning the earth and bringing a new day. There was a light breeze blowing off the ocean, and I breathed the salt laced air deeply into my lungs. I felt calm and the thoughts in my mind were still, as though I wasn't thinking at all.

After a half hour or more I looked upon the face of my mother and saw tears on her cheeks and a sparkle of light in her familiarly beautiful hazel green eyes. She gently took my hand and, nodding in silent appreciation to Ellen and Captain Tom, we rose to leave the place where sand meets sea and sea meets sky and the sun radiates its life, shedding beauty upon all things. Ellen got up and walked over to my mother and gently took her swollen hands and smiled. "Oliver is a special boy, Mrs. James. I have enjoyed his company a great deal. Thank you." My mom smiled and nodded her appreciation. Then Ellen turned to me and said, "I have gifts for you." She walked to where she had been sitting and reached into a bag and took out some items. She handed me a small blue book with the picture of a seagull on the front. The title said, *Jonathan Livingston Seagull,* by Richard Bach. "Read this book, Oliver. I think it speaks to your condition, and remember to read as much as possible. Reading is the gateway to knowledge; and you might consider writing down your thoughts in a journal. Take this notebook and put your thoughts and feelings into words, it helps one to become clear in heart and mind." The notebook was bound in blue leather and was thick with cream colored pages. She then handed me a black flute case with the word *Buescher* in gold lettering etched into the leather. "This was my very first flute," she said fondly as her hands stroked the case. "Open it, Oliver," she said excitedly. The silver flute was brightly polished and appeared brand new – as if it were never played before.

"It's beautiful!"

"It is not an expensive flute but it plays as well as any flute I've ever played or heard." She leaned close and whispered in my ear, "Take the flute your friend gave to you and return it to the school." I hugged her and thanked her as my eyes began to water. She affectionately said, "You will forever be my young *Ghetto Flower.*" She kissed me lightly on the cheek and without thinking I gave her a quick light kiss on her lips. At first she looked startled, took a small step back as she softly touched her fingers to her mouth and then she smiled.

Captain Tom rose from his comfortable spot in the sand and took my mother's hands and gently held them for a few moments as he gazed into her eyes and said nothing. He then turned to me and extended his large right hand, swallowing my hand, we shook and he said, "Remember what I told you about your family and how you ended up here in Stone Harbor. You may not fully believe my story, but does it really matter how much of the legend is fact or fantasy? Your family vacations in Stone Harbor, my daughter has become your teacher, we spent time together on my boat and today we shared communal worship. These things don't happen by mere coincidence my young friend." And then he laughed his familiar deep hearty laughter.

In this final precious moment as I gazed upon the ocean's horizon with my mother's hand placed affectionately in mine, I looked out at sea one more time and waves of thoughts flowed through my mind:

Stone Harbor, New Jersey! The enchanted land where my spirit is free and I dwell in a sanctuary from the worries of the world; a place where I experience parts of my personality that are mostly hidden when roaming the streets of South Philadelphia. Looking out upon the vastness of the ocean is like looking into the mind of creation. It is infinite, beautiful and mysterious. And now it is time to return to Philadelphia, which I anticipate with both dread and excitement. I am aware of a difference in how I feel at this moment and the way I am in Philadelphia. Although I have had many adventures in my South Philly neighborhood, deep down inside I often feel scared and alone. I don't have that feeling while in Stone Harbor. I am nervous about returning to an unfriendly public school and meeting up again with my neighborhood friends. In fact, I feel uncertain about what friendship truly is or, at least, my friendship with Ellen has taught me much about myself and the world – and playing the flute. Ah! And then there is my beautiful Italian-Irish Sandy - my half & half - and soon I will be playing my flute for her and, perhaps, she'll reward me with a kiss.

Sun, Sky, Sand & Sea

Thoughts placed upon the shoreline
Breezes move across the surface and sweep through my mind
Carrying each thought as grains of sand taken to another shore
Leaving this one empty to be filled with the horizon's expansiveness
And the beauty before me whispers of Nature's eternal embrace

My heart opens to the wideness of the sea and in its depths
The mysteries of life are there to explore
The yesterdays
The today
The tomorrows

All converge on the ebb and flow of time forever present
On the edge of mind, the ever changing line
Where sky meets sea and sea caresses land
And life's transitions spiral and ascend to continual new beginnings
Endless change while the basic elements remain the same

Do I make myself?
Anymore than sun, sky, sand & sea
For I am the same as these - perhaps more
Ever changing – ever changeless – for

I am as Nature created me

I am the sun
I am the sky
I am the sand
I am the sea

I am in Nature
Nature is in me
I am the mystery

Inseparable, like the lines that touch
Sun, Sky, Sand & Sea

Author's Novels

GHETTO FLOWERS
Dark & Light

The story of the Ghetto Flowers continues through their middle and high school years and beyond. The neighborhoods undergo radical change as the social and political forces shaping the country sweep through the narrow streets and influence the lives of these inner city youth, changing them and their culture forever. The forces within their neighborhood bring them to the razor's edge where the line between life and death is easily crossed with one decision, one small deed, where fate is determined and sealed. The Ghetto Flowers pass through the fires of racial violence, and make a giant leap over the hurdles of prejudice and ignorance. They apply what they learn to the circumstances of their inner city world, where poverty and cultural deterioration reach a peak of destruction - and illumination. Continue the journey with the Ghetto Flowers and experience the world through their eyes.

ISLAND ODYSSEY
Ghetto Flowers in Paradise

Island Odyssey is a novel set in the early 1970's in Negril, Jamaica, a pristine fishing village long before it became the thriving tourist resort that it is today. The international counter-culture generation that was seeking a simple life in a Garden of Eden paradise found this beautiful jewel in the Caribbean and lived out their dreams. Their innocence, ideals, and money influenced and forever changed the native people they had grown to love.

This was the era that gave birth to the worldwide influence of Reggae music and Jamaican culture, a phenomenon that attracted thousands of young people from around the globe to this beautiful island.

Two adolescent boys from the inner city of South Philadelphia travel to Jamaica and create a free spirited lifestyle full of adventure and romance. The process of creating a new life in an exotic culture takes them on a journey of exploration into the psychosexual, philosophical and spiritual domains of their inner and outer world. In the process they mature into young men with the support of a unique community of people from diverse cultures, especially the loving embrace of twin sister beauties.

Island Odyssey is a treasure that offers the opportunity to rediscover the hopes and dreams of a passing era. This story will stimulate visions of adventure, romance, and fascinating life challenges.

191

Novels can be purchased at the following on-line locations:

Ghetto Flowers Dark & Light

PRINT https://www.createspace.com/4323177

E-BOOK http://www.amazon.com/Ghetto-Flowers-Light-Francis-Oliver-ebook/dp/B00DJKWTY8

Island Odyssey Ghetto Flowers in Paradise

PRINT https://www.createspace.com/4258190

E-BOOK http://www.amazon.com/ISLAND-ODYSSEY-Ghetto-Flowers-Paradise-ebook/dp/B005TVG54A

GHETTO FLOWERS

The Early Years

Francis O. Lynn

25864611R00111

Made in the USA
Middletown, DE
12 November 2015